Bewilderness

Bewilderness

A Novel

KAREN TUCKER

Catapult  New York

Copyright © 2021 by Karen Tucker

All rights reserved

ISBN: 978-1-646220-24-3

Jacket design by Nicole Caputo
Book design by Wah-Ming Chang

Library of Congress Control Number: 2021933583

Catapult
1140 Broadway
Suite 704
New York, NY 10001

Printed in the United States of America
1 3 5 7 9 10 8 6 4 2

This is for those
who are no longer with us

Part 1

As soon as Luce's going-away party wound down enough for me to slip off unnoticed, I went outside and sat on the little wooden bench across from the restaurant. I guess I'd always known she was going to leave. Even before that first instant-release summer, when she was nothing more to me than a fellow cocktail server, alone and drifting, you could tell she was the kind of person who needed to scrape more out of life than most.

But Luce was also someone who liked to drag stuff out as long as possible, so of course she wanted to give one final hug to every last co-worker, from the waiters who always skipped out on their closing duties to the hosts who made sure to give you all the worst customers until you snuck them a coffee mug of wine. I figured I had time for a cigarette before she came out and caught me. I hadn't smoked in months but the past couple days had been more stressful than usual and in a moment of panic I'd bought a pack off one of the dishwashers. It wasn't my brand, but that didn't matter. Times like this were when all the old urges came swooping back in. I dug around in my bag for my lighter and though it took a few tries, I got the flame going. Once that first hit of nicotine roared into my blood-stream it felt like some broken-off part of me finally righted itself and slid into place.

By the time Luce came outside, all bundled up in her giant

green parka, I'd burned through three Marb Reds and part
of a fourth and my head was swimming way up above me.
She called to me from the door. "He's still not answering. You
didn't hear from him, did you?"

I dropped my cigarette in the snow before she could see it.
"Wilky?"

She ran her eyes over me. "Who else? Said he'd pick us up
by eleven at the latest."

I hoisted my purse over my shoulder and trudged back toward her. "He's just caught up in his own going-away deal. Bet
he's standing on a chair and making a big speech or something. You know how he is."

That earned me a faint smile, but you could tell by the stiff-
ness in Luce's jaw that she didn't believe it. She got out her
phone and called him again. When Wilky still didn't answer,
her cheeks went splotchy with anger. "Dude better have a good
explanation."

"It's okay. I don't mind walking," I said.

Luce and I rented a tiny clapboard bungalow a little less
than a mile from the restaurant. Neither of us had a car.
Or actually Luce did: an old Chevy Impala that needed at
least a thousand bucks in repairs before she could drive it
and which was busy decomposing in the side lot, next to
the skeletal remains of a tractor the previous tenants had
wisely abandoned. When the weather was halfway decent
we rode bikes to work. But it had been snowing on and off
since morning, so even if we'd been able to make it up-
hill to Broad Street during daylight, biking back down on

slick roads wasn't our idea of a choice evening, not after the night last winter when Luce hit a patch of ice, tumbled over her handlebars, and fractured her elbow. She lost almost a month of shifts and even then she had to learn how to carry trays left-handed.

At least she had Wilky. They'd been together over two years and lately he'd been working nights at a nearby bar, the kind with painted-over windows and the stink of urinal cakes wafting out of the bathroom. Although me and Luce always started our shifts a couple hours before him, if it was raining or snowing or we just didn't feel like biking, all we had to do was shoot him a quick text and he'd come give us a lift. Wilky was a sweet, low-key guy who'd gotten himself bounced out of the army for an incident that wasn't his fault, not really. Which is to say that in some ways he was also incredibly dumb. Don't get me wrong, Wilky had a head packed full of brains and a college education to go along with it and that's more than you can say for anyone else in our circle, myself included. But at the same time he was someone who always went around trusting everybody on the planet—no matter how little they might have deserved it.

"Maybe we should check on him," Luce said, looking over her shoulder. Wilky's bar sat way down at the south end of Broad, past even the sketchy 24-hour laundromat and the motel that had been shut down after being declared a public nuisance. Even on the clearest of nights you could barely make out the neon sign in the distance.

"Forget it. We're not walking anywhere extra. Will you

listen to yourself?" Already Luce's breath was struggling out of her in soft little wheezes. Her asthma liked to flare up in cold weather.

"Fine," she said.

We picked our way downhill. The sky had that weird purple color it sometimes took on right before midnight and every so often you could hear the territorial hiss of a barn owl or the cranky honk of a tree frog. On a nearby mountaintop, the abandoned Anklewood Mill rose out of the fog like some low-rent haunted castle that was more depressing than scary. As always, I tried not to look. It wasn't until we rounded the bend that a pale blue moon appeared above us like a giant 30 just waiting for someone to reach up and snatch it. A bit freaky, yes, but not surprising. One of the biggest battles you face when you're using is the constant shortage of goodies—and yet the moment you swear them off forever, pills start materializing all around you like some kind of sick joke.

The exact same thing had happened a couple nights earlier. Luce and I were out by the woods that pressed against the rear of our house, shooting BBs at a row of empty Monster Energy cans I'd strung up with clothesline. It was a good way to relax after a rough shift of waiting tables, especially now that our old stress-relief method was no longer an option. When I pointed out the 30mg moon dangling above us, she gave me a sour laugh of recognition.

"What's so funny?" Wilky said. He'd stopped by after work like always.

Luce lifted the air rifle and squeezed a shot off. "Just Irene being Irene." She reached for the box of pellets, started reloading.

"I'm serious," I said. "You can even see the numbers. Nice and tight. Purdue quality."

"Sounds like somebody needs a meeting," Luce said. She snapped the barrel back in position and passed the rifle to Wilky.

"Having some bad thoughts?" Wilky said to me. "Maybe you should hit up Greenie. She won't be mad you skipped her 1:30 and you'll feel a lot better once you tell her what's happening."

I told him I could miss our stupid home group every once in a while if I wanted and besides that, I felt amazing. To prove it, I took the rifle out of Wilky's hands and nailed one two three cans in a row. I pushed the gun back toward him. "Your turn," I said, smiling. Despite his time overseas, I'd always been a better shot than he was.

Wilky looked from me to Luce and back again. "Actually I think I'm done for the night. I still have a lot of packing left. Probably should get to bed early."

"You're kidding," I said. "We're just getting started."

"And anyway, I want to be up for the 8 a.m." He swung around and headed back to the dumpy little house Luce and I rented. Secretly, I was glad. I was pretty tired of him and Luce going on and on about their big move to Florida. Now me and her could hang out a little. Just the two of us, like old times. I should have known she'd go hurrying after Wilky, leaving me alone in the dark with nothing but a plastic gun and a dollar-store flashlight.

Wilky. He won that round.

Which is why I decided not to revisit the whole pill-in-the-sky situation. I didn't want Luce thinking about Wilky any more than she had to. Besides, the two of them had plans to load the truck first thing in the morning and hit the road right after, and his no-show had gotten her all worked up and jumpy. The added stress didn't do her asthma any favors and even in the short time we'd been outside her breathing had turned harsh and ragged. I wanted to tell her it would be okay, that everything would work itself out like always. No matter what happened we'd get through it, her and me. I pictured the two of us somewhere up ahead in our future, sitting at our kitchen table, maybe eating cake with our fingers and drinking huge mugs of hot sugary coffee and laughing about all the stuff we'd gone through since we first met each other. Not just the guys, but also the string of restaurant jobs, the side hustles, all the trouble we'd managed to kick up before we got clean.

"Yo, check it." Luce's voice came out of nowhere. She was stopped in the middle of the road, squinting up into the dark. It wasn't the moon that had caught her attention, but a bunch of bats zigzagging above us. They seemed confused, panicked even, as if their radar systems had gotten jammed and needed rebooting.

I looked at her. "I thought they hibernated in winter."

"Exactly," she said. "Remember all those dead ladybug husks we found? The box turtle? I'm telling you, Nature's in serious trouble." She hesitated. "You don't think it's a sign, do you? What if something happened to Wilky."

I told her he was just screwing around with his stupid work buddies. "I was you, I wouldn't be worried, I'd be pissed. You have a lot to do tomorrow. Get the U-Haul, load the U-Haul, realize you can't leave me stranded here all by my lonesome, unload the U-Haul."

"Haha," Luce said. She snuck an embarrassed look in my direction. "What if he's changed his mind about Florida and he's too scared to tell me."

"You mean like runaway-briding you?"

She nodded and let the air out of her lungs with a spooky rasp.

"Yeah, no," I said. "I mean he's got his issues, but that's not one of them. Now for real, where's your medicine?"

She stared at me as though she wasn't sure what kind of medicine I meant exactly and then she lowered her head and began scrabbling through her purse. At last she found her inhaler, and she shook it up, put it in her mouth, sucked in chemicals. Like some kind of magic trick, her lungs opened and she gulped in air. I'd seen her do it hundreds of times, but it always made me nervous. What if one day the trick stopped working?

"Much better," she said with effort.

We were pretty quiet the rest of the way home.

Once we got ourselves tucked safe inside, things mostly went back to normal. I cranked up the thermostat the way Luce liked and the heat started roaring. We changed out of our uniforms and into T-shirts and sweatpants. While she

microwaved a plate full of tater tots and shredded cheese
and mixed up her special blend of ketchup and hot sauce, I
turned on the TV, boosted the volume, and messed around
with the rabbit ears. Living on the outskirts of civilization
like we did—even in its heyday, Anklewood only had a few
thousand residents—there weren't but a couple channels that
didn't come in all blurred and distorted. Still we took what
we could get and while a boozy late-night host sweated his
way through an interview with some factory-issue blond
we'd never heard of, we sat on our couch and tore through a
mound of potatoes and melted cheddar. Our nightly routine.
The one good thing about getting your driver's license suspended and having to walk everywhere is you can eat whatever you want.

All in all it wasn't completely terrible, especially when you
consider that Luce and Wilky were leaving the next morning.
Only bad part was she kept checking her phone to see if she'd
missed a call from him, a text, something. Made me edgy.
Got on my nerves too, I have to admit. They were this close
to moving away so they could spend their whole entire life
together, so you'd think she could put him out of her mind
for half a second and pay attention to the person sitting right
there beside her. But you can't ever say anything like that.

After the tater tots came giant bowls of ice cream. Chocolate syrup, Cool Whip, rainbow sprinkles. The blond had been
replaced with something billed as "The Lip Sync Battle for the
Ages," which featured a couple actors who kept smirking at
the camera and the host who'd clearly been powdered down
during the commercials. It didn't look too promising but the

music they chose was a lot of old-school stuff we used to listen to back when we were baby waitresses. Soon we were singing along despite ourselves. Of course as soon as the music ended, she just had to text Wilky. No answer.

"Relax, will you?" I said. "He'll get here when he gets here."

She went and retrieved the bottle of Hershey's and wordlessly topped us off.

It wasn't until around one or so, maybe later, when headlights raked our front window. "Finally," Luce said. She hurried to the door, looked through the peephole, swung back to face me. "It's Nogales."

I stared at her in confusion. Nogales never stopped by, not since the two of us called it quits the year before. "Is he alone?"

"Yeah, but he's in uniform."

Out of habit I gave the room a quick once-over. "Probably heard you were leaving. Wants to say goodbye or something."

"It's just an excuse so he can see you. Want me to give you some privacy?"

"Very funny," I said.

She opened the door and invited him in, smiling in that Luce way of hers, all sweet and friendly as if she'd been hoping Nogales would decide to show up on our doorstep. Behind her, I gave him the finger.

"Irene. Nice to see you too," he said. His voice sounded odd, like he'd tried to swallow something and it had gotten stuck in his windpipe. He coughed a little. "Sorry, I think one of those moths that are always swirling around your porch lamp might have flown in my mouth. Mind if I have a glass of water?"

I met his eyes. "You know where to find it."

"It's okay, I got you," Luce said.

She headed into the kitchen and he moved toward the sofa. At least he didn't try to sit down and instead he stood there, hands jammed in his pockets. Except for the cop outfit, he looked pretty much the same as the last time I'd seen him. Cropped black hair, clean-shaven, friendly paunch on his belly. The kind of guy you're sure you can trust completely until it's way too late. When Luce came back with his water, he drank it with a loud greedy gulping.

"There something you want?" I said at last.

"Actually." He wiped his mouth. "You don't have a cigarette, do you? I could use one."

"She quit ages ago," Luce said. "You remember."

Nogales gave me one of his classic know-it-all looks, like he understood everything about me and then some. "Sure she did."

"All right," I said. "You have a big farewell speech planned for Luce, go ahead and make it. Otherwise, why don't you get back in your little cruiser and be on your way. It's late, we're tired, and no one's in the mood for your special brand of horseshit."

A moment passed between me and Nogales and soon the smug little grin he liked to cart around with him fizzled out altogether. He looked flustered. Scared, even. As if he'd gone from knowing everything on the planet to knowing nothing at all. "Thing is, something happened."

"Okay," Luce said. "What is it."

Nogales turned a funny greenish color.

My stomach flopped over. "Where is he," I said.

In a strangled voice, Nogales managed to say that someone had found Wilky slumped over his steering wheel a little before midnight. He was in the rear lot of his bar, parked next to the dumpster. ODd.

"Oh my god," Luce said, all wheezy.

"They called 911 right?" I said. "Where'd they take him? First Memorial?"

"EMS got there in minutes," said Nogales. "Hit him with Narcan a bunch of times, gave him oxygen."

"Long as they didn't take him to the VA," I said. "So where's he now? Poor guy must be hurting."

Nogales hesitated. Carefully he rested his hand on his stomach. "You don't understand. He didn't make it."

"Oh my god," Luce said again. Her jaw hung slack like it had broken off at the hinges.

I didn't know what to say.

It wasn't unheard of for someone in Anklewood to fall out on a fent press or a hidden hot spot. The way things had been going I'd figured it wouldn't be long before someone we loved went down for the count and never got up. And yet now that it had actually happened, it felt like nothing I'd ever expected. A sucker punch out of nowhere.

"Irene." Nogales's voice drifted over.

"What is it."

He jerked his chin in Luce's direction. "She okay?"

While he got her onto the couch, I ransacked her purse

for her inhaler. Her lips were a scary blue color and her gaze was fixed on a spot somewhere above her—but the worst part was her wheezing had stopped completely. Nothing going in or out. At last I found the thing zipped up in an inside pocket and I hurried over, got it into her mouth, pumped. Though she managed to inhale a tiny bit, no more than a shudder, she wasn't getting anywhere near the air she needed. I've never been someone who buys into all the Higher Power junk they're always pushing in meetings, but you better believe I was praying my face off.

At least Nogales had the brains to radio for assistance and it wasn't long before two paramedics had Luce laid out on a stretcher. While one of them fitted her with an oxygen mask, the other rigged up a spike and slid it into the back of her hand. Ketamine hydrochloride, he said when I asked him.

"As in K?" I said. "She can't. She's sober."

"Reduces anxiety. Helps with bronchodilation." He leveled an insinuating gaze at me. "It actually has a medical use."

It didn't take long for them to get her stabilized, though she was pretty loopy afterward. "It feels like I'm floating," she kept saying over and over. When they informed her she ought to go to the hospital and get checked out further, she nodded yes with a dreamy smile. "Tell Wilky where I am. I don't want him to worry."

Nogales coughed into his fist. "Luce—"

"Of course I will," I said. "I'll text him right this second."

I gave Nogales a warning look to shut up already and after a momentary bit of confusion I found her phone on the couch right where she'd left it. I typed out a message to a dead man and hit send. I turned to Luce. "It's going to be okay. Just promise me you'll keep breathing."

She slid a nervous glance at the oxygen tank looming behind her, like she thought it was some kind of robot assassin sent to finish her off altogether, and then she looked at me all walleyed and hazy. I wanted to ask the paramedics if this was normal or should I be worried, but one of them was bent over a clipboard of paperwork, chewing her lip in annoyance, and the other was yawning and rubbing his eyes with his knuckles as if this was just another call in an endless line of calls that night, week, year. Maybe they'd been the ones who'd tried to save Wilky. Once again my stomach curdled.

When I turned back to Luce, her face wobbled in panic.

"Hey," I said. "You had a tiny asthma attack, nothing serious. Probably didn't even need to call anyone, but I wanted to play it safe. You know who I am, don't you?"

"Irene," she said, swallowing.

"Exactly. Your best friend. You're going to be fine, I promise."

A moment passed and she nodded in agreement. She stole another look at the oxygen tank. Then she struggled up on her elbows, motioning me closer, and all at once I sensed she was about to confide a powerful secret. Something she hadn't told Wilky, something important, and already I could hear her saying how she'd never wanted to leave me in the first place, that the whole Florida thing had been Wilky's idea top to bottom and from this point on the two of us were going to stay here together, for as long as we wanted.

"It's okay," I said, trying to keep my voice steady. I didn't want to sound too eager. I leaned over the rails of her stretcher and smoothed her hair out of her face. "You can tell me anything. Always."

She gazed up at me with all the old wonder. "It feels like I'm floating," she said.

I FIRST MET LUCE TWO AND A HALF YEARS EARLIER at a shady little pool hall on the far side of the mountain. She worked the day shift from noon to seven and I came in at seven and stayed till one. All we did was ferry drinks from the bar to the tables. If the crowd wasn't spending enough we'd put out little saucers of peanuts to make everyone thirsty and if someone was getting too ripped and starting to make trouble we just had to signal the bartender and boom, they were cut off. It's not like the customers couldn't have walked a couple extra steps and ordered their own beer or liquor, but the owner—a well-muscled brute of a woman with knuckle tattoos that read YOUR NEXT—had decided the place could do with some decoration of the female kind.

Everything was under the table. No hourly wages, no paychecks, not even a time clock to keep track of our comings and goings. After tipping out the bartender, Luce and I got to keep whatever else we could wring out of the customers, tax-free. I'd just turned nineteen and before that I'd run the register at a horrible little convenience mart out by the highway that paid minimum wage and stank of boiled hot dogs. I wouldn't say my new job was any kind of spiritual experience, far from it, but the first night I strolled out of that pool hall with a hundred dollars cash in my pocket, it felt like I'd encountered the mysterious workings of some minor god.

Of course Luce and I weren't paid for anything so easy as bringing alcohol to alcoholics. The way I saw it, we did that part of the job for free and putting up with the rest was what earned us our money. A guy trying to cup your butt when you had a tray in one hand and a beer in the other. His buddy grazing up against your backside while you waited for the bartender to finish making your drinks. The owner, Kaycee, who could lift a full keg over her head like it was nothing, flashed her knuckles at anyone you asked her to—but I tried not to ask if it wasn't important. If I caused too much trouble she might decide to hire someone more accommodating and then I'd have to go talk the Quik Chek manager into giving me my old job back. He'd do it, sure, but it wouldn't come easy. At least at the pool hall, the perverts tipped.

I didn't know Luce yet. She'd grown up north of Anklewood, in a tiny unincorporated town called Ribbins. For the first week or so we just passed each other in the restroom during our shift change and gave each other careful smiles of assessment. While I shimmied into my denim shorts and tank top—the closest thing we had to a uniform—she tallied her cash on the bathroom countertop, tucking some into a well-worn Hello Kitty wallet and hiding the rest in the back of an eye shadow palette, the kind that lets you pop out the bottom to change shades or add refills. "In case my mom tries to help herself to my tip money," she said.

At the time I felt sorry for Luce. Not only did she look a bit on the delicate side, it was clear that days didn't pay near as good as nights did. Pair that with a mother who'd steal from her own daughter and she had it way worse than me. Not that my life was perfect. The motel I'd had to move into a couple months prior wasn't the Mountain Paradise its name promised, and my car, a battered green Plymouth I'd inherited from my father, had begun letting out evil clouds of white smoke every time I hit the gas. Then again, working days meant Luce didn't have to tolerate all the crap the p.m. freak show dished out on a nightly basis. Fair's fair, I told myself.

One evening I came rushing into work, almost half an hour late thanks to my car overheating while trying to chug up the mountain in August. By the time it cooled off enough for me to make it to the pool hall, the room was swarming with customers. No sign of Luce anywhere. I hurried into the restroom to change as fast as possible, hoping Kaycee hadn't noticed that no one was on the floor taking orders—and walked in on Luce and a guy. He had her up against the wall next to the towel dispenser, shoving his tongue in her mouth and dry-humping her pelvis. My first thought was I'd barged in on a private encounter. I'd once invited someone I'd been seeing into the Quik Chek bathroom and although our little get-together hadn't exactly been worth repeating, maybe Luce was into that kind of action. I started to back out, murmuring an apology. Seconds later, Luce up and elbowed the dude in the throat. She must have nailed him right in his Adam's apple because he began choking and gurgling, making all sorts of ugly noises. Luce wasn't breathing so well either but she managed to grab hold of my wrist and yank me out of the restroom.

"Mother . . . fucker," she said between gasps.

With me close behind she went straight to the bar where

Kaycee sat huddled up with the bartender, a man who—despite possessing a giant horseshoe mustache and elaborate skull tattoos that ran from his wrists up past his biceps—went by Alice. Alice turned and looked us over.

"Ladies," he said. "You okay?"

"This . . . guy . . ." said Luce. She jabbed her thumb at the restroom behind us.

She was having a hard time getting the words out, so I took over. "Scrawny white dude. Rattail. Jean jacket. I saw the whole thing. He's little enough we could hold him ourselves till the cops get here."

"Cops." Kaycee swiveled around on her barstool. "You're kidding."

Luce stared at her for a long moment. "You're right. Forget it."

"For real?" I said. I couldn't believe it.

Kaycee shot me a look so fierce I took a step backward.

"It's okay, I get it," Luce said. She aimed a weak smile in my direction. "Seriously, it's no big deal." She went behind the bar, got her pink backpack, exchanged a few words with Alice. He gave her an encouraging clap on the shoulder and went back to polishing glasses.

Before I could say anything else, she was gone.

My shift that night wasn't what you'd call pleasant. For starters, Kaycee didn't even bother to 86 Rattail and he ended up camping out at the bar for hours, nursing a whiskey and chewing a toothpick, trying to chat up any fool who had the misfortune to sit down beside him. Every so often he would rub his throat and wince, which I admit gave me a twinge of pleasure, and yet whenever I glimpsed that scraggly little braid snaking down the back of his jacket, my insides knotted up in disgust. At one point he looked straight at me and licked his lips, leaving behind a repulsive film of saliva. Then when it looked like he was finally getting ready to leave, Alice had to go and put another drink in front of him. "On the house," he said, smiling.

Fuck these fucking guys, I thought.

It wasn't until last call that Rattail finally hauled himself off his stool, swaying like he'd slurped down a whole handle of Old Crow instead of a few measly ounces. He left a crumple of bills on the bar and gave Alice a parting finger gun.

"Race it home," Alice called after him.

Rattail didn't even bother to look back.

After work, I walked alone to my car, half sick with fury. Now that my mom had gone and moved to Winston to live with her sister, I no longer had any reason to stay in Ankle- wood. If I could hang on for a few more months I'd have enough money to fix my car and get out of this place alto- gether. One good thing about serving, I'd come to realize, is someone somewhere is always hiring. After you've got a little experience behind you, you can pretty much find a job wher- ever you want. I was debating the merits of Charlotte and At- lanta when a figure stepped out of the shadows.

"What the shit?" I said, jumping backward.

"Relax. It's me."

It was Luce. Instead of the pink halter top and white cutoffs she'd worn earlier, she had on a black Metallica T-shirt, black jeans, black sneakers. Her hair, a short blond do she typically gelled into submission, was sticking up in angry-looking spikes.

"Can you give me a hand with something?" She motioned toward a dinged-up Impala she said belonged to her grandmother.

I told her I'd always had terrible luck with cars and she should probably get Alice to take a look at it. "He's counting the drawer. Should be done in a few minutes."

"It's not my car I need help with. Besides, Alice already did me a favor." She aimed a key-chain flashlight through the driver's-side window.

Stretched across the back seat was Rattail, out cold.

Soon all three of us were speeding toward the other side of the mountain. Trees roared past us, wild and distorted. The night sky hung low and had a faint rubbery odor as if we'd gotten trapped under a giant tarp. After an awkward minute of silence, Luce turned up the volume on a mix CD full of thrash metal. While she howled along with the lyrics I alternated between looking back to see if Rattail was awake yet and fixing my eyes on the road ahead in an effort to not get carsick, an embarrassing habit leftover from childhood.

Where was Luce going? When she first asked if I wouldn't mind giving her a hand for a quick half hour, I'd agreed right away, glad to get whatever revenge we could on that scumbag. But already the initial buzz of adrenaline had faded and in its place was a vague queasy sensation—the kind I always got when something was about to go sideways. Luce glanced at me. "Don't worry. It's not like we're going to kill him," she shouted over the music.

It didn't exactly ease my mind.

We passed the discount mart where my mom used to pull her returned-merchandise scams until they caught on to her. The old Revco where we'd once filled my father's heart med prescriptions before it went out of business, which was now E-Z Title Pawn and Payday Loans. After that came a string of boarded-up buildings, including the piano store where I'd taken weekly music lessons when I was little, the J & L Cafeteria where we used to eat after church service on Sundays, and the KinderCare I'd attended back when my parents were both full-time loomers—back before the Ankle brothers shuttered the mill without notice, raided the health insurance fund, and skedaddled to Mexico, a move that almost destroyed Anklewood altogether. Slowly all these places fell away behind us, growing smaller and smaller until at last I could no longer see them. Swallowing hard, I glanced at Rattail. He was still asleep, his knees curled up into his stomach, breathing through his mouth like a little kid.

We turned onto Old Road, which wasn't much more than a pitiful thread of tar that wound around in a senseless maze before finally joining up with the highway. No lights anywhere, not even an old mercury streetlamp or a bare bulb at a gas station. We drove past a dead raccoon lying belly-up on the shoulder, his tiny hands spread wide as if he'd been trying to fend off disaster. We passed a weathered cross with depressing plastic flowers wired to the wood. At one point we tore around a curve and almost rear-ended a shuddering brown hatchback going about two miles an hour. Luce leaned on her horn as we skidded around it. "Sleep with one eye open!" she shouted.

Rattail let out a groan of complaint and rolled over.

"Yeah fuck you too," Luce said.

At last we turned onto 109, heading north toward the Piedmont. If we kept going in this direction long enough, we'd eventually get to Winston where my mom was living. She hadn't handled my dad's passing as well as she could have and it was probably healthier for her to be with her sister instead of stranded up on our broken-down mountain with no one around to talk to but me. Even so, I missed her like crazy and as Luce and I raced toward the foothills I found myself pretending I was going to visit. I'd take her out to one of those breakfast buffets she loved, the kind where you could get custom-built omelets and boiling hot coffee and orange juice they squeezed fresh into a glass right when you ordered it. Afterward I'd take her to her noon meeting and clap louder than anyone if she shared her story. Maybe later we'd roam through the dizzying aisles of plants at Lowe's nursery and plan out all the flowers we'd have when we finally got our own house and garden, the way we used to do. And when I had to leave and come back to Anklewood, my mom would ask if I would please bring her home with me, saying she'd made a huge mistake and couldn't stand living apart from me a second longer. Of course, I'd say.

So when Luce took the next exit into Ribbins instead of keeping on to Winston, the old anger and disappointment needled into me like a poison. I scrunched deeper into my seat, wishing I'd never agreed to help out with whatever stupid payback Luce thought we were going to get from old Rattail.

Anyone with half a brain knew payback never worked out the way you wanted it to.

We followed an unmarked service road for several miles until at last we reached a turnoff. "Are we almost there yet?" I said. I knew it sounded childish but I couldn't help it.

Luce turned down the volume. "We're going in the back way. Might want to roll up your window."

Moments later we were trundling down a skinny dirt lane while clouds of pink dust billowed around us. It was impossible to see beyond the reach of the headlights and though I'd cranked up my window as fast as possible, the mineral taste of red dirt filled my mouth and throat. At one point, we hit a monster pothole that leaped out at the last second. The impact must have knocked the muffler loose, because after that it sounded like we were dragging a metal body behind us. Luce let out a curse, low and guttural.

Last thing we needed was to get stranded here.

When a white mailbox blasted into view, Luce braked hard and flicked off her headlights. She turned into a gravel driveway, killed the engine. As the dust settled around us, a house materialized in the distance. Beyond that, a dark, shimmering lake. I didn't know anything as civilized as a lake existed in the area since all we had in Anklewood was a bunch of helter-skelter creeks with razor-sharp rocks at the bottom. And my god, the house! Picture a huge white beast of a mansion, with gothic columns, rippling glass windows, multiple chimneys, and a lone attic porthole that peered out at the world like a giant demon eye. The wraparound porch sagged with expensive outdoor furniture that was far nicer than anything my family ever had inside and was surrounded by thick hedges of Queen Anne roses—the kind my mother longed for. Even from the car I could smell their rich, drunken odor.

"You know where we are?" said Luce.

I shook my head in confusion.

She nodded at Rattail, who was still snoring bubbles. "Meet Ronnie Ankle," she said.

We worked fast. Luce grabbed his wrists, I held Ronnie Ankle's ankles, and together we lugged him up the driveway. We laid him in the grass as gently as possible. Luce eased off his socks and sneakers, his acid-washed jacket. Off came his T-shirt and belt. It wasn't long before he began to whimper in his sleep, as though some part of him understood just what we were up to and by the time we managed to relieve him of his jeans and underwear my back was slick with perspiration for fear he was going to wake up and see us. While Luce went through his pockets, I kept a close eye on him. His junk looked so soft and helpless lying there in its nest of fur.

It wasn't until Luce let out a low whistle that I glanced up. She opened her hand, revealing what appeared to be little more than a hunk of plastic, and pushed a button.

The blade of a tactical knife sprang out at us. We stared at it, unmoving.

"Help me get him onto his stomach," Luce said.

Together we rolled him over, exposing his sad white buttocks. My chest thumped and thumped. Luce leaned down and spoke into Ronnie Ankle's ear. "Don't worry, sweetheart, you won't hardly feel it."

"Hold on," I whispered. "You're not going to hurt him, are you?"

She gave me a chilling smile. "Watch."

With an artful stroke, she sliced off his rattail. Unable to help myself, I busted out laughing. Old Ronnie Ankle didn't even flinch. Only when Luce held the braid up in the air like a trophy did he roll over on his side and protectively hug his knees to his chest.

As for Luce, she collapsed the knife and tucked it into her back pocket, along with his car keys and a tin of breath mints. After motioning for me to gather his clothing, she crumpled the money she'd found in his wallet all around him as if it were payment for services rendered and flung his nasty little rattail into the Queen Annes. She leaned over and gave him a parting smack on the bottom. "Next time it'll be way worse."

We sped back toward Anklewood, her mix CD blaring, our spirits higher than ever. Now we were both singing and banging the dashboard in time to the music. We tossed Ronnie Ankle's clothes into the dark, piece by piece. Nothing could get to us, not the choking clouds of pink dust, not the potholes springing out at us from nowhere, not the old scenes from childhood rising up like goblins. Even when the Impala's muffler fell off with a noisy clatter, Luce simply put the car in reverse, zoomed back toward it, and tossed it in her trunk to be soldered on later.

Only then did it strike me that—for the first time in a long while—I was happy. Or no, not happy. Not exactly. It was more like Luce had introduced me to my own mysterious power. The kind nobody else had ever thought to look for in me. She got in the car, hit the gas, and as the two of us rocketed into the distance, I sank back into my seat and let its intoxicating warmth ripple all through my bloodstream.

By the time we reached the pool hall, the cicadas that had been screaming earlier had downshifted to a husky rattle. The damp air quivered around us, jellylike. Luce parked, cut the engine, and set about emptying her pockets of Ronnie Ankle's possessions. The knife she hid in the Impala's glove box. The keys she bounced gently in her hand, as if weighing their possibilities, before sliding them back into the rear of her jeans. She popped open his tin of breath mints. "Fucking A. I knew it."

"What?"

Eyes gleaming, she held the tin out.

At the time I had no idea what I was looking at, but inside was what turned out to be a dozen or so 30s. Carolina blue with a sturdy little *M* stamped on top.

"Cool," I said, trying to hide my confusion.

"Here, give me your hand." She shook half the pills into my palm and glanced at me. All at once her face went soft in a funny way I couldn't decipher. A look of tenderness, I decided. "It's okay, we deserve it," she said.

I peered down at the jumbled blue tablets. They really did look about as harmless as breath mints, and yet even I knew I was at the edge of a strange, enchanted forest. The kind of place kids thrill to in late-night stories, spooky with magic—or at least that's how I would have described it back in those days. That night, when I met Luce's eyes in the dim of her beat-up Impala, an old metal ballad playing low-key in the background, the stink of our armpits rising into the air, I sensed she understood me better than anyone, including my own mother. A long moment passed between us. Together we walked into those woods.

I RODE WITH LUCE IN THE BACK OF THE AMBULANCE. The paramedic in charge of the ventilator, a dark-haired rockabilly type who kept thumbing her phone instead of watching the numbers, refused to acknowledge my questions no matter how nicely I asked if Luce was going to be okay and if she was in any real danger. Meanwhile Luce was winking and nodding at the oxygen tank that hummed alongside her as if they'd worked out their earlier disagreement and were now involved in some sort of private romance. When I tried to interrupt them, she cut her eyes at me in a way that suggested I ought to mind my own business. At last I gave up and focused my gaze on the back window. It being nighttime, you couldn't see out of course, but I kept my face as still as possible and pretended otherwise.

We pulled into the hospital parking lot and they hurried Luce through a side entrance I'd never noticed in all the times I'd visited. The moon had vanished, leaving nothing but a powdery blue smear across the horizon and a few scraps of light way down in the valley. I hung back for a bit, saying I was going to make a few calls, get in touch with Luce's family, but the truth was I needed to try and get my mind right. Already the snow was crusting up something fierce and once the paramedics left I crunched my way toward the rear of the hospital where I could think stuff through a little. I leaned on the guardrail and tried to pick out the house Luce and I shared

down below. We'd been burglarized a year or so earlier and
ever since she'd insisted we keep the porch lamp on all night
to warn off intruders. But I must have gotten turned around
on the ride up the mountain, what with all the curves and
switchbacks, because I couldn't find where we lived.

When the cold got too much I went inside to hit up the
front desk for info. It took some doing, but at last I learned
they planned to do a full workup and keep Luce till the end of
the day, maybe longer.

"Really?" I did my best not to sound alarmed. "How bad
off is she exactly?"

The receptionist and his big square head didn't even bother
to glance up from his paperwork. "Too early to say. Go home,
get some sleep. Someone will call you."

His dismissive tone made my bp spike even higher. You
could tell he was hiding something. Something a best friend
ought to know. As calm as I could, I leaned over the counter.
"Hey buddy. I'm not leaving till you give me some actual
answers."

The receptionist looked up from his clipboard. "That
right?" He picked up the phone, pushed a button.

When the buzz of the automatic door sounded behind me,
I turned around expecting to see one of those juiced-up overnight techs striding over—the kind they hire for hospital security and unruly patients. You can almost hear the Vitamin
S rattling around in their pockets.

"That was fast," the receptionist said.

But it wasn't a juicer—it was Nogales, still wearing his stupid police outfit. He wiped his boots on the mat and scanned

the lobby. When he spotted me by the desk, he took a deep breath and motioned me over.

Reluctantly I made my way toward him. We were alone in the waiting area, but Nogales still went and sat on a row of molded plastic chairs way off in the corner like he thought the two of us were going to get cozy.

I took the chair on the far end.

"So," he said. "How's she doing."

"Couldn't be better. Bombed out of her mind, stuck in the hospital. Boyfriend's in the morgue, toe-tagged and cooling."

He held my gaze. "I'm sorry."

We sat there not speaking for a good bit.

At last Nogales appeared to shake off some invisible burden pressing down on his shoulders. He straightened up, ran his fingers through his hair. "Listen, can I ask you a question?"

"As a cop?"

"As a friend. I'm off duty."

"Then no," I said. "We're not friends. Never will be."

He held up his hands. "Okay, so we'll keep it official."

"Great. You got a warrant?"

"Irene," he said. "I came here to check on you and Luce, maybe learn a little something about Wilky's family. We've got to notify them, you know. I'd be talking to Luce if she was up to it."

An electronic honking started up at the far end of the hallway. It sounded urgent, like someone had gone into cardiac arrest or stopped breathing, and for one terrible moment I was convinced it was coming from Luce's room. Then I remembered ICU was on the ground level, maternity was on second, so she'd be on the third floor most likely. Even so, when a nurse in blue scrubs strode out of a room and around a corner, it took a great deal of restraint to keep from hurrying after him. At last the honks stopped and all that was left was the evil buzz of fluorescent lighting. Like someone was drilling a hole through my skull and into the soft parts.

With effort, I turned to Nogales. "Fine. Ask away."

But once I agreed to talk, he turned strangely quiet. There seemed to be some unpleasant question on his mind and he was trying to dig out the courage to ask it. Or no—it was more like he'd already asked the question and it was the answer itself that kept tripping him up.

Then he caught sight of the vending machine next to the restrooms, the one that sold little containers of sludge marketed as coffee. "I know. What do you say we perk ourselves up with a cup? My treat. We could use it."

Sometimes he was so pathetic you almost had to feel sorry for him.

"Why not," I said.

I should have known better. Nogales was so careful about feeding coins into the slot and selecting the proper buttons you'd have thought he was trying to deactivate a bomb in the building. While we waited for the coffee to pour, he launched into this ridiculous lecture on the history of vending machines. Something about them being invented by Egyptians back during the Jesus era and how if you put in a shekel and pulled a lever, you'd get a few ounces of holy water. When he handed me my drink, he acted like he was presenting me with a sacred treasure.

I glanced into the cup. "Yeah, I don't like that much milk. Upsets my system."

Nogales's face went slack. "Really? You used to. Okay, hold on, let me get you another."

But the thought of dragging things out with him any longer made my insides feel hot and stabby. I held the cup away so he couldn't reach it. "Never mind, it'll do."

Manny Nogales and I had our own history. The short version is the two of us used to see each other sometimes, back before Luce and I quit using. I even liked him for a while there, which for me is kind of unusual. I don't get along with just anyone. Then one night something happened and thanks to him, everything blew up in our faces. Basically he had a choice between acting like a friend or acting like law enforcement— and guess which one he chose.

And though Luce and I managed to squeak by without any jail time, not counting the overnight, we still got our licenses suspended, big fines, and a couple hundred hours picking up trash on the highway. Meanwhile Nogales had the nerve to try and apologize. Texts, calls, notes left in our mailbox. Even showed up at the restaurant one night during the rush, holding a cone of flowers wrapped in brown paper and wanting to know if he could pick me up after work so we could talk things over. Just seeing him there at the hostess stand, chatting up customers and waving roses around like a real prince charming, made me break out in angry welts. I turned my tables over to Luce and told our manager at the time, a pro-level fuckhead in his own right, that I had to clock out early due to a family emergency. In the moment he didn't give me any hassle, but when the next schedule got posted he'd bumped me down to lunches, a move that pretty much halved my income. It took me over a month to get back on dinners, and only after I hooked him up with a half sheet of 10s.

I decided to get Nogales's questions over with fast as possible. I told him Wilky was from High Point, or was it Greensboro maybe, and he'd earned a degree in business at UNCG before hooking up with the army. "Of course we all remember how that ended."

"Which wasn't my fault," said Nogales. "You know that."

"And afterward he decided it was time to get clean. Meetings every day. Twice even sometimes." I hesitated. "Between us, I thought he'd be the last one of our group to slip."

Nogales asked if I knew how to get in touch with Wilky's family.

"You're going to have talk to Luce. I'm pretty sure his parents are still around, but beyond that who knows. They cut him off after his Big Chicken Dinner."

"All right then, let's check if she's awake." He stood and held his hand out.

"Yeah, I tried already. They're not letting anyone see her."

"That right?" There was that smug little smile again.

I followed Nogales back to the front desk. He propped his elbows right on the counter and informed the square-headed receptionist we needed to talk to Luce. "Should we find her room ourselves or you want to escort us?"

Now the receptionist was all polite and attentive. "I'm sorry, officer, but my supervisor said no visitors. The patient is supposed to be resting."

"If she's asleep, we won't wake her," said Nogales. "But I know that supervisor of yours doesn't want to mess around with law enforcement any more than she has to. If you want I could talk to her directly."

The squarehead's mouth formed a hard line of anger. "Third floor. First room on the left when you get off the elevator."

Nogales looked at me as if to say, See that wasn't so hard.

When we finally found Luce's room—we should have turned right—she was so pale and quiet my first thought was to rush over and lay my head on her chest to make sure she was still ticking. There wasn't any machine keeping track of her oxygen or even a nurse clogging around in the hallway. The air smelled faintly of potted lilies, which set off a bunch of unhappy memories from the Anklewood funeral home. I was this close to sticking my head out the door and yelling for a doctor when Luce rolled over. Her lungs made that faint scraping noise that always sounded so painful. For once, I was glad.

And yet as I watched her breathe, all nice and regular, I couldn't shake the sense that she was still floating around in that dangerous realm between here and nowhere. The news about Wilky had sent her reeling in a way I hadn't expected, as if some vital cord that kept her tied to earth had snapped. Once again I felt dizzy and soon little spots of light began swirling around me—like I too was drifting alone in the ether.

"I knew it," Nogales said from somewhere behind me.

I turned back to face him. There had been a time when I thought maybe the two of us had a future, but now anyone could see that a million miles had sprung up between me and Nogales. No way we'd get past it, no matter what happened. Not even if we wanted to. There are some things from which you can't ever recover.

"Knew what?" I said.

Nogales studied me for a long moment. "Nothing. Just that visiting your girl would cheer you up. See? She's getting some rest. No reason to worry."

When I didn't say anything to that, he came over and rested a hand on my shoulder. I couldn't decide if there was something comforting about this gesture or if it felt like the work of a self-righteous blowhard who thought he understood far better than you did how to live your dumb sad life. I stared up at him, trying to will the pathetic lump of muscle that lived in my chest into submission.

"Irene," he said.

"What is it."

"How about we get you home."

B Y THE TIME WE GOT BACK TO ME AND LUCE'S, THE temperature had sunk so much that a lace of frost covered our front windows. The paramedics' footprints had frozen themselves into the snow, an ugly reminder, and even from inside the patrol car you could see a slick of ice lying in wait on the porch steps. Despite the blast of the Crown Vic's heater I couldn't stop shivering.

"You okay?" Nogales said.

"I'm fine," I said, struggling with the seat belt. "What idiot designed this thing anyway?"

He leaned over and released me with the push of a button. "There. Now I want you to go inside and get some sleep already. She'll be home before you know it."

For the briefest of moments, I considered asking him to keep me company until I calmed down a little. Despite his many faults, Nogales was someone you could count on in the worst situations and the idea of being alone in that house was making me feel weirdly off-balance. Then again, being alone with Nogales was another kind of problem. A bigger one maybe.

He gave me a hopeful smile. "I'll keep my phone on in case you need something."

"You do that," I said, climbing out of the car.

But inside, the house was so cold and quiet that it wasn't long before I regretted not asking Nogales if he wanted to join me for a quick mug of hot chocolate or something. I turned on the TV thinking that would be a decent distraction, but the only thing showing at four in the morning was an old black-and-white sitcom with a bunch of creepy mechanical laughter. I turned it off, went into the kitchen, and ate some of the gummy vitamins Luce was always pushing. They didn't do what I wanted, not by a long shot, but after a couple minutes my nerves began to settle. I breathed in and out, the way Luce had taught me to do. Then I glimpsed the photo of her and Wilky on the fridge and the room tilted hard on its axis. I had to grab the counter to keep from falling.

Not today, I told myself.

Once the kitchen's seesawing slowed down a little, I made my way back into the main room, lay on the couch, and curled up with Luce's afghan. She'd crocheted it last spring, back when we first quit using. The granny squares kept sliding all over but it wasn't so bad if I focused my gaze on the ceiling. I thought of what they always said in the rooms: stay busy, stay out of trouble. I wasn't any kind of crocheter, but I could at least make a mental to-do list. First up, cancel Luce's U-Haul. Next, call our manager at work, let him know she wasn't going anywhere and tell him to put her back on the schedule. Remind him to delete the help-wanted ad on Craigslist. Hit up the landlord in Florida and get him to refund her first month's rent and deposit, and then unpack her stuff, put her clothes back in her closet, and fix up her bedroom the way she liked it. As if none of this had ever happened at all. Somehow this made me feel better and it wasn't long before the granny squares settled into place and the walls stopped moving and even the stabby feeling I'd had since the hospital eased up into a few half-hearted twists and pinches. I pulled Luce's afghan tighter around me. If you closed your eyes and concentrated, you could smell her strawberry-kiwi shampoo.

Next thing I knew sunlight was burning holes in the windows. The clock over the TV said it was almost one. After scrambling around for my phone in a panic I called First Memorial to see how Luce was doing. Endless ringing and at last someone answered. As calmly as I could I explained why I was calling. "No news so far," a cheery voice said. When I asked if I could talk to her, I was told I'd be transferred. An abrupt click followed and the phone let out another maddening series of rings that went on and on forever until in a fit of anger I hung up.

After that I roamed around the house, jittery and restless. I needed to find someone who could give me a ride to the hospital, but ever since our licenses got suspended Wilky had always been the one to drive Luce and me around when we needed it. The thought of asking anyone else made my insides fill up with acid. Not to mention Nogales was the only one I could think of to call. I ate a few handfuls of Froot Loops out of the box, which helped a little, and then I went and stared into Luce's empty bedroom. That didn't work the way I hoped it would.

I was sitting on her bed, this close to texting Nogales, when the front door whined open. "Hello?" I said. "Anyone there?" No one answered, so I called out again, louder this time.

The only response was the door clicking shut.

I was positive I'd set the dead bolt, but after everything

that had happened it wasn't like I could trust myself exactly. The thud of footsteps made their way closer. They hesitated outside my bedroom before continuing down the hallway. My chest pumping gallons, I glanced around for some sort of weapon but everything in Luce's room was packed except her bedding. When her door swung open, I made a grab for her pillow and stupidly held it over my stomach.

It was Luce, wearing earbuds. Her face was blotched and raw as if she'd just finished crying and her breath came in unsteady wheezes. Clearly she'd remembered about Wilky's OD. She hit pause on her phone and looked me over. "What are you doing in here?"

I said I wasn't doing anything, just fixing up her bed so she'd be comfortable. "Okay, so what happened? What did the doctor say?"

"Who gives a shit," she said.

She went to her closet, which had nothing left but a few plastic hangers, and gazed inside with a puzzled expression. All she had on was her T-shirt and sweats from the night before and a pair of disposable hospital slippers. I asked if she wanted to borrow some of my clothes until we unpacked her boxes. Without answering she swung around and headed back into the main room. I caught up with her in time to see her grab her parka off the sofa.

"Where are you going?" I said. "You just got here."

"If I'm going to make the 1:30, I have to leave right this second." She zipped up her coat. "You don't have to come if you don't want to."

I reminded her she'd just gotten out of the hospital and she was supposed to be resting. "And how'd you get here anyway? No way you walked it. Not in paper booties."

She frowned at her feet as if trying to remember. "Teena." She went to the pile of shoes by the front window, sat on the floor, and began switching the booties for sneakers.

Once again I got that same seasick feeling, like the ground was bucking and heaving beneath me. As discreetly as possible, I reached out and steadied myself on the wall.

Teena was our former dgirl and a serious grade-A hustler. The kind of person who would have talked the Virgin Mary into using if she thought it would make her a few dollars, and a real celebrity in certain Anklewood circles. You can't help admiring high-level talent like that. When Luce and I got clean, we had to cut her out of our lives completely.

"Oh yeah?" I said. "How's old Teena doing?"

Luce stood up and put on her sunglasses, a huge plasticky green pair that gave her an alien appearance. "She didn't give me anything, if that's what you're asking. She just happened to be the first person that texted back. Look, I'm going to lose my shit if I don't make this meeting. You coming or what?"

"I already said I was," I said.

We headed toward the church at the base of the mountain. Every so often Luce would pull a tissue from her coat and dab up under her giant sunglasses, but the rest of the time she kept her head down, her hands in her pockets. I tried a few different lines of conversation, but she either gave me brisk one-word responses or ignored me completely and at last I fell silent.

Luce and I had been attending twelve-step meetings in the basement of the United Methodist church since the previous February. We were a few short weeks away from getting our one-year tags. We already had the yellow nine-month ones of course, but the year ones were something special. They were glow-in-the-dark for starters, which even the most hard-hearted among us thought was pretty nifty, but it went beyond that. I don't know, maybe not using for 365 days in a row doesn't sound like much of an achievement to most people, but it wasn't so long ago that the idea of putting any real clean time together had been unimaginable to me and Luce. We'd even picked out the outfits we were going to wear when we accepted our tags and grocery store sheet cake. Hers was a vintage Metallica T-shirt she bought off eBay, which she planned to pair with an electric-pink skirt she'd made from a bolt of velvet she found on the sale table at Sew Happy Fabrics. Mine was just a stupid flowered shift dress my mom had left in her closet way back when. It wasn't very flattering and it sure wasn't stylish, but I guess it reminded me of her or something. Like in some small way she would be there with me.

We got to the church, went downstairs, and pushed through the double doors and into the fluorescent light of the basement. Folks were still milling around the ancient percolator in the corner, loading up their little Styrofoam cups of coffee with sugar and powdered creamer. There was the familiar buzz of conversation, punctured every so often by a squawk of laughter, and soon our sponsor, a bosomy old-timer named Greenie, caught sight of us. She lumbered over from the circle of folding chairs and gave us each a crushing hug.

"Called the second I heard but it kept going to voice mail.

I still can't hardly believe it." She took a step back, looked us over. "How you girls holding up?"

Luce gave a weird little shrug and adjusted her sunglasses.

"All right I guess," I said. "It came out of nowhere."

Greenie nodded. "Just yesterday he was right here in this room. Exchanging numbers with everyone, saying he'd be back up to visit come springtime."

Luce lowered her head, got out her tissue.

Greenie ran her eyes over me again. I got the sense she wanted to ask me something, but she must have thought better of it what with Luce standing right there beside us. "Let's talk after," she said, holding my gaze. She gave Luce's shoulder a regretful squeeze and headed back toward the circle, where she made a big production out of easing herself into the saggy yellow armchair she always sat in at meetings: her signal that it was time to get started.

A former supervisor at the mill, Greenie had run the 1:30 for as long as Luce and I had been attending. She'd also been in the game since before we were born, as she liked to remind us, and she was the only person I'd ever met who had a twenty-year medallion, which was no joke. As a result, she had the uncanny ability to sniff out bs when it came to addicts. It was a talent that had saved most everyone at our meeting at least once, me and Luce included, and if you were even starting to think about using, you could pretty much count on one of Greenie's trademark visits—the kind that would whack some sense into you with all the subtlety of a tire iron. Naturally we loved her for it right up until the point we tried to put something over on her and then it was a gift we could have done without.

Greenie started things off with the Serenity Prayer, followed by a moment of silence for Wilky's passing. "He was
a regular in the rooms and like all of us he had his ups and
downs, his struggles. I think we can probably also agree that
he had one of the biggest hearts of about anyone who ever
walked through these doors. You're not alone if you're having
some thoughts you don't want to be having. Just remember,
one day at a time. Let go, let god."

I glanced at Luce to see how she was doing. She was still
wearing her sunglasses, and what little you could see of her
face was so stiff and drained of color it looked like it had been
molded out of candle wax.

There wasn't a speaker scheduled, so a few volunteers took
turns reading chapters 9 and 10 of the Basic Text aloud, passing the book back and forth between them. "Just for Today—
Living the Program" and "More Will Be Revealed." After
that, people took turns sharing. Carmela talked about getting
dumped by her ex after he caught her going bare with their
dealer to get free product. Boz told about how an infected rig
once gave him an abscess the size of a baseball and brought
him this close to losing his arm. These war stories weren't ever
pretty, but if you could let go of the idea that they were supposed to lead you to some big epiphany, the experience could
be strangely soothing. They'd walked through the burning
forests of hell and not only had they lived to talk about it, they
were mostly doing all right for themselves.

At last the drug-a-logues petered out and the room fell silent. Greenie turned to Luce. "Anyone else feel like sharing?"

Luce didn't move, didn't even seem to notice anyone had

spoken. When I reached for her hand she flinched like she thought I meant to hurt her.

"All right then," said Greenie. "Basket time."

The final part of our meetings involved collecting donations for coffee supplies and acknowledging milestones. While the little wicker basket made its way around the circle, Greenie held up the box of key tags and gave it a shake. By and large this was a formality, since we all knew each other so well that we had everyone's dates pretty much committed to memory, and if one of us had been due to celebrate a birthday, Greenie would have already had a cake set up next to the percolator. "I don't guess anyone needs a new one of these babies?"

Luce gave a start like she'd been jolted back into the present. "Hi, I'm Luce and I'm an addict."

"Hi Luce," said everyone.

"I'll take a Day 1." Her voice caught a little, as if the words had hit a snag somewhere on their exit.

"Come on," I said as quietly as possible. "That K they gave you doesn't count and besides—"

"Yes it fucking *does*." Even with her sunglasses on she was able to give me a look so icy it sent shivers all down my backbone.

The room held itself perfectly still.

At last Greenie pulled herself up out of her chair, made her way over, and handed Luce a Day 1. "Girl, it's okay. You got this. Anyone can do it, you can."

Luce didn't say anything, just tucked the scrap of plastic into her coat pocket. She spent the final minutes of our meeting with her mouth set tight, her hands fisted up beside her.

As soon as the group hug ended, she slung her purse over her shoulder and made straight for the double doors. When Greenie called her name, Luce sped up until she looked like one of those mall speed-walkers and by the time I made it outside, she was already at the end of the driveway, past the church mailbox.

I called out to her to hold up a second. She didn't stop, though she did slow down enough so I could catch up if I hurried. But once I fell in beside her, she refused to talk to me, not even when I asked if she had her inhaler.

"I'm just worried is all," I said. "Last night was scary."

I can't say for certain, but it sounded like she gave me a snort of disgust.

We were almost home when Luce finally broke her silence, saying she needed to ask me a question.

I told her of course, anything she wanted.

She stopped walking and turned to face me. "Were you and him selling again?"

"Jesus," I said. "Are you serious?"

"Well why else would he have that crap? You know how much his recovery meant to him." Her breath came in ragged little puffs that hung briefly in the air before dissolving. "No way he would have been messing around, not unless someone dragged him back into it."

"Luce." I tried to stay calm. "We weren't selling, I promise. We only did that a couple times anyway. He slipped and that's all there is to it."

"Bullshit," she said. "Me and him were this close to getting free of this place. Starting over."

I got out my phone and pushed it at her. "Check my texts. Check my purse, my pockets. Go through my room if you want. And you're right, staying clean meant the world to Wilky. Only thing stronger than him was the disease."

I let that work on her for a bit before continuing. "Listen, I know it's hard to hear this, but moving in with someone is stressful. Starting over is stressful. Getting a new job, leaving home. I'm not saying it was the whole Florida thing that caused this, but we both know Wilky was in a vulnerable place. One slip, his tolerance is down, and it's all over."

She let out a choked little gasp.

For a good half minute we stood there until at last the wind rose up, urging us onward. We turned back to the road, started walking. Luce withdrew her soggy crumple of tissue from her coat. When I looked over, she was crying and you could tell from the way she pressed her hand to her chest that her lungs were on fire. Once again I hated myself.

I told her I was sorry and the last thing I wanted was to upset her.

She shook her head. "I'm the one who's sorry. I know you're not selling. It's just this whole thing has me completely fucked up. The thoughts going through my brain right now? Like back in the old days."

My breath caught in my throat.

"Look," she said. "Can you keep an eye on me for the next week or so? I'm not feeling too strong at the moment."

I tried to tell her she was doing pretty great, considering. "One day at a time, remember?"

"Maybe." Now it was Luce's turn to get out her phone. "But

you better hold on to this just in case. Put it somewhere I won't find it. I'm scared I'll text someone I shouldn't."

I hesitated. "I guess I could. If it'll make you feel better."

She put her phone in my hand and wrapped my fingers around it. "There's only one thing in the world that could make me feel better."

I knew exactly what she meant.

THE FIRST WAVE HIT RIGHT AS WE PULLED INTO the fairgrounds parking lot. Almost three months had passed since the Ronnie Ankle episode and at last Luce and I had our system down: suck off the coating, crush the raw pill between a couple of spoons, parachute the powder on an empty stomach. Instead of having to wait for a controlled release dragged out over twelve hours, we'd get the full dose roaring through us in fifteen minutes, tops. Within the year of course, all the anti-abuse folks would get Purdue to reformulate their product and inject an evil polymer matrix throughout the tablets, making them almost impossible to crush, even in a fancy electric spice grinder. Parachuting didn't speed up anything and if you were foolish enough to try to chop them into little chunks and rail them, you'd end up with a nose full of glue. Sure, you'd be okay if you could get your hands on the old OC 80s, but it wasn't long before dudes were trying to charge a hundred bucks per, which is total lunacy. On principle alone Luce and I refused to pay it, unless we were in dire straits.

But this was back before the world went spinning out of orbit and burned up around us. It was October in the Uwharrie Mountains, the most beautiful place in the world I'd wager, and everywhere you turned there was nothing but toasted golds and reds and soft fuzzy yellows. Luce and I floated out of her car all carefree and happy as if god herself had swept down from the sky and wrapped us in warm velvet blankets. The air was so clean and sweet that even Luce, whose lungs were scarred from a lifetime of improperly treated asthma, was gulping in oxygen like it was free. When a pink sun went rolling by, her face went slack with astonishment.

"Isn't life amazing?" she said.

That year, Luce and I were all kinds of lucky. Although our jobs at the pool hall had gone belly-up when the place lost its liquor license in August, we turned around and got ourselves hired as legit food servers at a chain restaurant that had just opened the next county over. This place was the real deal. Paid training, an official employee handbook, shift meals, our own personal computer codes. If a customer so much as thought about putting his hands on you, you just told the manager on duty and right away they sent one of the male servers to take over your table. There was even a sexual harassment hotline that went straight to corporate in case there was any trouble in-house. While it was true that we only got part-time hours so the company wouldn't have to spring for health insurance or, god forbid, sick leave, the money was decent if you knew how to hustle, and of course Luce and I did.

On occasion we'd pick up odd jobs for extra cash, which was how we found ourselves working the county fair that autumn. The woman who hired us, a middle-aged brunette named Pandora who kept squirting Afrin up her nose all through the interview, assured us the job was a no-brainer.

"You girls are going to have so much fun you probably ought to be paying me," she said. "Just collect the tickets and give them to my partner at the five-thirty shift change. Name's

Paulo. Shaved head, lots of puka shell jewelry. Round as a sphere. Acts tough but he's mostly a nice guy unless you mess with his money. Oh and word to the wise. Don't let him talk you into helping out with his side business."

Luce's eyes snapped into focus. "What kind of side business."

Pandora eased a tissue from the box on her desk and discreetly dabbed at each nostril. "Some sort of import thing I think."

She assigned us to the Buck-a-Dog booth. In exchange for one ticket, which cost a dollar at the front entrance, customers got to throw a little metal token at a bunch of plates that were balanced on the heads of giant plush beagles. If the token landed on a plate and didn't go sliding off into oblivion, they'd win one of the matching dogs that hung from above. It wasn't a completely impossible feat, said Pandora, and in fact it was good if a couple folks won in the morning because they would carry the dog around the fairgrounds all day, which was free advertising.

"But don't let more than a few people win if you can help it. Every so often you're going to want to wash the plates and tokens in this bath oil mixture I keep under the counter so everything stays nice and slippery. And make sure all the stuffed animals that hang overhead are as low as possible so the customers can't get a good arc. I buy the dogs from a discount outfit in Myrtle Beach and you can tell by the way some of them stink they're probably filled with nothing but garbage, but even so they cost real money. Paulo and I need to make some coin on this operation."

"Word," said Luce.

Pandora looked us over. "If you girls don't let go of more than five dogs all day, I'll give you each a quarter per ticket. Otherwise, it's a dime. You think you can do that?"

Luce slid a look at me. I did some quick math in my head. If business was halfway decent, we could probably walk with a hundred bucks each, as long as we didn't have too many winners. I gave Luce a nod of approval and she turned to Pandora.

"We got you," she said.

The day started out great. While I washed all the plates and tokens in a plastic bus tub, marveling at how delightful cold greasy water could feel under the right circumstances, Luce practiced tossing tokens so she could demonstrate how simple the game was to prospective players. Her first throws went sliding all over the place, which at the time felt like the funniest thing ever, but after she took a break to eat some of the watermelon Sour Patch candy we'd brought with us—our favorite snack while partaking—she discovered it was a lot easier if your token was sticky with corn syrup. Add in an old-lady pitch ("Now sir, you're not going to want to do it like this, but I have a messed-up shoulder and granny style is the only way I can throw these suckers") and bingo, she could nail it almost every try. By the time noon rolled around we'd collected almost fifty tickets like it was nothing. Even better, we hadn't forfeited a single dog.

It must have been when our high started to get a little frayed at the edges that it occurred to me to calculate our earnings. Of the two of us, Luce pretty much had all the talent when it came to just about anything, but the one skill I had some sort of natural advantage in was math. I'd even won a couple of competitions at the county level back in high school and there'd been a time when I'd wanted to go away to college and actually do something with it. "My girl's a mathlete," my dad used to tell all his nurses, his face blotchy with pride.

So even though my mental faculties weren't quite up to snuff in that moment, it didn't take long to realize what was happening. "What time is it," I said, looking up from our box of tickets.

"Time?" Luce glanced at me. She was busy chatting up a couple of army guys decked out in head-to-toe camouflage. "I don't know. One? Seven? Four a.m.? Let me guess. You got some big appointment."

The three of them laughed and went back to talking. I remembered I'd stashed my phone in Luce's bag. I got her purse from its hiding place under the counter, checked the clock, did some quick figuring. "Uh, Luce? Can I talk to you for a second?"

She wasn't pleased with the interruption, but she came over. "Dude, what? I'm working these fools. Turns out it's Military Appreciation Day and a whole bunch of them are here from Fort Bragg for some sort of exhibition. If we can get them all to visit our booth, we'll rake in tickets."

"I hope so. Cause at this rate we're barely making three bucks an hour."

She held my gaze for a long moment. Her pupils were tiny black holes that could suck you in if you weren't careful.

"All right," she said. "It's on."

We decided to let the army guys win so they'd spread the

word with their buddies. While I dealt with the rest of the crowd, Luce took Privates Frick and Frack aside and advised them to throw with an underhanded pitch, keeping their arm straight and the disk as flat as possible. When they still couldn't manage it, she gave them her special Sour Patch token to use. It took an embarrassing number of tries, but at last they both stuck the landing.

"Hooah!" said the one with the stupid high-and-tight haircut. "Nailed it."

"Thanks miss," his companion said, turning to Luce. He had the kind of politeness that could only have come from a small-town upbringing. "Couldn't have done it without you."

"Hey, I got you covered. Most of my folks are military." Luce held up the devil horn sign. "Army Strong."

The men headed back to their recruitment booth, the dogs tucked under their arms like war spoils. Sure enough, business started to pop. A few other army guys came by, eager to prove their own talents, but mostly it was regular civilians who'd seen the giant beagles being squired down the midway. The growing crowd around our stall attracted even more customers and soon tickets were flying at us so fast we could barely keep up with demand. It was like those rarest of days at the restaurant when your gears were humming and your blood was singing and people not only slipped giant cash tips into your apron pocket, they waved the manager over to tell him you were the best server they'd ever had. That kind of magic only happened when Luce and I had adjacent sections, which wasn't often since she almost always got the coveted row of booths along the front window and I generally ended up with the wobbly two-tops back by the restrooms. According to our manager I needed an attitude adjustment, but really all I needed was to work next to Luce.

"Yo Rainman!" she said. A sour gummy hit me in the shoulder. "How we looking?"

I did some quick calculations. "Nine forty an hour and climbing."

"Yes!" Luce broke out a few celebratory air guitar licks and sang along. She didn't exactly nail the pitch, but you could tell by the lyrics it was "Master of Puppets."

"Best song ever," a guy said from the sidelines. He opened up his jacket to reveal a faded Metallica T-shirt from the Damage Inc. tour. "Saw them back in the day at the Knoxville Civic."

"No way," Luce said. She went over and inspected the shirt more closely. "Man, whoever drew that skull is a serious genius. Like it's completely gorgeous and also completely scary."

"Check out the back." The man took off his jacket and turned around to show her. Instead of just one yellow-fanged skull staring at you, it was a whole pile of them. "It's the real deal too, not one of those reproductions."

"So tight," Luce said. "Knoxville. Wasn't that one of the shows when Marshall filled in for Hetfield?"

"True true, but it was still awesome. Screamed so much I couldn't talk for a week. Course that was years ago, when my hair was down to here and my knees had cartilage. Now then." He put his jacket back on and gave her a strip of tickets. "Wish me luck. My kid'll go bonkers if I bring her one of these big old dogs next weekend."

"Sure, but hold on a sec." She leaned toward him.

Next thing I knew he was tossing his token like a goddamn nursing home patient. I cleared my throat in a stagy manner.

"What?" Luce gave me a look of annoyance. "He's one of us."

After that we were down three dogs, which meant we only had a couple left before our earnings per ticket sank from a quarter to a dime. I set about rewashing all the plates and tokens in bath oil to make them slippery as possible. It wasn't so fun now that the high was fading. Meanwhile Luce remembered she had a tube of suntan lotion leftover from summer in her purse. After smearing some on her arms she started greeting every customer with a handshake—making sure their fingers got a hefty dose of Coppertone slime.

For the next hour or so, the pace chugged along nicely. Lots of players and no winners. So far, so good. Yes, there was a dip in business once the military parade started, but to our delight the army guys Luce had befriended not only secured their beagles to the roof of their Humvee, they even tied those little U.S. flags-on-a-stick to their paws so it looked like they were waving along in patriotic solidarity. Moments after the show ended, a whole new crush of customers showed up with tickets. Luce slung an arm around me. She smelled like coconuts and orange blossom flowers, but the chemical sunscreen version. "God bless America," she said.

Everything would have been perfect if all the rest of Fort Bragg hadn't decided to pay us a visit. Even that might have been okay—the insanity of lunch rushes had taught Luce and me how to haul butt when necessary—but Private Frick, the high-and-tight one of course, had gone and shared our trade secrets with his buddies in an effort to outdo the Marines and Air Force. Soon all the army guys were winning. We couldn't get the dogs down from their hooks fast enough. It was like one of those waiter nightmares, the kind where you're running around trying to refill coffee with an empty pot that's burned on the bottom and everyone's screaming at you for a to-go box or asking you to make change for a dollar. By the time it was all over, we'd completely run out of beagles.

Luce and I stared in disbelief at our plundered booth.

"Holy shit," she said. "Old Pandora's going to have to hit the slopes hard to recover."

"What are we going to tell Paulo? He's supposed to be here before too much longer."

We both stifled a yawn—the sign that the pills were almost out of our system—and exchanged uneasy glances.

"What's wrong, miss?" a voice behind us said.

We turned to see one of the original army guys eyeing us with concern. Not Private Frick, but the tall one with the small-town manners.

"Well look who it is," said Luce. "Hope you're proud of yourself. Thanks to you fuckers, our boss is going to go apeshit."

His face went still as though he'd been mortally offended— and just like that he turned around and left. No apology or excuse or anything close to it.

"Yeah, suck my dick," Luce called after him.

We'd planned to wait until the ride home to enjoy our last couple 30s, but the way things had gone down we decided we owed it to ourselves to eat early. Maybe Paulo wouldn't be so intimidating if we were faded. Luce announced she was going to swipe a couple paper napkins from the funnel cake stand a few booths over for parachuting purposes. We could use tokens to crush the pills instead of spoons. "You get our stuff together so we can make a run for it if we need to," she said over her shoulder. She turned back and almost collided with a giant stuffed dog. "What the—?"

"Sorry bout that," said a pink-cheeked man in fatigues. He thrust the animal in Luce's direction. "Here."

Within seconds we found ourselves surrounded by various army personnel, all of them carrying the stuffed beagles they'd won earlier. "We're not allowed to take them on the bus," one of them said. They took the liberty of going into our booth and hanging them back in their places and soon all the dogs were strung up on hooks except the one we gave to the Metallica fan.

It was Luce who spotted the tall polite soldier watching the scene from a distance. "Dude! Is this cause of you?" When he gave a sheepish nod of assent, she motioned him over. She squinted up at the name on his uniform. "Rowland. Hey thanks, man. I mean sorry, is that Private Rowland or Corporal or what? Like for real, you totally saved us."

"Actually I just made Staff Sergeant a few weeks ago. But if you don't mind, I'd rather you called me Wilky." He gave her a smile so raw, so tender, that my blood started galloping in panic as if some part of me already knew what was coming. Even Luce, who was as hard-hearted when it came to men as anyone I'd ever encountered, took a wobbly step back.

They started talking. Shyly at first, but it didn't take long for them to start jabbering like a couple of little kids, excited and eager. Wilky started telling some story, moving his hands all around and not taking his eyes off Luce for a second. Meanwhile Luce was laughing so hard I thought for sure I'd have to get her inhaler. She didn't wheeze once.

I tried to focus on counting tickets, but I kept losing my place and having to start over. It was like my brain couldn't concentrate on anything for more than a few seconds without an ugly thought muscling in. I recalled my father, boasting about my accomplishments to anyone who would listen while hospital machines whirred and beeped all around him. And here I was, working a rigged Buck-a-Dog booth and struggling to tally a bunch of greasy tickets. For one awful moment I had a flash of gratitude that my dad couldn't see how far I'd fallen, but that only made me feel worse.

"Ireeeene," said Luce, using the voice she reserved for restaurant guests who looked like they might be 20 percenters. "Would you mind holding down the fort for a minute? Me and Wilky are going to get some cotton candy before he has to head back. Oh and could you finish doing the numbers while you're at it? Thanks to him, I bet we set some kind of record." Together they headed off toward another part of the fairground.

I went straight to her purse and chewed up our last two pills.

I'm not quite sure how much time passed, thanks to the 30s that were sliding their way through my system, but at some

point Luce came back arm in arm with Wilky, lit up like someone had just changed her batteries. They kissed right in front
of me—a gentle exchange that hurt to look at—until at last
he pulled away and murmured something into her hair. This
elicited a throaty giggle from Luce, a sound I'd never heard
her make in all the time I had known her.

"I'd love that," she said, peering up at him. Another kiss,
and they exchanged reluctant goodbyes. As he vanished into
the crowd, I was struck with the peculiar feeling that something in my own life was slipping away too.

"Oh. My. God." Luce swung around to face me. She
wrapped her arms around herself and swayed back and forth.
"Is he a dream or what?"

I lowered my eyes, hoping she wouldn't notice the telltale
size of my pupils. "Yeah, he seems pretty great."

"Saturday night he's picking me up and taking me out to
dinner. For once it'll be me sitting down at a table instead of
having to stand up and take orders from some stupid slut and
her boyfriend."

I tilted my head at her. "You know we're both working
doubles on Saturday."

"So I'll go home after lunch," she said. "After today I can
afford to take a night off if I want to."

I reminded her she still had to get her shift covered. "It
won't be easy on such short notice."

"Guess I'm calling out sick then," Luce said, grabbing her
crotch.

In an effort to change the subject, I told her I'd gotten our fi-
nances squared away in her absence. One good thing about 30s

was they could always restore me, at least temporarily, to my former self. I started rattling off how many tickets we'd sold, our gross, our net, how much we'd earned per hour—

"Good god, cut to the chase already, will you?"

"We're each going to walk with a hundred and sixty-two dollars."

Luce threw back her head and let out a whoop of triumph. "Fuck yeah. You ready to celebrate?" Without waiting for my response, she headed straight for her purse, her fingers twitching in anticipation.

"About time," I said.

If you've never pretended to help your best friend find the drugs you stole from her while trying to conceal a high that makes you almost dizzy with happiness—you can count yourself among the more fortunate humans condemned to wander this planet. After digging through her bag in a frenzy, the sight of which forced me to bite my lips to keep from laughing, Luce upended the whole thing right on the counter. Crap went everywhere. When her Altoids tin still didn't turn up, she lifted her head and gazed at me, stricken. "We've been robbed."

This also struck me as terribly funny, though I couldn't let her know it. "That's ridiculous. It's got to be here." I tried to sort through the chaos of makeup, wadded-up receipts, coins, cellophane wrappers from the mints she liked to nab from the host stand. My hands felt like they were immersed in a vat of warm Jell-O and several times I felt a loopy grin bobbing up to the surface. It took all my concentration to push it back down.

"What the fuck?" Luce said, once it became clear that our stash wasn't going to materialize from the rubble.

"Maybe one of the army dudes that was back here took it," I said. "I bet half of them are on something just because of all their injuries."

"No way. I was watching. I'm not stupid."

"You sure you didn't leave it at home? In the kitchen maybe?"

"You know I always triple-check that shit. Besides, I saw it when I got the sunblock."

"Must have fallen out then," I said. That led to another few minutes of us scrabbling around on our hands and knees, looking for the little metal box I'd tossed in the garbage can a couple of booths over. The whole thing felt like a sketch from one of the sitcom reruns we'd sometimes watch in the afternoons before work and at one point I had to stop and press my hands to my cheeks to keep from yelping in laughter.

"Hold on a second," Luce said. "Look at me."

I didn't see any way around it, so I lifted my head and stared right at her. Even then I had to repress a round of childish giggles.

"Goddammit. You fucking ate them," she said.

"What?" I tried to sound insulted. "You really think I'd do that to you?"

"Don't bullshit me. Your eyes are pinned out like crazy." She stood up and began tossing her belongings back in her purse. "I can't fucking believe it. Leave you alone for one second. Guess I know who not to trust in the future."

Now I really was insulted. I pulled myself to my feet a little too quickly and almost fell over. "Yeah? Why don't you try looking at your own eyes for once. They're just as bad as mine, leftover from this morning."

She stared at me. "You're really going to double down on this."

I picked up her compact and held it out. "Look."

Luce reached for the mirror. A couple more seconds and she would know I'd not only stolen her drugs, I'd lied right to her. Her eyes looked perfectly normal. Nothing pinned whatsoever. Instinctively I braced myself.

She flipped open her compact, gazed into it. Lifted her eyes and peered into my face. Slowly the muscles in her jaw grew tight, the way they always did right before she lost her temper and already I could see her screaming her head off about how I'd betrayed her.

So when Luce's anger dissolved into nothing, I didn't know what to make of it. She kept watching me, her face blank as a tablet. Neither of us moved. At last she closed her compact—a sharp little click that seemed to signal something much larger.

"You're right. I'm sorry," she said.

I stared at her, uneasy and skittish. Clearly it was me who'd messed things up between us. Was Luce's apology some kind of trick? At least if she'd yelled in my face, I would have known where we stood with each other.

"It's okay," I said at last.

After that, we were pretty quiet. We tidied the booth and finished organizing our tickets. The evening crew showed up to replace us—a couple of girls our age with matching Hollister sweatshirts and flat-ironed hair and rhinestone nose studs that were supposed to make them look edgy. The kind of people who always go to happy hour, consume huge amounts of half-price drinks, and tip a dollar. You could almost hear them mewling for another glass of pink wine. I hoped Luce would try to screw with them in some way, maybe give them bad advice about running the game so they'd lose all the beagles, or at least knock the pan of greasy water all over their stupid sheepskin boots, but she just kept wiping circles of Windex into the counter as though she hadn't noticed the sudden stink of Victoria's Secret body fragrance. It was a little depressing, even with the 30s, to say the least.

Paulo came by and paid us. Cash as promised. Sure enough, he kept dropping hints about a lucrative side business he thought the two of us might be perfect for, especially after he saw our numbers, but Luce was so far off in her own thoughts that his little insinuations and coded language didn't register so much as a blip on her radar. He had the majestic planetary proportions that Pandora had mentioned, with an old Ron Jon *Spring Break 2009* tee stretched across his belly even though it was autumn. Pale linen trousers, leather flip-flops. A stack of shell bracelets rattled gently as he followed Luce around our booth. When it became clear his wooing methods were going nowhere, Paulo gathered up his sack of tickets and gave Luce a regretful look over his shoulder. "You ever change your mind, you call me anytime. Day or night, I mean it."

She zipped up her hoodie and shrugged past him. As I hurried after her, the Victoria's Secret girls let out a scornful laugh.

It wasn't until we were walking back to our car that Luce began to snap out of it. She turned to me. "Listen." Her voice was small and unsteady. "I'm sorry again about what I said before. Thing is, I don't exactly have a great track record when it comes to friendships. Somehow or other I always fuck them up. But I don't want to ruin things with you, so . . ." She snuck a cautious glance at me. "Can we maybe forget everything and pretend it never happened?"

I thought of Wilky, and the way he and Luce looked at each other. I thought of my father smiling up at me from his hospital bed. I thought of the rolling pink sun that morning, and all the other incalculable losses I knew were rushing straight toward me.

I slipped my hand into Luce's and held it tight as possible.

"Already forgotten," I said.

AFTER LUCE ASKED ME TO HANG ON TO HER PHONE, she kept everything on the level. Attended every 1:30 meeting. Daily one-on-ones with Greenie. No one sketchy showed up at our house unannounced. And yet I had zero doubt that she was thinking about using. Of course she was! Believe me when I say that if someone you love ODs and doesn't survive it, more than anything you'll want to medicate yourself out of that particular torture—even if it means dosing yourself with their exact same poison. There's more than one way to get close to someone.

It was me who found Wilky's online obituary, which set things rolling down a different hill altogether. The two of us were at the kitchen table drinking our morning coffee. Luce kept turning to stare out the window, unable to keep up a conversation for more than a few seconds despite my best efforts. At last I gave up and started messing around on my phone. I told myself I only wanted to find something funny on Reddit so I could make her laugh a little, but I guess part of me was also thinking about Wilky. It wasn't long before I found myself typing his name into my browser. Bam! Up popped his obit. Without thinking, I read it aloud. There weren't any details about what happened, as if the way he'd died was somehow humiliating or shameful. All it talked about was his cheerful personality and how he was always helping others. His military service, his college degree. Instead of flowers, mourners were asked to donate to the Melanoma Research Foundation, which seemed like a sneaky way of implying he'd died of skin cancer instead of addiction. At the end were the names of surviving family members. No mention of Luce.

The funeral was listed as private, but a memorial service was being held that Sunday. His parents were hosting it in their home in Greensboro. As soon as Luce heard that, she announced we were going to borrow a car and drive ourselves up there. Never mind she'd never met his family or that Wilky hadn't talked to any of his relatives since getting his Bad Conduct Discharge. As gently as possible, I suggested we might want to sit this one out. Getting caught behind the wheel could land us in some serious trouble since we still had suspended licenses, not to mention his mom and dad might not be all that eager to meet us.

She set her coffee mug down with an angry thud. "Fine. I'll go without you."

As fast as I could, I told her I wanted to go, of course I did. More than anything. "It's just we weren't invited. I don't want to upset anyone, is what I'm saying."

"It's a memorial for fuck's sake! People are supposed to be upset. Besides, no one sends out invites, you're just supposed to show up, cry, eat some macaroni salad. It's called being a human being!"

By this point I was scrambling to open up Google Maps. "Okay, you're right, we'll take a bunch of back roads to get there and avoid all the state troopers. We'll make this work. You want me to ask Boz about borrowing his car? Or maybe Carmela."

"We're not asking anyone from the rooms. Greenie finds out we're driving, she'll make us do a bunch of step work." Luce looked at me. "I know. Call Nogales."

"No way," I said. "Forget it."

"Knowing him, he'll probably want to drive us up there himself. It's perfect."

"I already said no!"

"Okay okay, don't get all worked up," Luce said. "Give me my phone then. I'll text Lonny. He owes us."

An alarm somewhere inside me began beeping. Not super loud—more like your microwave letting you know your tater tots are ready. A relic from our former life, Lonny was a skinny old Gulf War vet who had the highest tolerance I'd ever encountered. Never sold his meds, except maybe a few tramadols on occasion. Still, I didn't want him getting anywhere near Luce. "I'll hit him up. You've got enough to deal with."

A moment passed and Luce relented. "Fine." She angled her head toward the window and soon she was drifting back to the place she'd been before the whole obituary weirdness, wherever that was.

Once he heard the situation, Lonny agreed to loan us his old Mazda coupe on the condition we return it first thing the next morning. It was American-cheese yellow—not great for dodging law enforcement. Luce insisted on driving, which I wasn't crazy about either. Even before getting popped for possession she had two speeding tickets on her record and that's not counting all the times Nogales or one of his buddies let her off with a warning. But the Mazda was a stick shift and I sucked at stick shift, so that was that.

The morning of, we woke early and took our time getting ready. The only black dress I owned was the one I'd worn to my dad's funeral a few years earlier, but if I didn't let myself think about it, it wasn't too upsetting. Luce's only black dress was a strappy lace mini, which she paired with her favorite high heels. Neither of had us black coats, so we made do with our army surplus parkas, and after checking the taillights and brake lights to make sure they were in order, we got in the car and set out for Greensboro. I was in charge of navigation, and between watching my phone and looking for cops and thinking about Wilky, it wasn't long before the low-level nausea I'd had all week ramped up into high digits. I glanced at Luce. "You sure about this? It's not too late to turn around if you want to."

She took one look at me and went back to driving. "You better not barf all over this car."

Despite the endless looping side roads and spotty cell service and the sheriff's deputy who tailed us for four sweaty miles before turning onto an access road, we made it to Wilky's parents' place without any problems. A two-story brick house at the end of a cul-de-sac, it looked harmless enough. Black shutters, red door, a chimney with pale smoke curling skyward.

You could tell by the sweetish odor in the air they weren't burning any old trash-tree firewood either and had gone for something fancy like applewood or cherry. They'd also sprung for a valet service, but it wasn't so hard to find a spot for the cheese-mobile a couple streets over. As we walked back to the address, Luce kept pulling at the hem of her dress, trying to yank the fabric a few inches lower. I told her everything would go great and she should try not to worry. "I mean let's be real. They're just people."

"Hope you're right," she said with a final tug.

Once we got inside though, their home felt cozy, welcoming even, despite being huge and built for rich people. Sunken living room with a fireplace at one end and a grand piano at the other. Built-in bookshelves that ran floor to ceiling. A fat brown leather sofa with a bunch of fat leather armchairs to match. On the rear wall hung a giant painting that was nothing but a bunch of crude slashes of green with a few muddy splatters, so hard-core in its ugliness you could tell it was worth a fortune. Maybe one day Luce and I would have a painting like that.

We hung our parkas on the rack by the entrance, hiding them among sleek wool trenches and satiny puffers. After spotting the buffet set up in the dining room, we decided a little something on our stomachs might help us relax. You should have seen the spread these people had going. We loaded our plates with everything from shrimp-and-grits shooters to miniature chicken-and-waffles to bite-size pieces of salmon carved into roses. Rich people sure must like tiny food. Luce, who could really put it away when she was nervous, wrapped a bunch of raspberry thumbprints in a napkin for later. When she slid them into her purse—a fake Louis with greening hardware—a woman with a cropped bristle of hair peered down at us over a pair of fancy black glasses. Definitely not the kind of person who bought purses out of the back of a Pontiac Grand Am. She took a step closer. "I don't think we've met. I'm Wilky's aunt Nora."

Luce glanced up at her, her face softening with pleasure. "Oh my god, it's so nice to meet you. I'm Luce. Wilky's girlfriend."

As Aunt Nora took this information in, her expression shifted from the whole scolding-professor vibe to something else entirely. Like she'd just encountered something she felt a little disgusted by. Without saying anything else she headed toward what I guessed was the kitchen. Even her backside looked confused and angry. I turned to Luce. "Maybe we should try to find his mom and dad."

Nearby, a guy with a floppy brown topknot and an Ultimate Catering apron was pouring wine behind a little portable bar set up for the occasion. From the way he was struggling to fill a tray of plastic cups without spilling, you could tell he was pretty inexperienced as a server. Either that or he was pretty baked. I motioned to Luce and we made our way over. "Excuse me," I said. "Can you point out the parents?"

He blinked at us. "What parents."

"You know," I said. "The reason we're here in the first place?"

"The guy who ODd," Luce said a little too loudly.

"No way," he said. "What happened?"

Instead of answering, Luce plucked a cup of wine off his tray and sniffed it. "Wow, someone busted out the good stuff. Nice legs too," she said, giving it a swirl. She looked close to tossing it back in a single swallow and as calmly as I could, I took the cup out of her hand, put it back on the tray with the others, and led her over to the piano where it was less crowded.

We stood there eating in uncomfortable silence. All around, you could feel glances sliding over our bodies. It's true my old funeral dress could have been let out a few inches and Luce's stretchy black mini and teetering stilettos weren't exactly going unnoticed. She leaned into my ear. "Is it me, or is this place Puritan Central?"

"Episcopalian if I had to guess. Listen, we hit the road now, we can still make the 1:30."

"For your information," she said, examining a mini–crab cake, "I'm not going anywhere. Not until I meet Mr. and Mrs. Rowland."

I looked at her. Damp eyes, red nostrils. The bloom of chin acne that arrived like clockwork every twenty-nine days. Something in my chest went hot and spiky. There are people in this world you'll do anything for, even if you know you'll regret it later.

"Okay, sure," I said.

I was scanning the room for potential Wilky parents when a man's voice came out of nowhere. "Pardon me, can I ask you girls a question?"

We looked up in a single motion. It was like the future silver-haired version of Wilky had materialized right there before us. Luce's hand flew up to her mouth and even I took an uneasy step backward.

The man introduced himself as Wilky's father. "I'm told one of you is Wilky's girlfriend?"

Luce nodded, her face rumpling with sorrow.

"Nice to meet you, sir," I said. I told him our names and offered our condolences.

"Thank you, dear," Wilky Senior said. From the tender-looking pouches under his eyes you could tell he hadn't been sleeping and from the sickly-sweet odor of whiskey that radiated all around him it was clear he was pretty drunk. He turned to Luce. "I'm so sorry we never got to meet before this. I feel absolutely terrible about it."

Luce wiped her cheeks with her wrist and did her best to smile up at him. "Same."

They started chatting. Cautiously at first, but it wasn't long before they were sharing all sorts of memories about Wilky, exchanging stories. They even worked up a small laugh at one point. It hit me that if I could just find his mom and bring her over, we could wrap up this whole memorial business and still have time to make our meeting. I excused myself, telling Luce I'd be back in a minute, but she kept her eyes fixed on Wilky Senior as if I didn't exist at all.

I headed past the wine station and the buffet and into the white-hot lights of the kitchen. Maybe Aunt Nora, who must have steered Wilky's dad in our direction, could point me toward his mom. But the room was empty except for a gloomy-looking woman standing at the far end of a butcher-block island. She was only a few years older than Luce and me. She had a wineglass in one hand and a bottle of red in the other.

"Can I help you?" she said.

I told her I was trying to find Wilky's mother. "You don't happen to know where she's at, do you?"

The woman looked me over. She had on a skinny black suit and one of those short fashiony haircuts where the top part is longer than the sides and bottom. Sort of like a fancy crest on a bird. "Sorry, but how do you know Wilky exactly?"

Not wanting to get into details, I said we'd met back during his days at 82nd.

The answer must have satisfied her because she lowered her gaze long enough to take a hefty swallow of wine. "She stepped outside for some air. I'm Kit, by the way. Wilky's sister."

"I'm so sorry for your loss," I said. "It's awful."

She nodded. "Want some?" She waggled the bottle.

I told her no thank you.

"More for me then." She topped off her glass.

For a few minutes, Kit and I made small talk. Turned out she was the co-owner of a steakhouse in downtown Greensboro—the kind of place where servers wore jackets and ties instead of greasy aprons and the prices ended in even numbers instead of 99 cents. When I told her I waited tables she brightened in pleasure.

"I bet you're good at it too. I can tell by looking, you know how to hustle."

"I do my best," I said. "Yes sir, I'd love to pick all the raisins out of our carrot salad for you. More ranch coming right up. Split the check eighteen ways with eighteen different credit cards? I'd be delighted."

"Half sweet tea, half unsweet?" said Kit. "You ever get that one?"

"You have to make a whole special pitcher just for their refills," I said. "Last week a woman came up to me at the computers and asked if I'd stir a packet of Equal into her White Zin before I brought it to the table. Like what kind of person does that?"

"A sociopath," Kit said.

We were still laughing about that when a weary gray-faced woman came into the kitchen, struggling to carry a large cardboard box. "Give me that," Kit said, hurrying over.

"I'm fine." The woman heaved the box onto the counter. "This keeps up, we're going to need a second freezer."

Kit lifted the flaps and peered inside. "Green bean, tuna, macaroni. Oooh, is this King Ranch Chicken?"

"Courtesy of the book club. Take anything you want for you and Tiana. Right now even the littlest whiff of casserole makes me sick."

Although the woman was a lot shorter than Kit, on the petite side even, she had a sturdy, no-nonsense way about her that made her appear much bigger. Broad-shouldered, zero makeup, hair pulled back in an efficient knot. Even the way she was unloading containers of food onto the counter had a military sort of precision. I took a step forward. "Mrs. Rowland?"

She glanced up. "Yes dear?"

I introduced myself and said I was sorry for her loss, that I was a friend of Wilky's.

On hearing that, she paused long enough to give me a forlorn smile. "My goodness, you kids have all grown up so much I can't keep track of you. You went to Greensboro Day together, right? Or was it Montessori."

"Actually I didn't meet him until a couple years ago. I'm here with Luce. Wilky's girlfriend. She's been wanting to meet you."

Mrs. Rowland stopped unloading the box altogether and turned to me with renewed interest.

"We're heartbroken about what happened," I said. "The whole thing was a total shocker."

Kit came over and slid her arm into her mother's. "We can put the food away later. Why don't the two of us go check on Dad." She tried to lead her mom out of the kitchen.

Mrs. Rowland pulled herself free, her face white with anger. "Get the hell out of my house," she said to me.

Next thing I knew she was backing me out of the kitchen. "You understand? Go find your little friend—"

"Mrs. Rowland—"

"—and leave before I have you arrested for trespassing."

"Please," I said. "We're not here to cause trouble."

Mrs. Rowland stared into me with wild electric eyes. "You're telling me you didn't get my son back into drugs, you didn't get him kicked out of the army, you didn't give him those goddamn blue pills they found in his jacket?"

We were out by the buffet table at this point, me walking

backward, trying not to topple over in my stupid Payless wedges, Mrs. Rowland bearing down fast. "Just let me find Luce and we'll leave right this second."

"You let him die alone in his car! What kind of monster does that?" Her voice spiraled into a frightening new register.

"I'm so sorry." I held up my hands. "I mean it."

"I'm calling the police," she said.

I spun around, tripping over a case of wine sitting next to the bar, and went down hard on my knee, twisting it in a complicated angle. Pain zinged from one end of my leg to the other. When I looked back, Mrs. Rowland was on her phone. With Luce and me being on probation, the last thing we needed was to get arrested. I pulled myself to my feet as best I could and scanned the room in a panic. Luce and Wilky Senior were still by the piano, flipping through what looked like a photo album. I hobbled over and told her in a low voice that there'd been a tiny incident and we should probably get going.

"There you are," Luce said. "You're missing all the best stories. Oh my god, check out this picture of Wilky in a sailor suit. How old was he here, Mr. Rowland? Three? Four?"

Wilky Senior leaned back from the album, squinting stiffly at the photo. You could tell when it came into focus because his face went loose with grief. "My sweet baby. My poor sweet baby." He lowered his head, weeping.

I took the album out of Luce's hands and put it on top of the piano. "We need to go. Now." I tried to steer her to the front door despite the grinding pain in my kneecap.

"Hold on. I still haven't met his mother."

"I'm right here," Mrs. Rowland said, striding over. She planted herself in front of Luce. "You have a lot of nerve coming here today. You druggie garbage."

"Oh my god," Luce said.

I remember telling Luce the police were on their way and we needed to leave that instant. I remember Wilky Senior looking at us in teary confusion, clutching the photo album to his chest. Meanwhile Mrs. Rowland kept saying how Luce and I were nothing but a pair of lowlife sluts and junkies and she hoped the police would throw us in jail and flush the key down the toilet. It wasn't long before a crowd gathered.

"Sweetheart, I don't understand," Wilky Senior said to Mrs. Rowland.

"Come on," I said to Luce. "Before the cops get here."

"You worthless trash," Mrs. Rowland said to me.

I managed to pull Luce up the steps and to the front door and for a moment it looked like we were going to get away without any more trouble. Wilky Senior had his arm around his wife, who'd begun blubbering into his shoulder. Wilky's sister, Kit, stood in the doorway of the kitchen, her face scooped out and empty, uncorking another bottle of wine. Then Aunt Nora, she of the fancy purses, took a step forward. "I hope you two are happy ruining my nephew's memorial!"

I reached for Luce's arm, but it was pointless.

"Yeah?" Luce said. "Where the shit were you when he got clean? He was the most amazing man ever and you cut him off when he needed you most. Fuck you and your fucking tough-love bullshit." She pulled a fur-trimmed parka off the coatrack and strode out the door and down the path to the sidewalk. I helped myself to a black leather jacket and limped after her.

We got in the car, headed back toward the mountains. Luce wasn't doing so hot. If she'd been blowing through lights in a rage and zooming around corners I would have felt a lot better, despite the risk of us getting pulled over. Instead her face had a scary far-off expression and she was driving slow as a zombie. Worse, every few seconds she'd squeeze her right hand into a fist and then splay her fingers. Her old tell for wanting to use. As for me, my knee was throbbing so bad it felt like it had its own heartbeat. For the briefest of moments I saw myself eating a couple of 30s—just to knock the pain down a little—but that only made me more disgusted with myself than usual. I pushed the thought away and turned to Luce to see if she wanted me to put on some music. There went her hand again.

We were maybe halfway to Anklewood when she asked me to keep my eyes out for a gas station. "Need to make a pit stop."

My insides rolled over. Back when we were using, gas stations had been prime real estate when it came to cold-copping. You'd be hard-pressed to find one anywhere nearby where we hadn't scored at least a few blues from randos—and often a lot more than that. "You think you can hold it till the meeting? You know how Greenie gets when folks miss the announcements."

"I started my period this morning. Don't want to bleed all over this shitty yellow upholstery."

"Okay," I said. "Sure."

But by some stroke of luck, there wasn't anything for three miles, five miles, eight, and counting. Luce squirmed around her seat. "I'm serious. Things are about to get ugly."

"Let me check the glove box," I said. "Might be some fast food napkins you can stick in your undies."

When she perked up at my suggestion, I felt bad for thinking she was lying. I popped the latch but all I found was one of those stupid one-hitters meant to look like a cigarette and an unopened pack of condoms.

"Once a tool, always a tool," Luce said. She scooped them out of my hand, flung them out the window, and we both started laughing. I felt better after that.

We were about fifteen minutes from Anklewood when we saw an Exxon sign ahead in the distance. Luce sped up so fast I whacked the back of my head on the headrest and soon we were pulling into the station. She put the car in park, threw the door open. "Want anything? A fruit pie maybe?" Again I felt bad for not believing her. I told her I was good and thanks for asking.

"Back in a flash," she said, taking her purse.

I wanted to follow her in and keep an eye out, but I knew it would make her angry, so I told myself if she wasn't back in two minutes I'd go in and pretend I needed to pee, buy some chips or candy. At least the parking lot didn't look too bad. I had a hazy memory of copping at this particular Exxon on more than one occasion, but back then it had been littered with burnt squares of foil and spent lighters, with any number of sketchy characters lounging around in the shadows. Maybe the place had gotten new management.

The only person in sight was a ponytailed blond pumping gas into a giant white Yukon, wearing nothing but yoga gear with a bunch of mesh cutouts. While she waited for her tank to fill, she launched into some stupid pose: one leg down, the other kicked out behind her, arms stretching forward like they were making a grab for something. Once she finished pumping, she made a big deal out of rubbing sanitizer into her hands as if she thought she was going to catch a disease from all the poors who also got gas there. At last she climbed back in her car and drove off, revealing a bumper sticker that read *Namaste Y'all!* in hot-pink letters. Good Lord.

Luce still wasn't out. How long had it been? The dumb yoga chick had gotten me pissed off and distracted. I grabbed my purse and hauled myself out of the car, which set off a whole new round of fireworks in my knee region. While I was hopping around in agony, it struck me I could tell Luce I came in to buy ibuprofen. She couldn't argue with that. Inside she wasn't anywhere, but I did see the restroom back by the coolers. No one else was in the store, which made me feel better, since there was no one she could have copped anything from. I found a travel-size pack of Excedrin in a rack by the energy drinks and brought it up to the clerk, a weathered old dude who looked to be somewhere in his fifties. He was watching a portable TV and eating pistachios. The shells were piled on the counter in a neat little mound. "Excuse me, sir? You see my friend come in here? Short blond hair, black dress?"

He didn't so much as glance over. "In the can."

A weight I hadn't been aware of slid off my back and shoulders. I put the box of Excedrin on the counter and pushed it toward him.

"Anything else?"

"Two Scratch-offs. Triple Winning 7s." I hardly ever bought lottery tickets, but all at once I was feeling lucky. Almost as good as if I was scoring real painkillers. Maybe Luce and I would hit the jackpot and we could quit our jobs and fix her car and move out of our crappy rental and into our own house. Not in Anklewood either, but an actual city. We could even relocate to Florida if she wanted. Buy a sweet beachfront cottage where you could hear seagulls and smell the ocean. Open our own restaurant—a cozy breakfast spot with amazing coffee and homemade doughnuts, the kind of place that had a line of locals out the door every morning and closed at noon or one at the latest. After that, Luce and I would have the rest of the day to ourselves.

The clerk took his sweet time tearing off the tickets. He rang me up, told me what I owed him. As I stuck my debit card in the reader, I felt his eyes crawling all over me like a couple of dung beetles. You can always sense when a guy is being a perv. I lifted my head and stared back, figuring he'd glance away in embarrassment. Instead he smiled like he knew something about me. Something personal.

"You looking too?" he said.

Next thing I knew I was pounding on the bathroom door, yelling for Luce to stop whatever she was doing. Pinpricks of light spun before my eyes and my ears were roaring. "I mean it, open up!" When she didn't answer, I kicked the door with all the force I could summon. It was like Greenie had taken her famous tire iron to my knee. Pain screamed through me like nothing I'd ever experienced and for a moment I thought I was going to pass out right there by the coolers. Then Luce opened the door, smiling and holding a carton of tampons.

"What's up?" she said.

Although I didn't find out exactly what she'd done until later (bought a bun, sniffed a bag, stashed the rest), I had no doubt she'd used. I told her we were going straight to our meeting and I didn't want any argument either. I tried to lead her outside but my knee hurt so bad I had to stop for a second.

"Whoa there," she said. "Put your arm around me. That's it, I got you."

As she helped me out of the store, the clerk didn't so much as lift his head. Instead he kept eating pistachios and watching his little TV program, as though he'd seen dramas like ours a hundred times over. If it hadn't been for Luce I'd never have made it back to the car.

She wanted to drive, but I convinced her to let me take the wheel, saying if she got pulled over the way she was, we'd be in real trouble.

"Yeah but your knee," she said. "You have anything in your purse? Some Advil maybe?"

Only then did I realize I'd left the packet of Excedrin next to the register, along with our lucky Scratch-offs.

My stick shift skills were even more herky-jerky than I remembered, but as long as I went slow and stayed in first, it wasn't unbearable. We'd be a little late to the 1:30, but Greenie would understand, considering the situation. People showed up loaded at meetings on occasion and as long as they weren't too disruptive, she never asked them to leave the circle. Slips happen. They're part of recovery. It's fine, it's fine. I believed it too, until I saw flashing lights in the rearview. It didn't help that Luce started laughing as if me getting popped was the funniest thing ever.

"Joke's on you," she said.

My hands shook so bad I had a hard time steering, but I managed to pull onto the shoulder. I cut the engine and asked Luce to please put on her seat belt and try and act normal. When a set of knuckles rapped on my window, I rolled it down, chest scudding with panic.

"Hello ladies."

It was Nogales.

Luce let out another delighted yelp of laughter. "Told you," she said to me.

He rested his hands on the door. "Last I heard you two weren't getting your licenses back till March at the earliest. Mind telling me why you're driving?"

"Officer Manuel Nogales," Luce said. "Will you please fuck off? We just came from Wilky's memorial."

He gave her a startled look. "Right. That was today. You know I would have taken time off and driven you up there. I've got plenty of sick leave."

"Who you calling sick?" Luce said.

Nogales could be a pain in the dick sometimes, but he

wasn't stupid. He saw in about two seconds that Luce was loaded. He turned to me, his face tight with worry. "You okay, Irene?"

I told him we were fine and we were on our way to a meeting.

"Yeah man," Luce said. "Give us a break for once. Come on, you owe us."

I suggested to Luce that she might want to be quiet for the next few minutes.

"Why? It's not like we have anything. Not this time." She opened the glove box and gestured inside like a game show hostess. "See? Just this lovely box of Playtex. Check it out if you want." She pushed the carton at him. "Isn't it gorgeous?"

"Keep it," he said, looking uncomfortable.

"Happy to," Luce said. She smiled down at the box, cradling it in her arms like a baby—and all at once I knew where she'd hidden her stash. I put my hands on the wheel to steady myself, but I felt shakier than ever.

"Hey did you hear me?" said Nogales.

I looked up at him.

"I said I'll let you two off. Even give you a police escort to your meeting." He nodded at Luce. "Looks like she needs one."

"Ireeeeeene." Already Luce was growing drowsy. "You heard him. Let's get a move on."

"Thanks," I said to Nogales. "I owe you."

He gave the top of the car two quick raps with his knuckles. "See you there." He got in his cruiser, waited until we pulled out onto the road, started following.

Seconds later, Luce's head bobbed onto her chest.

With one hand on the wheel and the other trying to shake Luce back into alertness, I drove to the church as fast as possible. Parked, waved goodbye to Nogales, and as soon as he left I pulled Luce out of the car. Slung her arm around my shoulder, which woke her up for the most part, and together we struggled toward the entrance. The basement stairs cleared her head even more and by the time I got her into the circle, she looked almost normal. She apologized to the group for being late, saying we'd just come from Wilky's memorial. When Greenie asked how she was doing, Luce gave a funny little shrug. "You know. Progress, not perfection. Easy does it."

I don't think even Greenie caught on.

But in the middle of a newcomer's share—he'd recently found Adderall XR in his daughter's backpack and lost a hard-won month of clean time—Luce's head started drooping. First a quick dip, and then a slow one, and then she tumbled sideways onto me. Although I got her upright in moments, it set off the newcomer in a way I hadn't expected. He gazed around the circle, his face pale and quivering, and said he should have known these meetings were useless. The steps were a joke and our prayers were horseshit. "I never believed in a Higher Power anyway." Soon everyone in the room was upset and angry and at last Greenie hauled herself up out of her yellow armchair, came striding over, and asked the two of us to leave.

Later that night I made a big pot of soup and spooned it up to Luce's mouth at our kitchen table. I sat beside her on our couch and listened to her say she had one tiny slip and I should try and relax a little. When I asked if I could hang on to her box of tampons for safekeeping, she got so mad she locked herself in her room and refused to come out no matter how hard I pleaded. Looking back, it was just another awful day in a string of awful days that not only stretched out behind us, but way out ahead of us too—so far ahead it was impossible to see where it ended.

What I wouldn't give to go back and live through every one of those days all over again.

WILKY AND LUCE HAD BEEN TOGETHER A MONTH or so, maybe longer, and it was becoming clear that this wasn't any basic hookup. Before, Luce's relationships always started out with the guy spending every moment possible at our place, lounging around with his shirt off and eating up all our groceries while the salty funk of sex wafted out of her bedroom. Soon they'd have their first argument—usually over one of them dipping into the other's stash without permission—which would launch a series of fights and truces that swelled into a lung-splitting battle until at last Luce would break up with him once and for all and swear off guys forever and announce she'd be perfectly happy living with me for the rest of her life.

With Wilky, it was different.

For starters, she talked our manager into giving her weekends off, even though that was when the two of us made all our money, so she could spend them holed up at Wilky's cushy off-post setup. Huge carpeted bedroom, TV with endless channels, an upstairs deck that looked out onto a lake. When she got hungry, all she had to do was nose around in his giant silver refrigerator where she'd find just about anything a person could wish for, and if she got tired of rolling around in bed all morning, she only had to smile up at Wilky and he'd take her wherever she wanted to go. It wasn't long before she began dropping me off at our house on Fridays once our lunch shift ended and speeding out to his apartment so that she'd be there waiting when he got home from base. Anyone could see she wasn't thinking straight and I finally told her she ought to take a time-out. Make him miss her a little. "No need to spend every second of your life over there, you know. Besides, you and me haven't hung out in ages."

"Dude, I see you all day before work and all night at the restaurant. I see you more than anyone." She put the car in reverse, started backing down the driveway.

"Work doesn't count," I said, jogging after her. "Come on, wait a minute, will you?"

It didn't do any good.

But the weirdest part was Luce started talking about quitting. Not the restaurant. The pills. I didn't take her seriously at first since every user talks about getting clean someday— it's part of the whole using ritual—but then she confided that Wilky had no idea about her habit. Not only was she sick of lying, she was scared if he ever found out, he'd break up with her no questions asked. Turned out he had his own unpleasant history with painkillers, thanks to an injury he'd gotten in Jump School, and it had taken him some serious effort to get free of its clutches. If Luce could quit before he caught her, he'd never have to know about it at all.

When Wilky had base duty one weekend, she decided it was her chance to go cold turkey. Made herself a kick-it kit of vitamin supplements, ibuprofen, lemon-lime Gatorade, Imodium. Put on one of the reality shows she loved to hate-watch and settled in on the couch. Friday and Saturday weren't cakewalks by any stretch of the imagination, but Luce white-knuckled it through the cramps and nausea and terrible sleeping, and to her credit she didn't have so much as a generic 5mg. But Day 3 is when all the nastiest withdrawals come calling—we're talking full-blown fever, the shakes, liquid BMs, you name it—and suddenly things weren't so easy.

"Maybe you should just have half a one," I said at last. "To take the edge off."

She was shivering on the couch, cocooned in a quilt, green-gilled and sweaty. Our mop bucket waited in arm's reach. I was curled up on the recliner, still in my pj's, scrolling through my phone and keeping her company.

"I'm okay," she said, wincing.

"Well sure you are. Anyone has the strength to quit, it's you. All I'm saying is I scored some sweet e8s at work last night, so just say the word and I'll go crush one up for you. To get you through the worst part."

When another freight train of cramps slammed into her, she ground her teeth so hard it sounded like she'd cracked a molar. She rolled over and faced the back of the couch, groaning softly.

I asked if she wanted me to do a little research, see what Day 4 was supposed to be like. Maybe it would give her something to look forward to.

She didn't answer, just pulled the quilt tighter. I started typing stuff into my phone. "Whoa, really?" I said after a moment.

"What," she said. "What is it."

I hesitated. "Okay, don't go freaking out, but WebMD has

seizures and death listed under common withdrawal symptoms. I mean rare maybe, but common?"

With effort, Luce rolled over. "Let me see that."

"Hold on, forget them." I kept typing. "Let's find someone who actually went through this. All right, here we go. On Reddit they're saying Day 4's not a complete nightmare. Far as I can see, nope, doesn't look like anyone's died. Mostly people are talking about never-ending barf-a-thons and stabbing pains in the belly. Napalm poops. Oh my god, fire-rhea this one guy calls it."

At that, Luce made a grab for the mop bucket and puked up yellow liquid.

"See?" I said. "Compared to them, you're doing great. Don't worry, worst-case scenario I'll call 911 and get you checked into the hospital. Better safe than sorry."

"Can you hand me that washcloth?" she said.

I climbed off the recliner and knelt by the sofa. Took the washcloth out of the bowl of ice water I'd made earlier, wrung it out for her, watched as she struggled to wipe her mouth. "But I guess I am kind of wondering why you're going cold turkey. Everyone says the best way is to stop little by little."

"I don't know," she said, sniffling. "All the twelve-steppers swear by it."

"I'm sure it works for some people. But I can show you a hundred threads right now that swear tapering's the way to go. No fever, no runs, none of that gross vomity feeling."

At the word *vomity*, Luce doubled over like someone had punched her right in the liver. I handed her the bucket (the slosh inside smelled something awful) and within seconds she was projectile hurling. You'd be surprised how much liquid the human body can hold. When she finished, she lifted her head and stared at me, and although the next day she would have purple bruises on her eyelids from throwing up with such violence, the only thing I noticed was her gaze, all shipwrecked and watery.

"Why don't I go make you a pickle and cheese sandwich," I said.

Since that idea only made her shudder a little instead of barfing, I figured her stomach was finally empty. I passed her the Gatorade and she took a cautious swallow. I reached in my back pocket, withdrew two blues, put them on the arm of the couch. "I'm going to leave these here just in case you need them. Be back in a second." I went into the kitchen to give her some privacy. Let her think things over.

When I poked my head in a few minutes later, the pills were gone.

Soon we were laughing like school kids and blasting *Master of Puppets* and playing competitive air guitar to an imaginary stadium full of people who loved us. One good thing about going cold turkey is even if you just make it fifty-three hours, your tolerance plummets. Only took Luce 60mgs, 90 maybe, to feel better—and we're not talking regular baseline well, but almost as good as it was back in the old days. It's true your first high is always the best. When we finally wore ourselves out, we lay on the floor and ordered a pizza and chewed a couple more blues while we waited. Luce often got chatty when we were using and she couldn't stop talking about what we should pick up next time. I gazed at the ceiling and let her words slide over me. All I could think of was how Wilky was about to be 86ed like all the others and soon the two of us could go back to our old perfect life together.

How very wrong I was.

What can I tell you about Wilky? I guess you could call him handsome, if classic good looks are what you're into. Tall, fit, standard-issue buzz cut. A scruff of hair poking out of his shirt if he left the second button open. Hands that could open any jar no matter how tight the lid was screwed on. And sure, his eyes took on a funny sadness late at night as if he was too tired to pretend any longer, but aside from that they weren't anything special. He never raised his voice, not even during the worst of it, and yet whenever he got upset or frustrated you could see his Adam's apple start to jump around in his throat. He liked to play guitar—mournful, old-timey ballads that would rip your heart out by its roots if you listened too closely—and before I ever heard a single note come out of his fingers in person, Luce had hummed his lonesome melodies around our house so often I could have joined in if I'd wanted. I never did, of course.

I don't know how Luce managed to hide it so well, but it took a couple more months before Wilky found out about her habit. It was the day before Valentine's, which I remember because she couldn't get the 14th off from work even though she'd put in the request way back in December. Our GM at the time, a weaselly little prick named Raymond, thought just because he had a college degree in hospitality he knew what it was like to actually work in a restaurant. Insisted we upsell at every possible moment and tracked our sales on a giant whiteboard he hung up in the bus station. Made servers do kitchen prepwork to save on cooks' wages and then overstaffed us so bad we'd fight over tables. The sort of guy who liked to hide in his office during the rushes, watching trashy videos and updating his POF profile. Even though Luce was always one of the top sellers, since she could talk anyone into just about anything, he took a special pleasure in dicking her over. The two of us had been filling out applications for weeks in hopes of landing a better setup, but so far things hadn't worked out in our favor. Turned out we were only a couple months away from getting fired, but we didn't know that yet.

Anyway on the 13th, Wilky brought Luce an armful of roses, took her to dinner at some fancy place up in Durham, and while they waited for dessert he surprised her with a silver bracelet. The kind where you can keep adding dumb little charms if you want to. Hers already had a heart, and Wilky had gotten them to engrave TRUE LOVE on one side like one of those Valentine's candies that taste like chalk dust. Luce being Luce got all teary-eyed when she saw it. Said she didn't deserve it—not the gift, not the dinner, not the flowers, and certainly not Wilky. Ended up telling him all about her habit while the ten-dollar hot fudge sundae they'd ordered melted into a slimy pool. Wilky, being who he was, took hold of her hands and listened to everything she was saying. Reminded her that he'd found himself in the exact same trouble after wrecking his leg during his first week as an Airborne instructor. Even though he'd managed to put together a year-plus of clean time, he surprised her once again by promising to stick with her no matter what happened. Luce surprised herself by promising to quit.

She told me she was going to do it right this time and taper. After consulting our favorite subreddit, she came up with a jump-off plan that had her cutting her intake week by week, nice and steady. If everything went as scheduled, she'd be gliding into zero by April 1. Not wanting to be left out, I said I'd join her. Our farewell tour, as she liked to call it, wasn't easy by any stretch but cigarettes and sugar helped a little. We even went to a couple meetings to see what the deal was. There really is something nice about circling up with a bunch of folks going through the same thing you are and for the first time in a long while I didn't feel quite so lonely. Yet there we were, sailing straight toward April. Once Luce got clean, then what?

It was mid-March when the three of us crowded into Wilky's trusty Subaru Outback and roared off to some no-name town on the edge of the mountain. Luce and I had decided to splurge on a bunch of pandas from an old woman who was supposed to be dying. Apparently she had an actual prescription due to her insides rotting and since she didn't have any income except for a Social Security payout that covered next to nothing, she'd taken to selling her pain meds.

"This is going to be a serious jackpot," Luce said, rocking back and forth in the passenger seat. "I can feel it."

This was the week we'd planned to top out at 60mg a day and since Luce had chewed up her whole share of four IR 15s that morning, she was feeling a lot better than I was. I'd decided to spread mine out from breakfast to midnight, so I'd only eaten one and a half.

"Hope you're right," I said, adjusting my seat belt. I couldn't get comfortable.

"I don't know," said Wilky, who'd eaten exactly nothing. "You sure there's no one else you can buy from? They prescribe those kinds of pills for a reason."

Luce turned to him. "Who are you kidding, Mr. Doctor Shopper? Mr. Pill Mill City. You know the reason. Cha-ching. This right here is what you call a win-win-win situation."

"I don't know," Wilky said again. He glanced at me in the rearview. "Seems to me ten bucks a pop is red flag territory."

Luce let out a guffaw of junky laughter. "You've been watching too many Vice videos."

"Oh my god, Vice is the worst," I said.

Despite his job teaching soldiers how to jump out of planes, or maybe because of it, Wilky was the sort of person who refused to take even the littlest risk unless he had to. Back when he was using, he wouldn't eat anything unless it came straight out of a blister pack or at least one of those orange pharmacy bottles. Lucky for him, it hadn't been hard to get multiple scripts since he had a legitimate injury and X-rays to go along with it, but when waiting in line at all the various Fayettenam pain clinics turned into a giant time suck, he still never went for the quick thrill of cold-copping at gas stations or dark web convenience or even trying the latest mystery pills from the local dgirl. So when Luce announced we were meeting some stranger she found on Craigslist? Wilky about lost his mind.

He looked at me in the rearview again and I thought for sure he was going to pull a U and call the plan off altogether. "Just promise we'll leave at the first sign of trouble."

"Cross our hearts," Luce said. "Right, Irene?"

"Of course," I said, leaning back in my seat.

Soon we were pulling up to a dirty white bungalow, tucked way at the end of a gravel lane all rutty with potholes. A bunch of newspapers lay piled up on the front steps like the place was abandoned and a hopeful FOR SALE BY OWNER sign was posted next to the mailbox. The phone number had been rained on so much it had turned into an inky smear. Right away my bladder got tight, the way it always did when a deal felt sketchy.

"Guys?" I said. "You sure this is the right address?"

Luce frowned into her phone. "Great. No service."

"Don't worry," said Wilky. "It's not like we're lost. This is one of those dead-end country roads. Only one way out of here."

We climbed out of the car and gazed around at the landscape. Although I didn't recall going downhill on our way over, we'd somehow ended up in a bleak little valley. There was hardly any grass, just a few patches of stubble. Bare, witchy-looking trees rose up all around us, their limbs reaching toward the sky like they wanted to rip holes in it or maybe yank it down once and for all. The wind had changed directions since we'd left and now it whistled in from the north, cold and metallic. On a nearby power line, a couple of scroungy yard birds huddled close together. You could see their tiny chests rising and falling.

"Smell that?" Wilky said. "Rain'll be here within the hour."

Luce zipped up her hoodie. "This fucker better show soon. It's freezing."

"You're in luck," said a nearby voice.

We swung around to find a scraggy middle-aged man watching us from behind a pair of giant tortoiseshell sunglasses. He had on camouflage coveralls, the effect of which was canceled out by a blaze-orange hunting vest. His blond hair was slicked back from his forehead and the way the long parts curled around his neck made me think of chicken feathers.

"Three of you, huh?" he said. "Was expecting just the ladies."

Luce gave him one of the teasing grins she reserved for big tippers and guys who were holding. "Yeah and you got us too. Only reason he came is I didn't know if my grandma's car would make it all the way out to east nowhere."

Chicken Feathers pressed his lips together so hard they turned purple. He walked over to Wilky's car. "You wouldn't be hiding anyone in here, would you?" He cupped his hands around his sunglasses and bent over to peer through the window—revealing a gun holstered on his hip. My chest got a weird skittery feeling, like one of those yard birds had gotten trapped in there and was trying to scratch its way out in a panic. Why hadn't I gone for the full 60 at breakfast?

"Nice cannon," Luce said. "Out hunting wabbits?"

Chicken Feathers turned back to face her, his jaw working in anger. "Do me a favor and cut the flirty crap. I hate that shit more than just about anything."

Even Luce, who once bloodied a dude's nose when he tried to short us, nervously shifted her weight from one foot to the other.

Maybe I could sneak another k8 out of my purse and eat it right there.

Wilky cleared his throat. "Look, if you're busy, we can come back later. No problem."

"What he means," Luce said, "is let's do this. You got what we came for, we'll be out of your life in thirty seconds."

"Brought cash?"

"Come on, dog." Luce patted her handbag. "We look like a bunch of dumb college kids?"

"Just got to ask," Chicken Feathers said. He explained that his mom had the pills, that it was her game and she wanted to run it. There were few rules we had to agree to. Head around the side of the house and go in the back way, since his mom didn't care for strangers tramping through the front parlor. Wipe our feet on the mat. No foul language. Say please and thank you.

"Sunday school," Luce said. "We get it."

"One more thing. Ladies only."

"Actually," said Wilky. "I'm not thrilled about the idea of them heading into a strange house all alone. Hate to say it, but I'm going to have to tag along with them."

Chicken Feathers unholstered his gun and aimed it at Wilky. "Hate to say it, but my mom insists."

All around, the sky went a funny green color. A gust of wind kicked up out of nowhere, whipping my hair against my cheeks and forehead. The temperature dropped and the smell of rain was so sharp I could taste it: a faint vinegar smear at the back of my throat.

"Hey, it's cool." Wilky raised his hands. "We're all cool here."

"The fuck is your problem?" Luce said. "Ever occur to you that bowing up on your customers is about the stupidest move ever? How about you put your dick away and try and act normal."

"At least point it somewhere else," Wilky said, watching the barrel.

"No can do," Chicken Feathers said. "Just think of your driver here like a security deposit. You girls play nice with my mom, you get him back, nothing missing."

Luce held his gaze for several long seconds. Her lungs were starting to whistle from all the excitement. She turned to Wilky. "You win. Let's get going."

"In through your nose and out through your mouth," he told her. "Nice and slow, like we practiced."

"I'm *fine*," she said. "Let's go."

Wilky hesitated. He ran his eyes over Chicken Feathers and then he turned and looked at me. "What do you think? Should we do this?"

What I thought was maybe Wilky had a bigger interest in ten-dollar pandas than he'd first let on.

I also thought the smart thing would be for us to cut our losses and head out before things blew up in our faces. When you got right down to it Chicken Feathers was frightened, and if there was anything I'd learned since getting into this racket it was frightened people were not to be trusted. You never know what they're going to do. I was this close to agreeing to scrap the plan entirely—and then I snuck another glance at Luce. There was no mistaking what she wanted.

I turned back to Wilky. "We've already come this far."

Soon Luce and I were standing at the rear of that miserable little cottage. While she knocked on the door, I crept over to a nearby window in hopes of getting a heads-up on what we were walking into. All the lights were off, but I could make out a few hazy objects. A refrigerator, two chairs, a kitchen table. Flashing digits on the microwave. I reminded myself this was only a sick old lady, no reason to worry. Seconds later the rumble of male voices rose up out of the dark. I hurried over to warn Luce right as the back door swung open. In its frame stood a skeletal old woman in a graying bathrobe. She had a familiar bottle of magnesium citrate in one hand and a remote control in the other. The voices, I realized, were part of a TV commercial.

"Not buying whatever it is you're selling," she said.

"Ma'am, we're here to buy from *you*," said Luce. "Your son sent us?"

The old woman looked us over. "Christ, this shit again."

We followed her into the dim of the kitchen, down an unlit hallway, and into the so-called parlor. It had a damp medicinal smell, which I recognized as a combination of iodine and menthol cough drops, with a top note of that depressing acetone odor bodies give off in their final stages. Still no lights, just a bit of watery sun leaking through the curtains and a dull glow from a TV set up in the corner. The picture was so scrambled you could hardly make out the scene. When she switched on a table lamp, a foldout couch rumpled with sheets and blankets jumped out at us. Her sickbed, most likely. It made me think of my father.

"Mind if I use your restroom?" I said.

The old woman's upper lip curled in displeasure. "We get this over with nice and quick, you can go shit in the road for all I care. Pills are thirty bucks each. How many you wanting?"

Luce's mouth fell open. "It's supposed to be ten. Your son said so."

"His cut's ten. Mine's twenty. You girls know how to add, don't you?"

"False advertising," Luce said. "Not cool, lady."

"You don't want them, say the word. People like you are ten cents a dozen."

Luce and I exchanged glances. On one hand, we had a personal rule about not letting ourselves get hustled by dgirls, no matter how senior. On the other, pandas/Opanas were basically the best thing out there, with a high so smooth and dreamy you felt like you were sailing through heaven on a first-class ticket. They were also strong enough that you needed far less to get you going, but as luck would have it they were pretty rare. The last time we'd been able to find them we had to deal with a real charmer named Harold who kept adjusting his nutsack during the whole exchange and asking if we wanted to party. Even then he charged forty per. And afterward, surprise-surprise, he started texting Luce a bunch of unimpressive crotch shots until in a fit of anger she deleted the contact and blocked his number. Only problem was when we ran out and wanted more, we had no idea where to find him.

We went all over town asking if anyone had seen a guy with two little beard pigtails sprouting from his chin and pentagram ear gauges and still we came up empty-handed.

After some deliberating, Luce suggested we spring for twelve total. "We stick to our taper, that'll get us through till d-day."

It was the best I could hope for. I nodded in agreement.

The old woman gestured at the coffee table. "Count her out."

Luce sat on the floor and took her time separating the ones and fives, putting some into tidy stacks and fanning out others. When she started up with a bunch of distracting patter I knew she was fixing to pull one of her shortchange scams. She explained the reason we had so many small bills was because we waited tables and our manager wouldn't let us trade our ones in for twenties since it made counting his bank deposit take forever. "Course dude has plenty of time to sit in the back, monkeying around with his phone, posting dumb pictures—"

"Save it," the old woman said, cutting her off. "Never did understand tipping anyways. I never leave extra unless they bend over backwards."

"All done," Luce sang. She scooped up the cash and held it out like a treasure.

The old woman fixed Luce with one of her spooky skeleton gazes. "I was you, I'd count that again. No offense, but you didn't seem to be paying attention."

When Luce started talking again, this time about how crazy it was that the restaurant could legally pay us two dollars and thirteen cents an hour, the old woman leaned over and smacked the coffee table. "I said shut up and count."

After that it was quiet except for the shuffling of money. My bladder was tight as a drum. I told the old woman I really needed to use the bathroom, and as if I'd jogged her memory, she took a long drink from her bottle of magnesium citrate—a laxative every opioid user gets to know at some point.

"Sister, you and me both," she said. "Ever since I been on these suckers, it's all kinds of problems. Nothing works, not coffee, not prunes, not molasses, not even this nasty lemon-lime stuff my boy got me this morning."

Luce looked up. "You mean you never tried G-777s?" She pulled a ziplock of green pills out of her handbag.

"You can stop right there," I said.

One of Luce's favorite hustles, and she had many, was saving the sugar pills from our birth control packets and bagging them up to sell on college campuses alongside whatever else we were middling. Dudes only, of course. So far we'd just tested it at Elon and High Point U, but both times we'd made a couple hundred bucks in less than half an hour. Next on our hit list was Duke, where we planned to charge some serious money. You'd be surprised how stupid educated people are. But here, with some gun-toting maniac outside? No thank you.

"You're right." Luce started to put the pills back in her purse. "Forget it."

"Not so fast. What are those exactly," said the old woman.

Luce broke into one of her waitress smiles. "Canadian laxatives. Instant release. Can't buy them here cause the FDA won't approve the green dye in the coating."

"Libtards," the old woman said in disgust. "I'm over here needing real medicine but they're too busy trying to regulate stuff that don't need regulating."

"I hear you loud and clear," Luce said. "You know we're all in trouble when hardworking Americans can't even go to the bathroom when they want to. This dinky bag of pills? Five hundred bucks on the black market. Never mind what my girl here had to do to get it."

"Thanks a lot," I said.

With a regretful look, Luce put the pills away and went back to counting. I hoped that would be the end of it, but you could tell by the way the old woman kept eyeing Luce's bag that she wasn't about to drop the subject.

"You think I can get a couple of them green pills? I'll throw in two extra on my end."

Luce turned to me. "Boss, how about it?"

"Maybe we better just wrap this up. I'm sure our *driver* wants to get going."

Luce's face flickered for the briefest of moments. You could tell she'd forgotten all about Wilky. A nice little bonus I hadn't expected. She gave the old woman a shrug of apology. "You heard her. No can do."

As she counted bills in silence, our host stewed in her juices. Meanwhile I had to go so bad I was about to head outside and squat in the grass. At last the old woman aimed her skeleton spook in my direction. "Look here, you need to use the facilities, go on ahead. Back through the kitchen, on the right. Me and your friend can finish up without you, can't we?"

"Course we can," Luce said.

I didn't trust either of them, but I also didn't have a good choice one way or the other. Bodies are such fragile things. I hurried into the bathroom, locked the door behind me. I peed and peed and peed. Once I finished I made sure to check the medicine cabinet, but there was only a tube of Zilactin-B for treating mouth ulcers and a box of Antivert—the stuff my dad had used to fight off nausea. I sat on the edge of the bathtub and crunched up the other half of my k8. When it didn't kick in as fast as I wanted, I chewed another, a whole one this time.

There it is, I thought.

It wasn't until I heard a distant pounding that I lifted my head and came back from my travels. I struggled up from the tub, cracked the door open. When I saw it was Luce I got so happy I threw my arms around her.

"Really?" she said. "You couldn't hold off for five minutes?"

I tried to explain, but before I could she hollered something over her shoulder.

What a mystery she was!

She pulled me back into the parlor. Parlor? I glanced around the room in confusion. Something sharp dug into my ribs. To my delight it turned out to be Luce's elbow and I followed it up her arm, past her shoulder, along her jawline. Entranced, I stared at the side of her face. A spot of red burned high on her cheekbone and her mouth was moving.

"Remember, you have to take them with liquid." She was talking to the old woman. "That magnesium drink you got there is about 99 percent water, so you might as well chase them with that. Nothing else, it'll keep your son happy."

The old woman shook her head in admiration. "Sure hope

he finds himself a girl like you someday. He was a tiny bit younger, you'd make a great couple."

"I'll take that as a compliment," Luce said.

She slipped her hand into mine and led me out of that funeral parlor. As soon as the door shut behind us, she leaned in close. "Dude, we just set ourselves a record. Got all twelve for free. Now zip it till we're in the car. Don't want to give our boy any excuses."

"Tick-a-lock," I said happily.

It had grown even darker since we'd last been outside and as we rounded the corner the wind pushed into us, cold and oily. Chicken Feathers was sitting on the hood of the Outback, resting his gun on his knee and gazing off into the horizon. Wilky leaned against the fender, his hands plunged in his pockets, the afternoon's strain playing out on his face. It couldn't have been easy to drive us out here, not if he was trying to stay sober.

"Wilky!" I threw my hand in the air. "We're back!"

He looked up, startled. His eyes went straight from me to Luce. "Finally. I was getting worried."

"Took you girls long enough," Chicken Feathers said. He slid off the car, made his way over.

Luce told him if he'd given us the right price from the get-go, we'd have been a lot faster. "This stuff of yours better check out is all I'm saying."

"Comes straight from Walgreens." He tucked his gun in his holster. "None of that pressed shit here. Should be plenty of it for the next couple months, longer if we're lucky." His voice trailed off into nothing.

"Copy that." Luce turned to Wilky. "You ready?"

Wilky nodded with visible relief and got out his car keys.

"Whoa, slow down," Chicken Feathers said. He reached in his blaze-orange vest, dug around in an inside pocket. With a flourish, he pulled out a bun. Little glassine bags of what looked like brown sugar, all rubber-banded together. "For you ladies, fifty bucks. Deal of a lifetime."

It was right around then I felt the first drop of rain.

"Yeah, we don't do the hard stuff," Luce said, glancing skyward. "Got to draw the line somewhere."

Chicken Feathers squeezed out a mean little laugh. "Had a pill every time I heard that, I'd have ODd long ago. Looks of you, I'd say you'll be hitting the powder by summer. Sniffing through fall, needles by Christmas. Probably be going bare for it come springtime."

Just like that my mood went from 14/10 to zero.

"Fuck you," I heard myself say.

Chicken Feathers turned to face me, taking off his sunglasses so he could size me up better. He was even rougher-looking than I first thought. Pale eyes with red veins worming all through them. Scar tissue across the bridge of his nose from a beating he'd once taken—a nasty one too, from what I could tell. He took a step toward me, his cheeks flushed with anger. "You got some kind of problem?"

"She's a little touched," Luce said, tapping her forehead. "Go on now, get in the car, sweetie."

But I wasn't going to let him talk to Luce like that. I informed Chicken Feathers it was clear from his idiot lowball prices he didn't know anything about anything and he really should leave the selling to the pros. "Else you're going to keep getting ripped off over and over."

Even Wilky, who had one of the most chill demeanors I've ever encountered, came up and took hold of my elbow. "Come on, hotshot. Time to get going."

"Ripped off?" Chicken Feathers looked me over and then he turned and faced the cottage. "Mom, get out here!"

He wasn't so easy to talk to after that, but even back in those early days I was a pretty good liar. Necessity is the mother of invention, after all. Most people think the trick is staying as close to the truth as possible, but instead you've got to look at it like any other hustle—by which I mean figure out what they want to believe and tell them that. By the time I was done with Chicken Feathers he was convinced I had an older brother who'd served overseas, started selling when our dad got sick, and was now pretty much running the game in Cumberland County.

"You two are basically twins," I said. "Your only problem is you don't know the right people."

"So give me your bro's number. Maybe we could team up or something."

"For a bill, you got it."

Chicken Feathers stared at me. "A hundred dollars. For a number. You're crazy."

I informed him it was a small price to pay for jumping right to the top rung of the ladder. "Course maybe you're the kind of person who doesn't like taking risks. But man, if you could see the house he bought our mother."

Before he could say anything to that, the front door to the

cottage swung open. The old woman came out on the steps, still in her robe. "You call me? I was on the toilet."

"Fuck me," Luce said under her breath.

Chicken Feathers told her never mind and to get back inside and to please put some clothes on already. "And drink some more of that stuff I got you. You'll feel better."

"Do this, do that," said the old woman. "Turns out I don't need your nasty drink. Thanks to those girls there I just took the best shit I had in ages." She went inside and shut the door so loud you could hear it echo all through the mountains.

Poor Chicken Feathers went speckled red.

"Chemo brain," he said after a moment. "She can't help it."

"It's cool," said Luce. "We all got parents."

"I know about chemo brain," I said. "My dad went through it."

Chicken Feathers turned to me. His face went soft like a little kid's. "It's the worst. All those poisons they pump through them. Is your dad still . . . you know."

I tried to laugh it off, but it came out kind of strangled sounding. "Nah."

This next part I don't like thinking about so much, so I'll get it out quickly. What happened was I told him the actual truth. Not the full-length version, just the teaser. VA hospital, wrong diagnosis, wrong treatment. The doctor wanting to discharge him even though he was so ill he could only suck on ice chips. Me and my mom stepping out to get a couple drinks in the cafeteria. And sure, maybe we stayed away a little bit longer than we should have, but when we came back to his room we found nothing but turned-off machines and an empty bed, a gray-haired custodian already sanitizing the handrails.

"He's gone, isn't he?" my mom said, a little too loud. She'd tipped a couple airplane bottles into her Pepsi.

Seconds later the clatter of nurse clogs broke out in the hallway and a frazzled redhead in pink scrubs appeared in the door. She had a bag of Flamin' Hots in one hand and a clipboard in the other. "I was just getting ready to call you," she said.

When I finished my story, I looked up to see Chicken Feathers wincing like someone had punched him right in his busted septum. "That's messed up. I'm sorry."

I told him it was okay, that it was a long time ago and I was over it.

"You say so," he said. "Listen, about that number. All my cash is tied up in medical stuff right now, which is why I'm even in this business, but if you want I could give you a few bundles to middle. Make your dough that way."

I pretended to think it over. "I guess it'll do."

He gave me three buns out of his orange vest and then he dug one of those old Razr phones out of his camouflage coveralls and told me to put in my brother's number. I typed in my mom's cell since she still hadn't bothered to change the factory-preset message on her voice mail, and besides that, I knew she'd never answer. If nothing else, months of me calling her over and over had taught me that much.

Even so, when Chicken Feathers said he was going to check it, the prickle of adrenaline went shooting all through my system. Beside me, I could hear Luce's husky intake of breath. He tapped the screen, waited a second. Tapped it again. Made a face. "Reception here blows. You sure this number's for real? No bullshit?"

I held his gaze without so much as blinking. "Swear on my father's grave."

And then we were racing away in Wilky's Outback. Luce was so excited about our scam that she kicked off her shoes, put her seat all the way back, and did a little sock-foot jig on the ceiling. Wilky studied the road unspooling before us. It had begun to drizzle pretty much the second he started the engine and now the rain was coming down so furious the wipers could hardly keep up. We'd scored a dozen pandas and approximately three grams of dope and all it had cost us was a little over an hour. Well, that and the story about my dad. I felt bad about trading on his death, like it had become nothing more than some flimsy trinket to use in a hustle instead of the hard black diamond I carried around inside me.

Luce turned around. "Hey, you listening?"

"Sorry." I sat up a little. "I think I missed the last part."

She leaned in and gave me a teasing punch on my shoulder. "Dude, you kicked some serious ass today! The way you worked that motherfucker? Amazing."

"What about you and your G-777s?" I said. "That was some pure uncut genius."

"Are we a good team or what?" Luce smiled so big you could see the funny dogtooth incisor she was always hiding. It was one of my favorite things about her.

"The best," I said.

We went back and forth for the next few minutes, jabbering about the low oral ba of pandas and how in this case sniffing would be better than parachuting and that it was actually a good thing the old woman had given us generics since these wouldn't gel up in our noses like the name brand would. By the time we got around to debating if we should sell our bags on campus or one of the gas station hot spots, you could tell Wilky was seriously upset. Despite the rain, he was hitting close to eighty in the straight parts and taking curves so fast we were sliding all over. At one point he hit a bump and Luce and I flew up and bonked our heads on the ceiling. "What the shit?" she said.

He didn't say anything for another minute, maybe longer, though he did slow down to a reasonable limit. The only sound was the wipers sloshing back and forth. At last he glanced at Luce. Said he was sorry. "I'd never want to hurt you in a million years. Thing is, I think I'm starting to feel all the old cravings. It's scary, to be honest."

"I'm sorry, baby," Luce said. "But just hang tight and this will all be over in two weeks. Right, Irene?"

I hesitated, weighing my options. I needed to get this next part right. "Two weeks, absolutely. And if you need to step away until then, we understand. You can't go risking your clean time."

"Wait, what?" Luce looked at me. "Step away? You're kidding."

"I mean, whatever's best for Wilky of course." I leaned

forward. "What does your sponsor say about the cravings? Or have you told him."

Wilky glanced at me in the rearview. I don't know why, but he always trusted me. "He'd probably say something like Meeting makers make it. Stick with the winners. That I might have another high left, but not another recovery. You know, the usual."

Luce stared at him, breathing from her mouth, the way she did when she was upset about something. You could hear her lungs squeaking from all the stress. "Okay, fine. Maybe a break's not the worst idea ever. But just until d-day."

When Wilky said he was also concerned about being a 13th stepper, Luce let out a choked little cry. Even we knew the famous rule against dating newcomers to the program. I leaned back and tried to keep my face from jumping around in triumph. Soon it would be just me and Luce again. The way it should be.

"So you're saying it's over," she said. "Like over-over?"

A pause so long we could have driven our whole lives through it.

"It's either that or start using again," Wilky said.

Years later I still think of that afternoon, the three of us heading home in the rain, sunk in our own private worries. In the front seat, Luce leaned against the window, weeping into the sleeve of her hoodie. Outside a blur of trees rushed by in a dizzying excitement until I wished I'd stolen the old woman's Antivert when I'd had the chance. Meanwhile Wilky turned on the radio, some of the easy-listening junk he was into. "Rainy Days and Mondays," I think was playing, poor Karen Carpenter, or maybe it was "We've Only Just Begun."

The next week, Wilky would tell his primary doc at Bragg's medical center that he'd re-hurt his knee on a practice jump and he needed a new prescription. The doctor-shopping antics would kick in soon after, the whole pain-clinic racket, and before long even that would balloon into something else altogether, something much bigger and far more terrible than we could have ever imagined.

Well I guess you already know about that.

Was there a turnoff we missed, a fateful guidepost? How did we not see where we were going? Even back in those earliest days the warning signs kept popping out all over—and yet it was like they had nothing to do with us or where we were headed. You believe what you want to believe. I guess it was just another hustle, is what I'm saying, except this particular hustle was one we pulled on ourselves.

That afternoon, as we drove up the mountain out of that sad rainy valley, the fog burned away around us and the sky opened back up with all of its bright, dazzling promise. We were invincible once again.

THERE'S A CERTAIN PARKING LOT AT THE EDGE OF Anklewood, right before the town peters out into nothing, where Luce and I used to go when the mood struck us. Wedged behind a seedy neighborhood bar, it didn't look like anything special. Its primary draw was a busted green couch that customers sometimes lounged in during smoke breaks and a couple of folding chairs tucked beneath a low metal awning. A Folgers coffee can full of sand, butts, ashes. An industrial work lamp you could plug in or not.

Because the bar never opened before seven at night, and even later in summer, we'd often head there during daylight hours. Plop ourselves on that shabby green sofa or maybe sprawl out on the old Holly Hobbie blanket Luce kept in the trunk of her Impala. For hours the two of us would gaze out at that empty parking lot. Also the field that lay beyond it, which was overgrown with pokeweed and thistles, and the woods that sat even farther out, waiting, waiting. This was back when we were still using, of course.

On occasion I'd retrieve the pack of cards I kept stashed in the couch cushions and we'd play war or rummy. Other times we'd just chill, maybe mess around on our phones. Later on, when Wilky joined us, he'd bring his guitar and we'd sing all the old songs from childhood. At some point Luce would get up and start dancing and next thing you knew we were spinning around light-headed with pleasure until she had to sit down on her blanket and let her breathing get back to normal. I miss those days.

The bar's owner, a stringy older woman with sun damage from when she ran a tanning salon back in the nineties, didn't mind us hanging out on her property. Despite her never having had children, you could tell a powerful streak of the maternal chugged through her bloodstream. I think she felt protective of us. Better to use in a familiar place than off in some remote, sketchy location. She'd known most of us since we were babies, had watched us grow up, attended our church picnics, applauded us at games and recitals. I'll never forget seeing her eyes well up at my high school graduation. Or how when my dad died my senior year she brought a giant pan of shepherd's pie to the house.

Later on, after Wilky got Big-Chicken-Dinnered from the army and moved out to Anklewood, it was she who gave him a job cleaning the bar every morning. Made him eat when he wasn't eating, talked him down when his parents cut him off without warning, promoted him to bouncer when he got his six-month tag. And while she treated all three of us with a kindness that was getting harder and harder to come by, it was clear she reserved a tender spot for Wilky. The phantom son who had at last materialized. I guess it almost makes sense that of all the shady nooks where everything could have blown up in our faces, it was there Wilky met his end that final evening, slumped in his car, ODd.

•

When I woke up the day after his memorial and saw Luce had vanished, that lonely scrap of land was the first place I thought of. I threw on my new leather jacket, got in the cheese-mobile, and drove up the mountain in the pale chill of morning. At least I'd had enough sense to hide the car keys from Luce. Up to Broad Street, past the Anklewood Mill and its unhappy reminders, past the restaurant where Luce and I waited tables. A handful of folks in line for the Anklewood Wellness Clinic. A slew of boarded-up buildings with FOR RENT signs. In front of the AME Zion church a man in a cheerful blue tracksuit unloaded Bibles from the rear of his hatchback. As I approached MJ's Auto Repair a car alarm went off in a frantic series of honks. Moments later a boy who didn't look any older than twelve or thirteen hurdled the shop's chain-link fence and sprinted in front of me, his arms pumping in panic. I had to brake hard not to hit him, which made a nasty burnt smell pour out of the heater, and though I leaned on the horn, the kid kept going and soon I couldn't see him any longer. A few seconds later the alarm fell still.

I pulled up in front of Wilky's bar and cut the engine. Ordinarily I would have parked in the lot out back, but if Luce was there I didn't want to startle her into running. As quietly as I could I made my way down the footpath that ran alongside the building. Pain bulleted into my knee. Already I could picture Luce asleep on that green couch, lungs wheezing in the chill of the morning—and for one ugly moment I saw myself too. Squatting down beside her, going through her coat pockets to check for leftovers, sniffing whatever I found before she woke up and caught me. As fast as I could

I pushed that thought back into the murky recesses it had crawled out of.

I rounded the corner to the parking lot to see a bulky object lying next to the dumpster. A bag of trash too heavy to toss in the bin was the first thing I thought of, but within moments the bag came into focus. Luce. I sprinted over as best I could, rolled her onto her back, and knuckled her sternum, a trick I'd learned from watching Wilky revive a woman I'd found passed out in a Hardee's bathroom a couple months earlier.

"Dude, what the shit?" Luce pushed me off her.

I stared at her. "I didn't think you were breathing!"

"That fucking hurt," she said, rubbing her chest. With effort, she sat up and filled her lungs with a dramatic whooshing. "See? Couldn't be better."

From the way the words lolled out of her mouth like jelly, I knew she'd sniffed another bag or more.

As calmly as I could, I sat down beside her and informed her that people who were sleeping outside in winter could definitely be doing better. "And why are you next to the dumpster?"

She gave me a look like this was one of the stupider questions I'd asked her.

"Wilky," I said in a rush of understanding. This was where he'd been parked the night he ODd. "I'm sorry. I get it," I said.

I asked her to please come home, saying that I'd make us a big breakfast once we got there. Eggs and home fries and buttermilk pancakes. A pot of superstrong coffee. "Cheesemobile's across the street, ready and waiting."

"Nope," she said. "Not tricking me into one of your meetings."

"What do you mean *my* meetings?"

She didn't answer, just lay back down, pulled her knees up to her chest, and wrapped her arms around them.

A full minute passed.

At last I couldn't take it any longer and I got out my phone to text Greenie. All I had to do was tell her what was going on and she'd be at the bar in minutes. If anyone could help Luce right now, she could. I was typing out my message, trying to strike the right balance of concern and alarm, when out of nowhere Luce's leg flew up and karate-kicked my phone out of my fingers. It sailed into the air and slammed into the side of the dumpster before hitting the ground with a clatter. Luce broke into one of the fits of laughter she used to get back when we were both using: a low whooping sound that started out in her belly before rising up into a convulsive squawk. I'd almost forgotten about that laugh—it felt like it belonged to a whole other lifetime—and hearing it again set off a hot spike of longing.

We went back and forth for several impossible minutes, arguing about Greenie and meetings and the whole entire program. Even though I knew it was pointless, I couldn't help reminding her of all the good stuff that had happened since we got clean. Jobs. Health. Our money situation. "Like when was the last time we had to steal food out of the walk-in?" I said. That sent Luce into a whole new round of junky laughter. I told myself I'd just have to ride it out.

I stayed quiet, drawing loops in the grime with my finger. Experience had taught me that Luce would cool off sooner than later and sure enough it wasn't long before she settled down and closed her eyes, lungs whirring gently. Soon I'd be able to lead her back to the car without any trouble, and though you'd think that would have eased my mind, it only made me more unhappy. I'd never noticed before, probably since I'd always been loaded right alongside her, but when Luce was nodding she was a bit less Luce-like somehow. And yet as I watched her sink back into that numb bliss we used to spend all our time chasing, another pang for the old days went flaring through me. So what if I was clean, if I was also lonely and frightened? Luce looked so peaceful lying there in the dirt.

We headed home. Looking back, we probably should have returned the cheese-mobile on the way and gotten a ride back to our place. For the past couple hours Lonny had been texting me over and over. I NEED IT FOR WORK! said his last message. But I was too busy dealing with Luce. Though she'd leveled off some and was sitting in the passenger seat all buckled up and acting agreeable, one wrong move could send her spinning. I'd just gotten her to promise she'd go to a meeting first thing in the morning.

"On one condition."

"Okay." I glanced over.

Turned out she wanted to stop at Quik Chek and get some ice for my knee. "You make the worst face every time you hit the gas pedal. I can't take it."

I told her we'd be back at our place in a few minutes and we had ice in the freezer.

"You used it all last night, remember? Trays are still in the sink where you left them." She paused. "Or don't you trust me."

"Stop," I said. "I trust you completely. But you know what they say. All this time the disease has been doing push-ups."

Now it was Luce who made a face. "Will you give it a rest with that twelve-step shit? Can't you let your best friend take care of you a little?"

I admit the idea was hard to resist.

We went to Quik Chek. No doubt she'd start bellowing about trust again if I went in with her, so I parked in front of the big plate-glass window. She said she'd be back in two seconds and slid out of the car. A guy in one of those aviator hats with the fake-fur lining was lounging by the newspaper stand and as soon as he caught sight of Luce, he jogged over and held the door open. She disappeared into a wash of fluo-rescent lights. If he'd followed her inside, you better believe I would have gone in right after, but instead he strolled back to his spot, checked his phone, and scanned the horizon, which made me feel a bit better. Anyone could tell he was waiting for his own connect to roll up.

The angle of the window didn't let me see inside the store the way I wanted, but to my relief Luce kept her word about being fast with her purchase. Even so, from the merry little tune she hummed as she plopped down beside me and heaved the sack of ice into the back seat, it was clear she'd scored something for later. Sometimes you just need to look at your gear to get that first rush of pleasure. I've seen more than one person drool at the sight of a loaded rig.

"Crushed was on sale so I got you that. Also, ta-da!" She held up a pack of gummy sours.

Of course.

I thanked her for the ice and the candy, trying my best not to sound suspicious. If she didn't know I was onto her, it would be easier to steal whatever she'd copped and flush it.

"Oh and I swiped you some of this menthol ointment." She pulled a box out of her coat and tossed it into my lap. "My grandma used to rub it on her joints. Said it worked wonders."

So now she was back to shoplifting. There went step 8.

By the newspaper stand, a high-school-age girl with a short feathery haircut approached aviator-hat guy. They did the handoff, parted ways in seconds. It's amazing how fast these things go down. I glanced at Luce. "I was thinking. How about I hit up Greenie and see if she'll swing by our place for a few minutes?"

All the energy bouncing around on her side of the car went flat. "Dude, why are you all up on me? I already said I'm going back tomorrow." Her hand drifted to her right pants pocket, confirming her goodies were still where she'd stashed them. A subconscious move we both made in stressful situations.

It told me all I needed.

"You win," I said.

By the time we pulled into our driveway, the sky had lost all its color and the air had an odd musty smell, sort of like wet newspapers. I checked my phone out of habit. Three more messages from Lonny. I started to respond, asking if I brought his car over now could he give me a ride back to my place.

"You better not be texting any twelve-step people," Luce said, craning over my shoulder.

"I'm not." I showed her my phone to prove it.

When she saw Lonny's string of messages, she shook her head in disgust. "Dude wants his car so bad, he can come over and get it. He's lucky I don't pop a couple BBs in him too. All the stuff we used to give him when he was hurting, he owes us a lot more than a couple days with this piece-of-shit beater." A moment passed and she met my eyes. "Listen, I'm sorry I was an ass before. You're trying to look out for me. I get it."

Despite everything, a warm liquid feeling filled up my insides. "It's all good," I said.

We went in our house and though it was coming up on noon, I made pancakes, scrambled eggs, fried potatoes with lots of salt and butter. I still felt pretty sick about the whole parking lot incident—never mind whatever she'd copped at Quik Chek—but I kept telling myself not to worry. Luce was Luce was Luce. She was the strongest person I'd ever met and if anyone could move past this little setback, she could, no question. Besides, you could hardly blame her. What with everything that had happened, you'd have to be some kind of monster not to slip.

After breakfast I suggested we leave the dishes for later, maybe watch a little TV and put our feet up and try not to think about anything for half a second. I still planned to steal her dope as soon as possible and since Luce often dozed off during crime dramas, I figured it wouldn't be long before opportunity came calling. Already her eyes had that thick muddy look they got during the tail end of a binge. It's nothing I'm proud of, but back when we were using I'd gotten pretty good at picking her pockets. At least this time it wouldn't be for my own selfish reasons.

While Luce emptied the bag of gummy sours into a bowl for us to snack on, I scooped ice into a baggie and began re-wrapping my knee. The clock on the microwave said almost one thirty, which of course made me think of our meeting. Then it hit me that I was supposed to be at work by four. No way could I wait tables in my condition and I sure wasn't leaving Luce unsupervised. Even though I'd called out sick the past two nights, I told myself I could probably get away with missing one more shift.

Because our manager liked Luce more than me (according to my monthly evals I wasn't a good team player) I asked if she'd go get my phone out of my leather jacket and call him. Hers was still hidden away in my closet and after this latest stunt, I wouldn't be giving it back in the near future. "Tell him you think my cold's turned into strep and you're making me stay home even though I don't want to."

Right away, Luce went trotting off. She loved pulling one over on people more than just about anything, and soon I could hear her pacing back and forth by the couch, going on about how my throat was so swollen up with infection I definitely couldn't talk to people, much less customers. I had to put my hand over my mouth to keep from laughing. There was no one in the world like Luce.

"You're all set," she called out. "Marshall says he hopes you feel better."

"Sure he does," I said, hobbling into the main room.

"Hopefully I can walk okay tomorrow or else you're going to have to get creative."

"You really don't want to use my insurance? All you need's my social. We could take the Mazda and drive out to an urgent care where they don't know us."

By some trick of fate, Luce was still on her stepdad's Blue Cross policy even though they hadn't spoken since the previous summer. I hadn't had insurance since my parents got laid off back when I was in high school, and like all the others, our current restaurant made sure no one got enough hours to qualify for their plan. Although the local walk-in clinic had helped me out in the past, Luce and I had been banned from the premises for trying to jimmy a cabinet.

"Better not," I said, lowering myself onto the sofa. "They'd catch on sooner or later and then we'd be on the hook for fraud and who knows what else."

Luce flopped down on the BarcaLounger. "Dude, we're seriously turning into a couple old ladies. We never have any fun anymore. Come on, maybe they'll give you some legit pain meds. We'll split them."

When I looked at her in surprise, she started laughing like it was the funniest thing ever. "I'm just fucking with you," she said.

We sat there for a while not talking, watching a *Law & Order* episode we'd seen a dozen times over. You know the one. Where the woman's been shot in the head, but if the doctors remove the bullet, she could croak right there on the table. The whole time I kept waiting for Luce to either conk out or else excuse herself to the bathroom so she could sniff in private, but when she just sat there gazing at the TV like she was actually following the story, it occurred to me that maybe I'd misjudged her. Some friend I was. I got out the menthol ointment she'd given me and squinted at the label and then I snuck another look at her: feet kicked up in the recliner, one hand resting on the mound of her belly, the other fanning herself with a Bed Bath & Beyond flyer. I thought of her crack about us turning into a couple of old ladies. Maybe it was true.

It wasn't until the next episode started up in that way they fold right into each other that I turned to see Luce hunched over the coffee table. For a split second I thought I was dreaming. She was using the Bed Bath & Beyond flyer to cut a line of dope! A jolt of electricity streaked through me like I'd been plugged into a socket.

She smiled at me. "Junk mail. Get it?"

"Luce." I didn't know what to say. When she sniffed up the powder, my intestines cramped so bad it was like I was going cold turkey. "Please. I mean it."

"You're right, I'm being an asshole." She held out the flyer. "Have a bump."

The TV went to commercial and a series of glossy middle-aged people started giving testimonials for a product I couldn't make any sense of. My knee ached like someone was driving nails straight through the bone. I tried to reason with Luce, saying she shouldn't be snorting anything, not with her asthma. "And where's your inhaler?"

"Inhaler, inhaler," she said. "I know. Why don't you try minding your own business?"

I looked around but I didn't see her purse anywhere. "Go get it, will you? In case something happens."

Instead of answering, she raised her upper lip and bared her teeth at me. Even that quick glimpse of her dogtooth incisor made my heart jump around a little. When she started chopping another line, it stopped and held itself perfectly still. "Luce. Don't. I'm not kidding."

With an icy smile, she leaned over the powder.

"Fine. I'm calling Greenie then." I got my phone off the coffee table where she'd left it. Quick as a flash she lunged in my direction and next thing I knew Luce was sitting on top of me, trying to pry it out of my fingers. "My knee," I said, gasping.

"You call her, I'll fucking hate you forever."

"You're hurting me!"

"Promise you won't call Greenie."

A knock came at the door.

If you've ever fought with someone you love more than anyone else on the planet, then I don't have to explain how you can feel like full-on murdering that person one second and then a second later be willing to throw yourself on top of a bomb for them. No doubt Greenie was checking up on us after we missed the 1:30. Showing up loaded to yesterday's meeting wasn't the smartest move ever. If she saw Luce was still using, she'd say this wasn't a slip but a full-blown relapse, which would lead to required twice-daily group meetings, one-on-one sessions, copying entire chapters of the Basic Text by hand, not to mention counseling at Journeys if Greenie was madder than usual. There was even a chance she'd ship Luce off to some state-funded rehab. No way was I letting that happen. What would I ever do without Luce?

The knock came again. "Come on, ladies. Open up. It's freezing."

Nogales?

I yelled for him to hold on a sec. "I just got out of the shower!"

"Dude never fucking gives up," Luce said. She rolled off the couch, leaned over the coffee table, and sniffed up the line she'd cut. "I know you two used to be cool and all, but this is turning into harassment."

Even though she was still a good ten minutes away from peaking, her skin already had the telltale flush of someone with junk in their system. Her pupils looked like tiny black poppy seeds. Sure Nogales had let her off the day before, but his goodwill wasn't endless.

In a low voice I told Luce to go to her room. "He sees you like this, he could report you for violating probation."

She gave me a mocking salute. "Aye aye, Captain."

"And leave the rest here." I held my hand out.

Luce inhaled. A soft ugly rasping. "I don't have any left, I swear it."

"I'll give it back I promise, but I don't want you doing the rest of it alone in your room."

She gave me a hateful look as expected, but at last she reached into her pocket and pulled out what remained of a bun. I could still feel the heat from her skin when she pressed it into my fingers. "There, bitch, you happy?"

"I love you too," I said.

After scooting her off to her room with her inhaler, I limped into the bathroom, wrapped a towel around my head, put on my robe, and tucked the dope in the chest pocket. I fought my way back into the main room and hid the empty glassine bags under the pile of mail. When I finally opened the door, Nogales didn't look happy.

"We need to chat," he said.

I let him inside, telling him not to track any crap in. If I'd been nice about it, he would have been suspicious. Even so, his eyes went straight to the coffee table as if he knew exactly what had gone down. "Bed Bath & Beyond, huh? You planning a little shopping excursion?"

"I have to get ready for work," I said. "Can we have this chat tomorrow?"

He checked his watch. "It's just now three. You don't have to be there for another hour."

"Good memory. Thing is, they sprayed for bugs last night and Marshall asked if I'd do him a favor and come in early to wipe the poison off the chairs and tables."

"Look at you. Doing favors." Nogales went to the kitchen and poked his head in. "Where's Luce?"

I said she was taking a nap, that Wilky's memorial had knocked the wind out of her.

He nodded. "She wasn't doing great yesterday, that's for sure. That meeting help any?"

"You know Greenie. Keeping us all on the straight and narrow."

Nogales held my gaze. "Hope so."

At last he got around to telling me that Lonny had called

the sheriff's office about his stupid Mazda. It took some doing, but Nogales had convinced him not to press charges. "Had to promise him a get-out-of-jail-free card next time he's pulled over."

"Yeah?" I said. "Funny, me and Luce never got one of those. Way I remember it, we got locked up in about six seconds. First-time offenders."

"Come on," he said, flushing. "You want me to say it again? I'm sorry, I'm sorry, I'm sorry, I'm sorry."

He meant it too, you could see it.

"Sure you are," I said.

While he went outside and radioed for a tow truck, my thoughts kept ricocheting between Luce holed up in her bedroom and the dope burning a square in my pocket. Even though I knew she'd hate me, I had to get rid of it before Nogales came back and figured out what was happening. I'm not saying he was some kind of psychic, but with me he always had an oddly accurate sixth sense. Back when we were together, it felt like part of whatever private connection we shared between us, and once I got used to him knowing what I was thinking, it was kind of nice having someone around who understood me. Comforting, almost. Now that we were broken up, it wasn't such a comfort anymore.

I was standing over the garbage disposal when I heard the front door open. I whisked the bags back into my robe quick as possible.

"Truck's on its way," Nogales called out. A split second later, he appeared in the kitchen doorway. "What are you doing in here? Thought you had to get ready."

"You know me. Coffee first." I pulled a couple of mugs out of the dry rack. "Want some? I was just about to make it."

"Sounds great," he said.

But as we stood there looking at each other, his face grew twitchy—not much, you would've had to look hard to see it— and I knew Nogales was having one of his mind-reading episodes. Although he covered it up quick, there was no denying he'd realized something was up, even if he didn't understand what exactly.

"Actually." He cleared his throat. "I better take a rain check. You know how busy Mondays get down at the station."

"You sure?" I smiled as best I could. "Won't take but a second."

Nogales was already heading to the front door. "Say hi to Luce, will you? I'll catch you two later."

And he was gone.

Almost an hour had passed since the tow truck pulled the cheese-mobile out of our driveway. Luce was back in the Barca-Lounger watching yet another *Law & Order*. I was stretched out on the sofa with a fresh baggie of ice balanced on my knee. The air stunk of menthol ointment and a second round of ibuprofen was making its way through my system. So far none of it had knocked the pain down any, but maybe something would kick in by the time they got to the courtroom section.

The good news was Luce hadn't asked for her dope back. I wasn't sure why—no way she'd forgotten I had it—but at least she wasn't acting all fiendy. I told myself I did the right thing by

not rinsing it down the disposal. That was Luce's job. We'd talk
it out and then we'd go into the kitchen together. I'd hand it over
and watch as she emptied it into the drain and pushed the button. Greenie always said you couldn't make anyone get clean unless they were willing. Until then, it waited in my chest pocket,
warm and steady. There was something calming about it.

When my phone buzzed out of nowhere, I flinched, causing
my ice pack to fall onto the floor next to the sofa. A call from
an unfamiliar local number. Before I could answer, whoever it
was hung up. Right away I knew it was Nogales, hitting me up
from a buddy's phone to trick me into answering. I turned to
Luce, planning to make some crack about needy dudes, only
to find the recliner was empty. She was by the door, pulling her
boots on.

"Mail came," she said. "Be back in a second."

I looked at her. "You expecting something?"

"Been getting a few condolence cards. It's not like I want
to read them, but I also don't want them sitting out there all
by their lonesome." She zipped up her new fur-trimmed parka
and spun around like a model. "Not bad, right?"

"You look great," I said.

On TV, Jack McCoy was heckling a witness and the Advil
was doing as much good as a children's chewable. I checked
my pocket, making sure Luce hadn't somehow lifted the bags
when I wasn't paying attention. But they were there, loyal as
ever. I glanced out the window. Luce was at the mailbox, flipping through envelopes. A painful fist formed in my stomach.
Some people look extra sad when they don't know they're being watched.

When my phone buzzed again. I expected to see the same number as before but instead it was the restaurant. Without thinking, I answered.

"Where are you?" said Marshall. "I got Fran doing your opening sidework and she isn't too happy about it. You almost here or what?"

"I'm sick, remember? Luce called you."

As if on cue, the front door opened and in she came. She took off her boots and went sock-wise into the bathroom.

"I haven't talked to her in days," Marshall said. "And hey, I know you girls are going through some stuff, but this no-show crap won't fly. I don't care how short-staffed we are, either you're here in ten minutes or you can take the rest of the week off right along with it."

"I'm sorry," I said. "I really am sick, I promise. Or actually the truth is I twisted my knee yesterday and it hurts to walk. You don't remember talking to Luce? I heard her call you."

"See you in a week," he said, hanging up.

I probably don't have to tell you that by the time Luce emerged from the bathroom, she was well on her way to Nodsville. She socked her way back to the BarcaLounger, plopped down, and reclined her chair with a slow crank of the lever. When I told her I just got off the phone with Marshall, she laced her hands over her stomach and closed her eyes. "Yeah? How's he doing."

The whole thing came together as if Junky Jesus himself had delivered it in a sermon on the mount. I leaned forward. "You texted someone on my phone instead of calling Marshall. They put your shit in the mailbox, rang once as a signal. Let me guess, it was either Teena or Marcella. Or no." I snapped my fingers. "Durl. Probably thinks he's got a shot with you after what all happened."

"Durl," she said, dragging the name out. "Anyone deserves to get hustled, he does."

"While I get a week's suspension for no-call no-show. Is this really how you want to play it?"

"Listen, I'll go to the 1:30 tomorrow, I promise, but can you please just let me enjoy myself for one fucking second?"

We sat there not speaking. It wasn't long before Luce turned her face away and began to snore—a gentle buzz that usually cheered me up whenever I heard it—but now only made me even more angry. I turned off the TV, hoping that would get her attention, but she just let out a shiver and rolled over. At last I hauled myself up and tucked the afghan around her arms and shoulders.

Outside, the sun had turned an overripe sort of color, like a peach right before it goes wormy. From my spot on the couch, I watched it sink lower and lower until it vanished behind the mountain. I reached up and pulled the chain on the gooseneck lamp next to the coffee table. A cone of light formed in the air. Only then did I realize Luce had her eyes open. She was watching me with a funny expression—as if there was something she wanted to tell me.

"What," I said.

She filled her lungs, let the air out slowly. "Look. People drift apart. It happens."

"Drift?" I did my best to smile at her. "Sorry, but you're too messed up to make any sense. Go back to sleep. We have a big day tomorrow."

"I'm serious," she said. "You're this close to getting your one-year tag and I'm about to take my second Day 1 in a week. Let's be real. We're in complete different places."

I told her how much time a person has doesn't matter. "You know that."

"Bullshit," she said.

This next part Greenie doesn't like so much when I share it. The regulars don't appear to be all that wild about it either and even the hot-off-the-press newbies tend to start squirming around in their chairs. But what they don't realize is it's one of the best, most wholesome parts of the story! Don't get me wrong, Greenie always helped me a lot and I respect her, just like I respect anyone else who has the guts to sit circled up in these rooms. Old-timers like her know something about life on this planet that most of us never come close to understanding—so you'd think she'd recognize that what happened next had nothing to do with loss or pain or failure. It was from an entirely different universe.

I reached for the mail on the coffee table. Got one of those postcards that are always advertising ten-dollar oil changes. Took Luce's stash out of my pocket, shook out a bag on the table, chopped it, sniffed up a rail. A warm fizz filled my veins and it wasn't long before my knee felt better than ever. The rest of my troubles faded into the dim, one by one. Soon the only thing left was the mysterious grace of god rippling all through me, along with a faint sour drip at the back of my throat.

And Luce. Luce glowing in the yellow haze of lamplight. Her glorious dogtooth incisor. Her lungs taking air in and out. Already I could see us walking into tomorrow's meeting, chins high, shoulder to shoulder. We'd pour ourselves cups of coffee and join the circle. Listen to stories. Maybe share a little. Reach in the box of key tags and take our Day 1s. Just the thought of it brought on a whole new rush of wonder and to celebrate I cut another line of powder. Luce and I were together again.

Part 2

FIRST THINGS FIRST: DON'T DO IT. MAYBE YOU think you have the willpower to be a tourist, to chip on weekends, on payday, when you're stressed out because your mom phoned you up asking you to send her another Money-Gram so she can buy groceries or because your manager keeps following you around the restaurant saying you might not have such a crap schedule if you'd just go out for drinks with him once in a while—but guess what? That gray glob of fat riding around in your skull works like every other human brain on the planet. It won't be long before that stuff owns you. Seriously, don't start.

And if you do start, don't eat/sniff/smoke/shoot/boof and drive. I know a woman who nodded off, smashed into a utility pole outside the Quik Chek, woke up to being Narcanned in an ambulance, and was taken straight to County where she got to go through withdrawal in lockup. Another guy I know railed percs in his bedroom one night, decided he just had to have himself a ten-piece McNuggets and ended up flipping his mom's Celica. Dude walked away with nothing more than a nasty bruise on his shoulder, thanks to Junky Jesus, but the car was totaled and of course his mom only had liability. A year later she's still taking the bus to work.

If you decide to drive, don't keep your stash in your glove box or your center console. You get pulled over, that's the first place they're checking. Even if they don't have probable all they do is pretend they smell weed and just like that your vehicle's being searched and you're being felt up by a rubber-gloved deputy sheriff. Do yourself a favor and hide it in your fuse panel. In the overhead light fixture. Depending on your personal situation, you can tuck it in your privates, but believe me when I tell you the pervert cops will be jamming their fingers in you in about two seconds flat. Luce's solution was to take out the padded inserts in her bras, which left a couple handy pockets for storage that no one ever found no matter how enthusiastically they groped her. Then again Luce was always lucky, for the most part.

Don't steal your grandma's pain pills, it'll haunt you forever. Don't steal her fent patches. Don't volunteer to drive her to her friend's house for their weekly cribbage tournament, ask if you can use the bathroom, and go through the medicine chest. Don't get mad at your grandma when she starts hiding her Dilaudid from you. Don't dig through her garbage so you can smoke the used patches. Don't take her cash out of her purse. When she asks you about the missing dough, don't lie to her face and make her worry even more about her failing memory. Don't steal her ATM card and try out your birthday for the password—she loves you so much that it will work. When she dies, you will 10/10 feel like a piece of shit for having been the worst kind of grandkid imaginable but even if it hurts so bad you think you might black out, definitely don't leave her funeral early and hurry back to her apartment and search her bedroom until you find her meds hidden in the lining of her old winter parka. You'll end up sharing that story at meetings for years and it'll never get easier.

If you can quit at this point, do.

Don't say dumb crap over text. Ask if the tickets are still available, if they can hang, if you can pay them the hundred bucks you owe them. Don't fuck people over. Always pay your debts. Don't wear good clothes or sit on a nice couch if you're a smoker because when you nod you'll wake up to find burn holes in the fabric. Don't ignore your gut—take off if something feels sketchy. Keep your eyes open. Never let your money walk.

It's true that Junky Jesus will often help out if you need it. I can't tell you how many people I know who've been sweaty and feverish and almost doubled over in pain, and then they look on the ground and find a legit OC 80 just waiting for someone to come along and eat it. A ziplock of roxies. A strip of a215s still in the blister pack. Once Luce and I were so sick we thought we were going to die right there at the Chevron and of course the rain wouldn't stop and none of the regulars were around and no one was answering texts, not even the shady middles or the dudes who took pleasure in ripping girls off. When the cashier, a stocky redhead named Sharlene who used to babysit me when I was in kindergarten, came out and said she was going to call the cops if we didn't get a move on, my bowels cramped up so bad I thought I was going to poop my pants like a little kid. And then in rolls this beat-up Chevy Impala, same exact year as Luce's only this one is midnight blue instead of green, and a girl with candy-pink hair and a weirdly cool chambray jumpsuit climbs out and starts filling her tank, her head bobbing in time to some private interior music. She also has this giant corduroy purse she hugs close to her body instead of leaving it in the front seat like most people—and this is what tips us off. We go up to her and Luce asks if we could maybe get directions. Directions to where exactly, Luce doesn't say. The girl flicks her eyes over our gray sweaty faces and then she tells us to hold on a sec because she has to pee like a mother. Goes inside, comes out a few minutes later, hands us a plastic sack. "Got you a couple Gatorades, some Sour Skittles. Threw in a little extra something on me. A get-well treat you could call it." She slides into her car and goes zooming off into the distance. At the bottom of the bag are a half dozen dillies. Junky Jesus for the win.

If your girl tells you it's so strong that dudes are falling out all over, listen. If the pill looks faded or crumbly, if the numbers are blurry or the lettering isn't tight in the corners, do a test bump no bigger than the size of a match head. It's probably fent-pressed. If you're trying not to use, don't go on r/opioids and look at the dope porn because it'll just make you drool and put you at risk for slipping. If you need to cold-cop, buy a small amount at first so you're not out a lot of dough if it ends up being trash. If you get shorted, say something. You don't have to be a dick about it but stand up for yourself so you won't keep getting taken advantage of. If you decide the game has gotten too exhausting, too stupid, that it costs too much and gives you a whole bunch of nothing or worse in return, maybe go to a meeting and see what happens, just for today.

If you're sick and no one's answering, J.J. has also been known to work his miracles on Craigslist. Look for listings under roofing tar, missed connections named Roxy, or designer blue jeans size m30. Also some folks swear by the DNM. Install

Tor, get some BTC (localbitcoins.com), and check r/DarkNet for a good OPSEC guide and the names of a few reliable vendors. Although Luce and I never really got into that scene, even when we were flailing around in the snake pit, I'm told the quality can be off-the-charts fantastic and you can find rare stuff you'd never be able to get from your local dgirl. Then again now that the Feds have been seizing markets I hear it's turning into a real cluster. Nothing's as easy as it used to be. Still, imagine a package just showing up at your doorstep— you'd never have to leave the house if you didn't want to! Which is also risky. If you're able to get out of the game, try.

Make sure you and your friends have Narcan and know how to use it. If you can't wake someone or if their breathing is slow/shallow and their eyes are pinned, they might be in serious trouble. Call 911, stick the tip of the device into one of their nostrils, press down on the plunger. Sometimes you have to administer repeated doses before they regain consciousness. Also be aware that it basically puts the recipient into instant painful withdrawal so don't be surprised if they start howling in anguish. After a little time has passed they'll be forever grateful you were around to revive them—but in the moment they'll think they're about to go meet the great dealer in the sky. And since you can never predict when someone you know will slip after an extra-crap night at work followed by drinks with their pervert manager, or after a surprise visit from their mom during which an entire weekend's worth of tips vanishes out of their bag, or if you happen upon a stranger sitting outside the Food Lion in a dented blue Impala, slumped against the dashboard, circling the drain, you'll want to keep a box of the spray in your purse or backpack. There's a real crisis going on out there. Take it from a former high school mathlete: the real Junky Jesus = Narcan + someone who happens to care whether or not you pull through.

I'D SET MY ALARM SO WE COULD GET READY FOR OUR new Day 1s, but either it never went off or else I slept through it. It was almost noon when I woke up feeling more well rested than I had in ages. That was one good thing about using.

I got out of bed, took a step, yelped in pain and confusion. After rewrapping my knee and swallowing two Advil, I made my way into the kitchen. Luce was sitting at the table wearing Wilky's giant *Florida: Come Hell or High Water!* T-shirt, picking the mini-marshmallows out of a leftover box of Count Chocula with one hand and scrolling through her phone with the other.

"Where'd you find that?" I said.

"In the cupboard. Been there since Halloween probably." She didn't look up, just thumbed the screen over and over.

"Not the cereal, your phone. Did you go in my room while I was asleep and take it?"

"You gave it to me before bed, remember?"

I tried to think how the night had ended, but the last thing I could picture was me doing one last line and drifting into a warm froth of pleasure. "Okay, but you asked me to hang on to it for safekeeping."

"And now I don't need to be kept safe anymore." She put the cereal box down and started typing. The sound of a message being sent whooshed between us.

"Fine," I said. "We still on for the 1:30?"

"For sure." Before she could say anything else, her phone lit up with an incoming message. She read it and let out a low, earthy laugh. Right away she went back to texting.

I put my hands on the table and told her I was going to take a quick shower and then call Greenie to see if she'd drive us, since my knee wasn't fully recovered. "You think you can be ready to go in an hour?"

"For sure," she said again.

But once I'd showered and called Greenie, I came back to find Luce had moved to the sofa where she was watching a YouTube video with her phone propped on her stomach. A guy with an Adidas snapback worn low to hide his features was explaining how to break the time release on OPs.

"Man, we weren't even out of the game for a year," Luce said when she looked up and saw me. "Since then, it's gone total bananas. I'm not talking the old Dr Pepper soak or that Ped Egg horseshit. Just saw this one chick in a pair of swimming goggles grind up her pandas with an electric drill, toast the powder in her little Chefmaster, and then chill it and snort it up with a tube from one of those metal Zebra pens. I'm all, really bitch? That's what we're doing?"

"Sorry to interrupt, but you might want to start getting ready. Greenie'll be here before too much longer."

"And the prices. Be one thing if you knew for sure what you were buying."

"There's plenty of hot water left if you want to take a quick shower."

"Not to mention the dupe market is seriously out of control. You can buy a tablet press on eBay for two hundred dollars." Luce shook her head in amazement. "And you should see the mold die sets on Bonanza. Looking real as fuck. Used to be you could tell the fakes just by eyeballing them, but I guess that's over."

"Even if you don't want to wash up, you better eat something besides chocolate marshmallows. You want me to make you a sandwich?" I turned toward the kitchen.

"Hold up, you got to see this." Luce typed something into her phone. "Okay here, check it. Mall Santa nodding right in front of fucking Belk's. Now wait, wait for it—" She broke out in a fit of laughter. "Down he goes! I must have seen this thing twenty times and it still gets me. I mean seriously, who downvoted this, it's amazing!"

I had to admit it was pretty funny but at the same time it was completely sad. "Come on. We don't want to keep Greenie waiting. After your little performance, she's not going to be too patient."

"Calm down, will you? Takes me thirty seconds to get ready."

"Fine," I said, holding my hands up. She was right. Over the past two and a half years we'd been through all sorts of stuff and though Luce had given me quite the scare on any number of occasions, no matter what happened she always came through.

I went into the kitchen and made us each a grape jelly sandwich. I told myself not to worry, but I couldn't help trying to hear if she was still watching dumb junky videos. Of course she was. Back when I was using I often did the same thing and while it's true all the online stuff cheers you up in the moment—like discovering your real family right there at the tips of your fingers—in the end it just makes you feel even more alone.

I brought her a Gatorade along with her sandwich and set them on the coffee table, hoping a little nourishment would give her the jump start she needed. She was sitting up, which I took as a sign of progress, and as politely as I could I suggested that if she wasn't going to shower, she should at least put on a T-shirt that didn't stink to high heaven. Some deodorant maybe.

She let out a huff of annoyance and pulled the afghan around her shoulders.

"No offense," I said. "You're a bit ripe for a meeting is all I'm saying."

"Yeah, about that. I can't make it."

I stared at her. "You promised. Greenie's on her way over."

"Too bad." She raised her head and looked at me. "I'm busy."

With a shock I saw her eyes were pinned.

She hauled herself off the couch and walked toward her bedroom, her afghan clutched around her like a cape. I don't know how, but whenever Luce was breaking your heart, she always managed to look especially regal.

"Wait," I said. "I need to ask you a question."

The only response I got was the sound of her door clicking shut.

Seeing no way around it, I texted Greenie and said we were grabbing a ride from a neighbor so she didn't need to come get us. I definitely didn't want her anywhere near Luce. Greenie had an NA connection in Raleigh, some bigwig named Flo she'd once met at a conference, and in the eleven months that me and Luce had been going to meetings at least half a dozen relapsers had disappeared out of the rooms without warning. Thirty days later they resurfaced, thumping the Big Book and talking in nothing but slogans. If Greenie saw how bad things had gotten, she'd be on the phone to Raleigh in seconds. And sure, thirty days is nothing when it comes to rehab, but I couldn't imagine being separated from Luce for anywhere near that long.

From her bedroom came the sound of Tool blasting on the little boom box she kept on her dresser. Luce wasn't much into prog metal when she was sober, but when she was using she liked to nod to everything from power noise to surfer music to even that whiny shoegazer garbage. It wasn't too promising that of all the songs in the world, she'd chosen "Undertow" to play on repeat at earsplitting volume. I went to her room and pounded on the door. "I get it, the home group can be pretty stressful. You think maybe you could make the 7?"

When she didn't answer I decided to lie down on the couch, let things cool off a little. The spirograph of pain in my knee kept getting worse, radiating outward like some evil geometry. I came close to asking Luce for another bag—just so I could knock the pain down enough to walk to the meeting— but I managed to talk myself out of it.

Maybe if I could get Nogales to bring me a brace it would take the edge off. I got my phone out, composed a message. I hadn't even hit send when a car came gravelling onto our driveway. Pretty impressive, even for Nogales, but I guess some people just have a certain connection. I hauled myself off the couch and went to let him in. "You must be psychic," I said, pulling the door open.

"Comes with the territory," Greenie said.

I took a painful step backward and did a quick sweep of the room for any stray empties. "Sorry, I thought you were Nogales."

"Nice to see you too," she said. She pushed past me, holding a cardboard tray of three Dunkin' coffees. "Extra cream, extra sugar, the way you like it."

"Thanks, but didn't you get my message?"

"Course I did." Greenie sat on the couch like a detection dog that just alerted. "Want to tell me what's going on?"

In the calmest voice I could muster, I explained that Luce was having a rough day and she wasn't quite up for being around people. "We'll definitely be at your 1:30 tomorrow, no question."

"When she's upset is when she most needs a meeting."

"I know. I tried to tell her. You know how hardheaded she gets once she makes up her mind about something."

But Greenie had already stopped listening to me. She angled her head toward Luce's bedroom, where Tool was still blasting. You could see her trying to puzzle out the lyrics. Once she realized what Maynard was talking about, who knew what would happen.

"Actually," I said, "I was hoping you could help me get a brace for my knee. You have time to run me out to Walmart?"

Greenie flicked her eyes over me. "You're trying to hustle me out of here. I can smell it."

"Look!" I rolled up my sweatpants to help sell my story.

When she saw the mangle of tissue, Greenie turned an unflattering shade of white. She hauled herself off the couch, faced Luce's bedroom, and tilted her head back. "Lucille! Get out here now."

Although she didn't turn the music off, Luce lowered the volume—a testament to Greenie's power. A long moment passed and at last she came out of her room. Though she did her best to smile like things were normal, her cheeks were smeary and red as if she'd been crying. "Did I hear the voice of an angel?" she said.

Greenie informed Luce she had two choices. Either go to the 1:30 and stay for some serious one-on-one time after, or skip it and go straight to in-patient treatment. "One phone call to the Department of Mental Health and the rehab wheels get set in motion."

"Mental health," Luce said. "Concept."

"I take it you're choosing the meeting?" said Greenie.

Luce appeared to think this over. "Yeah, hard pass. You two go on without me. I got shit here to take care of."

"Okay then." Greenie got her phone out. "Actually you're making the smart decision. Considering all you've been through lately, going away is probably the best option."

"Can't fucking wait," Luce said.

I stared at her. I couldn't believe it. Was she really agreeing to a monthlong stint with the Big Book cronies? "Excuse me, but can we maybe discuss this on the way to Walmart? I got a real knee emergency."

Greenie spoke into her phone. "Hello, is Flo available?"

"Fine," I said. "If you won't drive me, I'll find someone else. Someone who actually cares about my well-being."

"Tell her it's about a new client," said Greenie.

"Teena," I said. "You remember her, right? From the old days?"

Greenie turned to me with a grunt of displeasure. She didn't want us talking to our former dgirls under any circumstances. "You know what, let me call you back in a minute."

I glanced at Luce, hoping she'd be impressed with my distraction tactics. She just went over to the door and began putting her shoes on. "Whatever, you win. Long as we take Irene to Walmart, I'll go to your damn meeting. I can't listen to her gripe about her stupid knee for one more second."

"Good girl," said Greenie. She checked the time on her phone and turned to me. "We're going to be cutting it close. You sure we can't get the brace after the 1:30?"

"Not if you're planning some big one-on-one session," I said. "Those things take forever."

"We could always skip that part," said Luce.

"Nice try," said Greenie.

Soon we were zooming east on 27 in Greenie's VW Beetle. Luce had her head stuck out the passenger-side window like one of those country dogs you always see riding shotgun in summer. I was in the back, my bad leg stretched across the bench seat. Even though Luce and I were finally on our way to a meeting, I felt off-balance and nervous. Maybe because the last time I was at this particular Walmart my mom got popped for sneaking a case of Progresso chili out through the garden center entrance. The security guard who nabbed her, a woman with a sticky-looking puff of yellow hair and what looked like those plastic aligners from the SmileDirectClub, hauled us both in the back, took my mom's photo, and made her sign a paper swearing she'd never again set foot on the property. Talked to her like she was a complete garbage-head even though my mom had been on a timeout from drinking since New Year's. Of course the timeout ended the second we got home. The whole thing was a real turning point for my mom, and in the wrong direction. I'll never forget the beaten look she had on her face while the security guard shamed her in front of her daughter.

We got to Walmart, Greenie parked, cut the engine. "You girls wait here. I'll be back in a jiffy."

"You sure?" I said. "I can go get it."

"With that knee of yours, it'll take all day." She looked around the lot. "Just stay in the car and roll up that window. Don't talk to anyone. I swear this place gets worse every time I come here. You'd think security would do something about it."

"Don't worry," Luce said. "Everyone knows this place is press central. We're not stupid."

A look of relief passed across Greenie's face. "Okay then, see you in a minute." She got out of the car and went lumbering toward the entrance.

The moment the automatic doors slid shut behind Greenie, Luce got out of the car. Without waiting to see if I was coming, she made straight for the bank of vending machines—Coke, Redbox, purified water—where a man in a too-small pink puffer was examining a slip of paper. I hurried after her as best I could. See, the scam goes like this: find a Walmart receipt someone lost or discarded and then go into the store, pull whatever they bought from the shelf, and take it to customer service. Get refunded cash if you're lucky, but chances are they'll hook you up with store credit—and every dealer I ever met will give you fifty cents on the dollar.

When Pink Puffer looked up and saw us, he gave us the classic chin nod as if he'd been expecting our arrival. "Gimme five minutes. Just got to find the vacuum section."

"Other way around," Luce said. "We're looking."

"Are you serious?" I said to her. "She'll be back any second."

Luce kept her gaze fixed on Pink Puffer. "Who around here's reliable?"

"I mean it," I said. "If we're not in the car, she'll completely lose it."

"So let her. She'll get over it."

Pink Puffer shook his head in amusement. "You ladies best figure yourselves out. You're still here when I get back, I'll make an introduction." Before either Luce or I could say anything further, he went hurrying down the sidewalk.

"Better be careful with that guy," a voice behind us said.

I hadn't noticed her earlier, but sitting on the ground nearby was a ruddy-faced woman who looked to be somewhere in her thirties, gripping a cigarette in her knuckles like it was the only thing left in the world that could save her.

"Why's that," Luce said, barely glancing over.

The woman exhaled two dragon-like plumes of smoke

through her nose. "Take it you girls are on your way to a meeting?"

That got Luce's attention. "How'd you know that?"

"Saw you pull up earlier. I'd recognize that green bug of Greenie's anywhere. Was in the rooms with her for a while, couple years ago maybe."

"Really?" I said. "You switch to a different meeting, or?"

The woman shrugged and went back to smoking.

"Hey, it's cool," I said. "We've been trying to stay out of the game for eleven months now. It's not easy."

"Don't go kidding yourself," said the woman. "We're all in the game. You, me, Greenie, and everyone else on the planet. Even the little tiny babies, so fresh and pure they don't have any idea who they are or what the hell they're doing. You see what I'm saying?"

"Sure," I said, trying to hide my confusion. "Absolutely."

"Okay then," she said.

Her name was Gayle Crystal, she went on to tell us. "Like the singer, but backwards. You know, the one whose hair went down past her butt. Would have been a singer myself, but my lungs are fried from asthma. Not to mention I used to be a sniffer, and now the doc says my chest is chock-full of scar tissue."

"I have asthma too," Luce said. "Ever since I was little."

"Yeah?" said Gayle Crystal. "You're not a sniffer, are you?"

A horn was honking somewhere in the distance.

"No," Luce said. "Or yeah, once in a while. But me and her are mostly clean now. Greenie's our sponsor."

"Greenie, Greenie, Greenie," Gayle Crystal said. "She was

half as smart as she thinks she is, she'd be a certifiable genius."

Before that moment, I'd never heard anyone say one bad word against Greenie. "What's that supposed to mean?"

"What do you think," said Gayle Crystal, watching me closely. Her face took on a folded-up, secret look. "So what's the deal with your knee? Spent too much time on it buffing pickles?"

Luce busted out laughing. I didn't get what was so funny.

"No, but seriously," said Gayle Crystal. "The three of us should hang out sometime. I'll show you how to rig a bendy straw so your lungs don't get all clogged with powder. How to sniff so you get the most bang for your dollar. Key words being *low* and *slow*. It's too late for me, but maybe not for you two."

"She has an inhaler," I said. "Does a pretty good job of helping."

"You kidding? Those things, you're squirting poison straight down your throat." Gayle Crystal turned to Luce. "You want, I'll hook you up with my personal doctor. He's got one of those pay-what-you-can deals. Your name's Lucille, right?"

I gaped at her in disbelief. "How'd you know that?"

Even Luce looked shaken.

Gayle Crystal gave us a knowing smile. "Irene, better not ask a question if you don't want the answer."

"Fuck man," said Luce. "Are you some kind of fortune-teller or something?"

"You could say that," Gayle Crystal said. "And I hate to be the one to tell you, but your fortunes just took a serious turn south. You didn't hear old Greenie bawling your names and blasting her horn the past couple minutes?"

In a single move, Luce and I ducked into the shadow of the Redbox dispenser.

Gayle Crystal mashed her cigarette out on the pavement. "I was you, I'd lay low till she comes to her senses. That temper of hers is something."

Another long horn honk, and then Greenie belted Luce's full name so loud I swear the sky tore right in two. Moments later her green bug zipped across the parking lot, almost nailing a dude in a yellow safety vest pushing a stack of carts toward the cart collector.

"Like a goddamn exploding sun," Gayle Crystal said.

She offered to give us a ride to her doctor. "We'll get him to check your lungs, make sure everything's working the way it ought to. While we're there, we could get him to look at your knee. He might even have some medical-grade painkillers for you, if that's one of your interests. We're talking rare high-end stuff. Pricey, but worth it."

Luce smiled so big you'd never have guessed how profoundly unhappy she was. "Why didn't you say you were a middle?"

"Never know who you can trust," said Gayle Crystal. With effort, she pulled herself to her feet. "Now then, break's almost over. Let me go tell my supervisor I got a family emergency, you two get some dough, and we'll meet up in ten minutes."

"Wait, you work here?" Luce said.

"Course. Asset protection." She unzipped her jacket. Sure

enough a Walmart security guard uniform was underneath. "Shoplifters love this place. Someone's got to stop them."

"What about that guy in the pink puffer?" I said. "You didn't try to stop him."

"My partner." Gayle Crystal gave me a slow grin of triumph. "I told you I got this game figured out."

After Luce and I withdrew a couple hundred bucks each from the MoneyPass ATM inside Walmart, the three of us headed north in Gayle Crystal's little blue hatchback. It didn't feel great to dip into my savings, but I told myself in the long run it wouldn't matter. Turns out once you're not feeding a habit, it's not so hard to put back a few dollars each week. Over the past eleven months I'd accumulated almost thirteen hundred bucks in savings just by picking up extra shifts, working doubles. As soon as we got our licenses restored the first week of March, it was all going to fix Luce's car.

Luce. I did my best not to worry. You're way less likely to OD from sniffing than needles, but I didn't want to take any chances. Maybe she'd listen to Gayle Crystal and her bendy-straw suggestion. Gayle Crystal, I was beginning to notice, had a funny singsong way of talking. All during the drive she kept up an endless jabber, her voice rising over the music, and soon I felt dizzy and light-headed, but in a good way. Sort of like how I used to get when Luce and me would sneak into the walk-in at work and do a few whip-its before tackling our closing duties. I should probably also mention that before we left Walmart, Gayle Crystal pulled a bag of dope out of her coat pocket and divided it up into three fat lines on the hood of her car. "A little pregame action to get us going."

"Gayle Crystal coming through," Luce said.

Was it Megadeth we were playing? Early Slayer? Anthrax? I don't remember for sure, but looking back I doubt it. More likely Gayle Crystal put on Waylon Jennings or Tanya Tucker or some other outlaw country singer that Luce and I would never have signed off on if we hadn't been faded. And although it took us close to an hour to get to the doctor, we hardly noticed. Car trips are so much better when you're feeling right. When we finally arrived, the office wasn't in some shady mini-mall like I'd expected, or in the back of a tattoo parlor full of dudes with wizard beards and big rubbery bellies. No, this was one of those massive office parks, the kind with professional landscaping and tidy lines painted onto the asphalt. Buildings that looked like they'd been cranked out of a giant machine. I tried to focus so I could find the place again in the future, but it didn't take long for me to get completely turned around.

We pulled up in front of a cluster of maybe eight units. Gayle Crystal said to give her our money and she'd be back in a minute.

"No way," said Luce. "We're going in. Our money's not walking."

"Yeah, that's not how my guy operates," Gayle Crystal said. "His number one rule is staying anonymous. Like he's an actual doctor and all. He's got a lot more to lose than most people."

"Tough shit. We got a lot to lose also."

With a regretful shake of her head, Gayle Crystal started the car, put it in reverse, backed out in silence.

"Okay okay," Luce said. "You can go in solo."

Up until that point I'd never seen Luce break her own rule about money walking. She must have wanted the dope pretty bad.

But Gayle Crystal wasn't having it. "Yeah, I can't work with folks who think I have shady intentions. Hurts my feelings."

"Look, I'm sorry, okay?" Luce turned to me in the back seat. "Give me your dough. Hurry."

Not wanting to upset her, I handed it over fast as possible. She dropped our cash in Gayle Crystal's lap.

With a final wounded look at each of us, Gayle Crystal counted our money. Once she was satisfied, she tucked the wad in her coat, parked again, and got out of the car. Approached the building and rang the bell of the corner unit. When the door swung open she gave Luce and me a jaunty thumbs-up before disappearing into the office.

A solid minute passed before either of us spoke.

It was Luce who broke the silence. "She's cool, right? We didn't just fuck up, did we?"

I hesitated. "She's a little off, but I think we can trust her."

Luce went back to watching the building. "Hope so."

Five minutes passed. Ten minutes. "Dumb bitch is probably blowing him for extras," Luce said. She reached over and pressed the horn. When that didn't get a response, she leaned out the window. "Finish him off! We need to get going!"

Even though I had a sick feeling in my stomach, I started

laughing. No matter how bad things got, you couldn't help being happy around Luce.

At fifteen minutes, she hauled herself out of the car and motioned for me to follow. The blinds were closed, but we put our ears to the side window. When we couldn't hear anything, Luce went around front and pounded on the office door. "Gayle Crystal! Let's get a move on."

Within moments, a petite older man opened up. "May I help you ladies?"

"Yeah," Luce said. "Tell Gayle Crystal to get her flat ass out here."

He gave us a puzzled look. "You didn't see her? She just went out the rear exit."

Behind us, a car engine sputtered and came to life. Seconds later Gayle Crystal was speeding away and giving us a middle-finger salute out the window.

"Our purses," I said. "Our phones. Your inhaler."

"Bitch!" Luce yelled. She swung back around to the doctor. "Don't tell me you two aren't in this together."

"Miss." He reared up stiffly. "I've no idea what you're talking about. Gayle's a patient. I hardly know her."

"Motherfucker, don't start with me," Luce said. She was only a little thing herself, but when she was mad she was downright scary. "For your information, a very good friend of ours works in law enforcement. You want us to tell him about your medical-grade horseshit? Get him and his pals nosing around your office?"

At last something in the doctor appeared to relent. "How

about I give you girls a generous helping of samples and we'll call it even. I'll throw in a taxi, since Gayle accidentally drove off without you, and then we can forget all about this unfortunate incident." He stepped aside and waved us into his office with a wrist so delicate a child could have snapped it.

Luce and I exchanged glances. Already I knew she planned to steal his drugs.

Under the harsh fluorescent lights, the doctor looked even more fragile. Elfin features set off by a pale, chalky complexion. Eyes a little too big for their sockets. He couldn't have been more than five one, five two, tops. With an apologetic smile, he gestured to a nearby cubby. "I hate to ask, but would you mind taking your shoes off? You can put them there if it's not too much trouble."

"Sure thing," Luce said, prying off her sneakers. "Hey, you think maybe your receptionist or whoever could get us some water? My throat's kind of scratchy."

"Oh, it's just me here right now," the doctor said. "But I'll be happy to get you girls a beverage. Is flavored seltzer all right? I'm afraid it's all I have at the moment."

"Perfect," Luce said.

While he stepped into another room to get our drinks and call a taxi, we sussed out the situation. For the most part the place resembled any other doctor's lobby. White walls, beige office furniture, a few waxy-looking houseplants. A whiff of disinfectant. The only item that seemed the least bit homey was the dog leash hanging on a hook by the door. Probably for some little poodle with ribbons. "I wish we had a dog," said Luce. Then she spotted the pair of filing cabinets tucked away by the window. The first one had nothing but a bunch of useless papers, but the second one was locked up tight as a bank vault. "Bingo," Luce said.

By the time the doctor came back in, we'd settled ourselves on the sofa. He placed a tray with two glasses of a foamy pink liquid and a saucer of shortbread cookies on the coffee table before us. "Your ride will be here shortly. Please help yourselves. I hope you like sparkling grapefruit. The slight bitterness I find to be quite refreshing."

Luce took several noisy gulps of seltzer. "Man, I needed that. Getting ripped off is a thirsty business."

"Again, I apologize." The doctor settled into an armchair. "I don't want any trouble."

"Let's see what we can work out," Luce said.

She proposed that he give us each two bottles of Dilaudid, scripts for ninety more, and three hundred bucks so we could buy new phones and purses. In exchange, we'd forget all about him and Gayle Crystal.

The doctor leaned back and gave a jolly little laugh. "Oh dear. I'm afraid you misunderstand. I'm a PhD, not an MD. I'm not qualified to write prescriptions and I certainly don't keep hydromorphone on the premises. My focus is research."

Luce looked at him. "So why the hell did GC drive us all the way out here?"

"Research as in research chemicals?" I said. They were pretty fascinating, from what I'd read on Reddit. Basically scientists would take an illegal drug and change up a molecule or two, creating a whole new substance that was technically legal even though it could still mess you up six ways from Sunday.

"Smart girl." The doctor turned to me with a smile of approval. You could hear a faint clicking in his little Keebler jaw. "The field is quite intriguing, with considerable untapped potential."

"Okay, now we're getting somewhere," Luce said. "How about hooking us up with some of that research."

The doctor studied Luce's face like she was under a microscope in a lab. "You're aware there's a risk factor."

"Come on," she said. "Everything on this whole entire planet is risky. I know two chicks who ODd in sober living. Another in rehab. Another one in her parents' house while they snored their heads off the next room." She took a bite of cookie and washed it down with a chug of seltzer. "This one guy? Clean for over eleven months, works the steps, goes to daily meetings. Eats a couple presses and poof. Gone forever."

I reached for her hand, but she tucked it under her leg before I could get there.

"Maybe he was right," she said after a moment. "Maybe that's the way to do it. Just slip away when nobody's watching."

"Hey," I said. "Don't say that."

"At least he's not dealing with this shit anymore." She drained the rest of her glass and sank into the cushions. "It's just. So. Fucking. Exhausting."

It struck me that I was pretty tired from everything too. Following her lead, I drank some more of my seltzer and helped myself to another cookie, hoping the sugar would kick in before too much longer.

"You girls do seem a bit low energy," said the doctor. There was that weird clicking in his jaw again. "I can give you something to help with that if you're interested."

"Sure man, throw it in the bag. Whatever." Luce's voice sounded drowsy and hoarse, the way it always got in peak allergy season.

I leaned toward her. "How you feeling?"

She gazed at me through the half-lidded eyes of someone about to fall out.

Clearly she was having a reaction to the dope we'd sniffed off the hood of Gayle Crystal's Corolla. Maybe it had been cut with ground-up Benadryl to make people think they were getting an extra good nod on. Maybe she'd hit a hot spot of fent. When a knock came at the door and a man's voice called out that the cab was ready, relief went zooming all through me. Forget the stupid research chemicals, we needed to get Luce home soon as possible. I tugged at her elbow. "Come on, our ride's here."

She didn't answer, just groaned a little.

"It's unlocked," the doctor called out.

The door opened and the cabdriver entered. White dude. Forties. Slicked-back brown hair, navy windbreaker, pleated khakis. A bulky canvas satchel tucked under one arm. He placed it on the coffee table, next to the plate of cookies, and then without being asked he eased off a pair of boat shoes and stored them in the cubby next to mine and Luce's.

I tried to pull myself up but my head kept bobbing onto my chest and my limbs felt stuffed with concrete. "Wait," I heard myself say. At last I fell back onto the sofa, useless. I must have hit a hot spot too.

From somewhere inside my body I watched as the cab-driver unzipped his satchel and withdrew several tubes of metal. He screwed them together, revealing a tripod. He pulled out a complicated-looking camera and selected a lens. "How we doing?" he said to the doctor.

"One down, one to go," he said.

I remember turning to Luce and seeing her head slumped on her shoulders, eyes closed, her mouth hanging open.

I remember the doctor saying I needed a refill.

I remember watching him top off my glass, sit down beside me, and hold the drink to my lips until I choked down a few swallows.

The lights dimmed into a briny green.

When the doctor got up from the couch, the whole room lurched sideways as if it had been thrown off-balance. The cabdriver leaned over and peered into my eyes. "Don't worry, we're just going to take a few pictures." He squeezed my bad knee like a cook testing meat for doneness.

When the doctor came back into focus, the dog leash was hanging from his hand.

r/opioids • Posted by **u/86thepervontable3**

14 hours ago

Need advice please

So my friend is having a rough time. What happened
was we were clean for 11 months but then her boyfriend
ODd and she slipped on K (asthma attack, not her fault),
we got kicked out of his memorial (also not her fault),
and we both ended up sniffing h. Then last night we got
roofied (don't want to get into that here) and afterward
things got even worse. Point is, I keep trying to get her
back to a meeting and she always says yes, but when
the time comes she backs out. Any ideas?

all 80 comments

---

sorted by: old (suggested)

Please keep discussion civil!

PLEASE READ THE RULES BEFORE COMMENTING!
NO SOURCING!

allbarredout89 31 points • 14 hours ago
No offense, but you what you need is to worry about your own self before you worry about her. Don't see a whole lot of taking responsibility happening.

  thegameisrigs 7 points • 14 hours ago
  was thinking the same thing haha

  86thepervontable3 3 points • 14 hours ago
  Did you even read the post? I am taking responsibility. I'm trying to get her to a meeting!

lungingtheairduster 19 points • 14 hours ago
You got kicked out the funeral? You show up wasted?

  86thepervontable3 2 points • 14 hours ago
  Memorial and no.

signmycardplease 12 points • 14 hours ago
IANAL but you might be able to get her detained if she's posing a threat to herself or others. Probably depends on where you're at. I know in Florida you can get someone Baker-acted without too much trouble. My parents did it to me twice. Only good for 72 hours, but if she's in bad enough shape you can get her involuntary rehab which is more longterm. Hard agree you need to take responsbility for your choices.

cheekingmymeds 5 points • 14 hours ago
in cali its called a 5150. been there done that, can be
ok if you know what your doing.

> **andthedishranawaywiththespoon** 8 points •
> 14 hours ago
> username checks out

86thepervontable3 2 points • 14 hours ago
Yeah, rehab is off the table. Not sending her anywhere,
thanks though

cottonsick 11 points • 14 hours ago
oh my god I was roofied once by someone I used to think
was a friend. Im so sorry that happened to you. Never
knew what he did to me exactly since I was in full-on
blackout but mentallyit fucked me up big time. Sending
big hugs.

> **86thepervontable3** 9 points • 14 hours ago
> Hugs back to you. Thanks.

needlesandpins 11 points • 13 hours ago
holy shit i'm sorry. Go the cops now so they can get
evidence. Getting your pubes combed isn't fun and
neither is court but at least the dude who assalted me
got jail time.

86thepervontable3 8 points • 13 hours ago
We weren't assaulted.

needlesandpins 12 points • 13 hours ago
OK but how do you know you weren't assalted if you
were roofied?

86thepervontable3 2 points • 13 hours ago
We were mostly blacked out but there are some
fuzzy parts I kind of remember (camera, dog
leash). I think they just took some fucked up pics of
me and my friend. Probably online already.

proboville 18 points • 13 hours ago
girl that happened to me once except it was my
boyfriend at the time who did it. only reason I
found out is cause a co-worker saw the shots for
sale on kik. kik is crazy, like no mods or anything.
still messed up about it

cottonsick 10 points • 13 hours ago
Dog leash? Fuuuuuck. Prob on some .onion site
by now. I'm sorry.

needlesandpins 31 points • 13 hours ago
THAT IS STILL ASSAULT. Please please report this
and get help. You need to focus on recovery and
your health rn. I've been there too and you can
get through this.
Edit: spelling

dudesfuckingsuck 18 points • 13 hours ago
This x 1000000000000

andthedishranawaywiththespoon
11 points • 13 hours ago
ding ding ding we have a winner!

86thepervontable3 3 points • 13 hours ago
um ok thanks for the advice, but no cops. Also,
can we stay on topic?

foilsagain 18 points • 12 hours ago
THEY?!!?

PharmaJohn 11 points • 13 hours ago
You know that story about the airplane masks? from the
rooms? put it on yourself first then your friend. Gotta
take care of yourself before worrying bout others.

86thepervontable3 1 point • 13 hours ago
I am taking care of myself! I'm the one keeping LE off
our back, I'm the one making sure we're eating, I'm
the one reminding her to use her inhaler so she doesn't
have another asthma attack. You don't know the whole
story!

PharmaJohn 10 points • 13 hours ago
My point exactly. Check out al-anon. You could use
some detachment. Good luck.

86thepervontable3 −3 points • 13 hours ago
JFC can you read? We're not drinkers. DoC is pills.
Edit: why the downvotes? I'm just being honest.

kratomredhead 9 points • 12 hours ago
try kratom. takes the edge off when you're tryin to quit.

igotthat50ioweyou 24 points • 12 hours ago
Maybe an intervention would work? Though honestly it
sounds like you have some control issues. Do you have a
parent who's afflicted?

  hookitupfat 8 points • 12 hours ago
  Totally thought the same thing when I read this

  86thepervontable3 0 points • 12 hours ago
  Not sure why I'm getting jumped on here. I'm just
  trying to help my friend.

snitchesgetstitches 14 points • 12 hours ago
What does your sponsor say? You told them all this right?

  coffinsup 2 points • 8 hours ago
  lol word

thegameisrigs 7 points • 12 hours ago
Set her up and get her arrested. If she's a first-timer
she'll probably get court ordered rehab.

allbarredout89 38 points • 12 hours ago
Only do this if she's white! If she's Black or brown forget it, she'll get jail.

> **getthempressies** 14 points • 11 hours ago
> would upvote this a thousand times. the system is fucked.

> **snowballerqueen** 13 points • 9 hours ago
> Can confirm. We have a rehab/work release program at my job (food service) and it's all white guys but one. Black people get locked up like always. This country is sick.

shitbangstough 4 points • 12 hours ago
hey its her life man. faster she hits bottom, faster she gets up. load her up with china white n see what happens

> **86thepervontable3** 2 points • 12 hours ago
> Wow. WTF is wrong with you.

> > **shitbangstough** 4 points • 6 hours ago
> > haha to much to get into here fam

kratomredhead 1 point • 12 hours ago
seriously tho try kratom. helps with the cravings and its legal

out4delivery 9 points • 11 hours ago
enough with the kratom posts. we get it. your into
kratom.

  kratomredhead 0 points • 11 hours ago
  this is my second kratom post?

    out4delivery 10 points • 10 hours ago
    user history says different

offpaperin6 13 points • 10 hours ago
imo kratom does nothing. only thing that ever worked
is subs but i'm tryin a wean myself off them too.

  southieskeezah 2 points • 4 hours ago
  where do you get subs. I don't have insurance

    offpaperin6 3 points • 4 hours ago
    you can buy them on the street if you wnt but
    some clinics have them. where you at?

      AutoModerator 4 points • 4 hours ago
      this post has been removed by autobot. no
      sourcing, no locations.

        southieskeezah 2 points • 4 hours ago
        wow really autobot?

snowwhite1010 7 points • 4 hours ago
Mod here. Read the sidebar. We have rules in
place so we don't get shut down.

southieskeezah 3 points • 4 hours ago
ne. that better mods?

offpaperin6 8 points • 4 hours ago
dont know about that. i'm westcoast

tylersmom79 18 points • 12 hours ago
Why do you think meetings are the way to go? My bf
went to plenty and he still ODd. Left me with our 2 yr
old kid. Actually he used to be on this sub pretty regular,
anyone remember u/waitingonapackage?

bluelightinthebathroom 9 points • 12 hours ago
Whoa yes, haven't seen him around lately. He passed?
When? Deepest condolences.

tylersmom79 17 points • 12 hours ago
December 26

iswearitsavitamin 8 points • 12 hours ago
.

mycathasdiabetes 8 points • 12 hours ago
.

morefentpops4me 12 points • 12 hours ago
oh my god i'm so sad. dude had the biggest heart and he
was so funny. RIP he'll be missed. I'm sorry for your loss

throwitallawayaccount 7 points • 12 hours ago
.

animalPharm160 5 points • 11 hours ago
.

buyingpissinabongshop 3 points • 11 hours ago
.

  ropeadopegirl 1 point • 10 hours ago
  sorry but what's with all the dots? newbie here

    buyingpissinabongshop 8 points • 10 hours
    ago
    Moment of Silence for someone who Died

junkyarddogbiteshard 4 points • 10 hours ago
.

yourabscessstinks 2 points • 3 hours ago
.

eatingcerealwithafork 4 points • 12 hours ago
why stop youre friend from using heroine if she wants?
its her life. shes an adult.

AutoModerator 2 points • 12 hours ago
A heroine is a female who faces danger or
adversity and displays courage. Heroin is a name
for diacetylmorphine which comes from its sale as
branded product by Bayer in the early 1900s.

*I am a bot, and this action was performed
automatically. Please <u>contact the moderators of this
subreddit</u> if you have any questions or concerns.*

> **pandorasboxxx** 1 point • 10 hours ago
> good bot

> > **B0tRank** 1 point • 10 hours ago
> > Thank you, pandorasboxxx, for voting on
> > AutoModerator.
> > This bot wants to find the best and worst bots on
> > Reddit. <u>You can view results here.</u>
> >
> > ─────────────────────────────
> >
> > Even if I don't reply to your comment, I'm still lis-
> > tening for votes. Check the webpage to see if your
> > vote registered!

cottonfever 4 points • 12 hours ago
My stepmom forced me to go to rehab and it saved my
life. Def doesn't always work though. No easy answers.

86thepervontable3 –7 points   •   12 hours ago
I SAID NO REHAB WHY IS THIS SUB FULL OF FUCKING
IDIOTS!

> **junkscience101** 9 points   •   12 hours ago
> Wow no need to smash the all caps. I know you've
> been through some shit but we're just trying to
> help you
>
> > **dontlabratme** 2 points   •   12 hours ago
> > facts
>
> > **86thepervontable3** –9 points   •   12 hours ago
> > [deleted]
>
> > **86thepervontable3** –15 points   •   12 hours ago
> > [deleted]
>
> > **junkscience101** 22 points   •   12 hours ago
> > Um, hey buddy. You got any landing gear over
> > there or?
>
> > **86thepervontable3** 2 points   •   11 hours ago
> > nvr mind people, all good now. tmrw is a new
> > day 1 :)

eatingcerealwithafork 8 points • 9 hours
ago
looks like op got some more powder lmaoooo.
good luck sis

looking4afiend 1 point • 11 hours ago
tar or #4

daddyl0nglegs 1 point • 8 hours ago
maybe shes just sad about her man. cut her some slack,
shell come around sooner or later. keep us posted. btw
get some narcan if you havent got it already

hairynodder 1 point • 9 minutes ago
Sorry if this is off topic . If I post a pic will someone tell
me if my shits pressed or not ?

IT TOOK SOME EFFORT BUT AT LAST I MANAGED TO roll over and pull myself up to a sitting position. Night air thick like a curtain. Jumble of voices off in the distance. Gasoline fumes, an idling engine. I was in a parking lot, I realized. A pair of headlights washed over my body and soon a chill wind rose up and I began to shiver. My new leather jacket was gone. When someone slid their hands under my arms and hoisted me skyward I tried to scream but all that came out was an ugly gurgle.

"Come on now, upsy daisy."

Luce.

With her help I managed to get to my feet, but my legs kept buckling. She held me by the shoulders and gave me a shake. Not rough or anything, just enough to get me to wake up a little.

"Stick your finger down your throat and make yourself barf," she said. "Go on, you'll feel better."

"You girls okay?" A man's voice. My body clenched up so tight it was painful.

"Doing great," Luce said. "Just got ourselves roofied, our shit stolen. Not bad for a Tuesday." She pulled my finger out of my mouth, stuck her own hand in and rummaged around and then I was vomiting onto the pavement.

"Gross," the man said, hurrying away.

It helped. Soon I was able to stand on my own and with

Luce's arm around me I could walk without too much trouble. She steered me into what turned out to be a convenience mart. Not one I'd ever been in before. One glance at the hot dog bar made what remained of my insides turn to liquid, but at least the bright lights made me feel safer. Luce propped me up next to the condiment station—the cheese sauce had a nasty skin on top and smelled like sweat socks—and called out to the clerk behind the register. "Hey man, sorry to bother you but can I use your phone for a second?"

He lifted his head so slow you'd have thought someone had to go back there and hand-crank the lever. "Got a phone booth outside. You walked right past it."

"Yep, we surely did," said Luce. "Which is how I know it's been vandalized. All you got in there is a cord with a bunch of sticking-out wires."

"Huh," the clerk said. "Guess I forgot. But you can't use ours. Store policy."

Luce gave him one of her smiles. "Come on, guy. Work with me a little."

"Okay, let me spell it out for you." He nodded at the ceiling behind us. "See that camera? My boss catches me letting customers use the phone, I'm dunzo."

The word *camera* made me feel woozy all over again.

Up by the Bartles & Jaymes display, a door I hadn't noticed before creaked open and a girl who looked to be our age, maybe younger, came gliding out of the restroom. She brushed past me, whisked a bag of Whoppers into her pocket, and went sailing out the exit. You could almost see the trail of smoked foil fumes floating behind her. It smelled like toasted marshmallows.

"I saw that," the clerk called after her. He turned back to Luce. "Now then. Where were we."

"Your phone?" she said. "Look, I get it about the camera but we all know they're not watching footage 24/7. Please? Me and her just got our bags stolen. We got nothing."

At that, the clerk's face shifted. He pulled a cell phone out of his back pocket, set it on top of the register. Ran his eyes up and down Luce. "You want to use mine, I'm sure we could work out something."

A moment passed, and then another. You could tell by the way Luce's face got all splotchy that she was trying her best to choke down her anger. Her fists tightened up into hard little buds. I took a deep breath and a fresh wave of nausea slammed into me with such force I had to grab on to the condiment shelf to keep from falling.

"Sorry, guy," Luce said. "You picked the wrong night."

"Hey now, you don't have to get all butt-hurt about it. It's just a fun little idea." He glanced at me. "I'd even settle for a couple pictures. Got a whole album going thanks to girls like you and Miss Whoppers."

That did it.

"Go fuck yourself," Luce said.

She headed straight for the exit. More than anything I wanted to follow her but I guess my hand had other ideas. I watched as it raked itself across the shelf full of hot dog toppings, sending all the metal containers onto the floor with a noisy crashing.

"Hey!" The clerk came out from behind the counter. "The fuck?"

As he stood gaping at the chaos of rancid cheese sludge, ketchup, pickle relish, the quivering blobs of mayonnaise that stretched from one end of the aisle to the other, Luce pulled me into the restroom and slid the dead bolt. I barely made it to the sink. There wasn't much left in my stomach, but what came out was a horrible shade of yellow and smelled like garbage.

"Good job," she said, rubbing my back.

She told me to rinse my mouth out and drink some water while she ducked in the stall for a quick second. By this point the clerk was pounding on the door and threatening to call the cops. Luce's response was to flush about a thousand paper towels down the toilet and once she got a good flood going, she poked her head out the door and informed the clerk there'd been a teensy accident. He went sprinting into the back room to shut off the water. Luce took my hand, led me over to the register, and snagged his phone.

We hurried outside and took off running. The one good thing about all the chemicals in my system was my knee didn't hurt and instead it just felt warm and prickly. Within a couple blocks we came upon an all-night laundromat. After tucking ourselves behind a wall of dryers, we tried to figure out who we could call to come get us.

"I know," she said. "Nogales."

"Absolutely not. Forget it."

"Why? For you, he'll speed right over."

"He's the last person I want to find out about this. Not to mention he'll make us take a drug test to see what that guy put in our seltzer. They find out we've been using, our probation's done for."

"Nobody's finding out shit," Luce said. "And anyway, they can't prove he didn't give us dope along with whatever else he snuck in there."

"No Nogales!"

"Okay," she said. "Chill."

The only other person whose number we knew by heart was Teena, our very first dgirl. We'd met her way back when we worked at the pool hall and though she'd pretty much been the worst bartender ever—she once asked me what was in a gin and tonic—she turned out to be a total pro when it came to dealing. Returned all texts, showed up when she promised, made a run down to Broward County once a month and came back with a suitcase full of orange bottles. This was back when Luce and me didn't mess with anything but legit pharms.

Only thing was Teena could be a real hothead when the mood struck her. We're talking the kind of temper that goes from ice to batshit with zero warning. One night I saw her hold a knife to a guy's throat after he accused her stuff of looking like presses. Another time she went after a dude with a baseball bat for shorting her twenty bucks. She never pulled anything like that on me and Luce, but when Teena got popped for distribution and landed in County, I was secretly glad we had to find someone else to buy from.

At least she got to the laundromat fast. Within minutes Teena's old Mercury Cougar was pulling into the lot out front, music pumping so loud we could hear it over the spin cycle. As we hurried outside, she gave us a couple toots of the horn.

"What's up, fellas? Been a minute." She held her hand out the window.

Luce slapped her palm. "Thanks for coming. We owe you."

"You know I got you. We go way back." Teena turned to me. "Hey Irene. What's in a vodka soda?"

At first I thought she was serious. We all had a pretty good laugh after that.

While we drove back to Anklewood, Luce told her what happened. Before we even got to the worst of it, Teena was rocking back and forth in her seat, saying how most dudes were complete monsters, even the nice ones. By the time Luce got to the part with the dog leash she was ready to drive straight to the sheriff's even though she hated cops more than just about anything. "Bro, you got to file a report, get the exam, start the ball rolling."

"Not happening," Luce said. "We already discussed it."

"Seriously?" Teena glanced at me in the rearview mirror. "These guys laid hands on you!"

"We're still on probo," Luce said. "Can't have any trouble."

"Okay. I hear you," Teena said. She stared at the road in grim concentration. "So we're taking care of this ourselves. You think we should round some folks up or can the three of us handle it?"

"Fuck man," I said, leaning forward. "She told you we're not doing anything! Just take us home already. We need some peace and quiet."

Luce gave me a look of warning.

"Easy now," Teena said.

We kept driving. Billboards ticked by us one after the other. ADULT SUPERSTORE NEXT EXIT. JESUS HAS THE ANSWER. WE BUY HOUSES—CASH OFFER! No one spoke. From the helter-skelter way she was driving, Teena was boiling with so much rage she could hardly control it. Beside her, Luce was playing some kind of game on the clerk's shitty burner. Even with the constant electronic beeping and booping you could hear her breath coming in harsh little rasps. All I wanted was to get in the shower, scrub myself raw, and try to blot out the images that kept flashing before me. The dog leash, the dog leash. Next thing I knew the interior light was on and Luce was turned around in her seat, telling me to calm down already. I think maybe I was punching Teena's car door or something.

"We're almost home," Luce said. "Try and hang tight, will you?"

"Sorry," I said, cradling my knuckles. I glanced at Teena in the mirror. "I didn't mean to."

She didn't say anything to that, just put on her turn signal.

Luce looked over. "Actually our place is a couple more exits. I mean you could go Old Road, but it takes way longer—"

"Yeah, we're making a quick stop," Teena said, glancing back at me. Her voice was flat, but there was no mistaking the fury rumbling beneath it.

"Okay," said Luce. "Sure."

We turned down a service road and pulled into a gravel lot with a squat little single-wide hunkered down by the entrance. GRIFFIN & SONS WRECKING, said a nearby sign. Teena swung her car around and used the headlights to scan the perimeter. Only then did I realize we were surrounded by piles of scrap metal that loomed up all around us. Huge silvery monsters watching us in the dim.

Once she was satisfied the place was empty, Teena cut the engine. Got out of her car, left the door open, which wouldn't stop dinging, and popped the trunk. Various sounds soon joined in the ruckus: the clank of a tire iron, a buzzing zipper, a plastic bag rustle.

I whispered to Luce. "She's not going to do anything, is she? I didn't mean to beat her car up."

Luce rolled down her window and stuck her head out. "Teena, you okay back there?"

The hiss of a vacuum-sealed bottle being opened. "Bring me my phone charger cable, will you?"

"I fucking knew it," Luce said.

She got out of the car and went around back with me right behind her. Teena's kit was laid out nice and neat inside the trunk. Bottle of water, rig, lighter, pinch of cotton. She was tapping a bag into a spoon. Luce said, "Can't you at least drop us off before you get started?"

"Hand me the water," said Teena.

"Come on. We just want to get home," Luce said. "You can do that at our place if you want. No one will stop you."

Teena got the water herself, dribbled some into the powder. "Relax, champ. This here is for you two. You went through some serious fuckery. Your girl was losing it back there."

"Sorry about that," I said. "I'm okay now."

Teena held the lighter under the mixture. "Bullshit."

I started to argue, but Luce cut me off. "What she's trying to say is, is me and her don't exactly do needles."

Teena glanced up. "No way. You girls are still pills only? What year is this?"

"We sniff a little too," Luce said. "You want to slice up some lines, great, let's do it."

"A sniffer." Teena shook her head in disappointment. "With your lungs. No wonder you were huffing and puffing the whole ride over. Here, take off your jacket."

Luce hesitated and shrugged off her hoodie. All she had on underneath was Wilky's Florida tee. "You sure we can't do this back at our place? Cold as balls out here."

Teena told her not to worry, that she wouldn't be cold much longer. After asking me to pass her the phone cable, she wrapped it around Luce's bicep and let out a low whistle. "Virgin veins. Haven't seen that in a minute."

"Hold on," I said. "Are we really doing this?"

"Relax, I'll tie you off too," Teena said. "And I'm only giving you a little cause I don't want you two yakking all over."

"You sure?" I said to Luce. I didn't feel cold, but for some reason I couldn't stop shaking.

Luce glanced at me. Her face had a funny torn-up look I'd never seen in all our years of friendship. She turned back to Teena. "Just do it already," she said.

Teena put the cotton in the liquid, drew up the shot, eased the spike into the crook of Luce's arm. When the barrel went red, she pushed down on the plunger.

A few seconds passed. Nothing. My chest thudded so hard I could hear it all around me. A few more seconds. Still zip. Maybe IV wasn't as powerful as people kept saying. Maybe it didn't have the usual effect on someone like Luce. Right when

I thought we might be getting off easy, her head bobbed a little and her eyes rolled back in their sockets.

"Fuck," she said, the word pooling out like syrup.

Teena turned to me. "You're up, sister."

And that was that.

LUCE WAS SITTING CROSS-LEGGED ON THE COUCH IN a rectangle of sunlight, scrolling through her phone and eating an apple. I was stretched out on the BarcaLounger, her afghan bunched down around my ankles. The sense that something ugly had happened the night before rippled all through me, but I couldn't think what it was. My head felt packed full of dirty wet cotton.

"Look who's awake," Luce said. "Listen, they're saying today's going to be super nice out. Might even hit 70. We should try and bike somewhere now that the snow's all melted."

Her voice had the knife's edge it always got when she was upset and didn't want to discuss it. I tried to sit up but my body had a weird spongy quality. It didn't hurt exactly, not even in my knee, though there was an odd pressure in my pelvic region. Sort of like a bruise, but on the inside. I glanced at Luce. She was still eating her apple, her jaw working in anger. I reached down for the afghan and drew it protectively up to my shoulders.

For the next few minutes I lay in my chair and tried to think what had happened. Slowly the night came back like a slideshow of humiliating photographs. The doctor. The cab-driver. The clerk behind the register. The needle sliding into Luce's arm. Me lying across the hood of Teena's car, laughing about how the Big Dipper looked like a giant cooker. I pushed up my sleeve and saw a reddish prick in the tender inside of my elbow. An insect bite, if I hadn't known better.

"We still on for a meeting?" I said.

"Most definitely," Luce said through a mouthful of apple. She set the core on the arm of the couch, wiped her hand on her sweatpants, and went back to scrolling. Her phone, I realized then, belonged to the clerk. "Whoa, check it. We have the same exact forecast as Palm Beach County. In February. I swear, Nature's as fucked-up as we are."

I asked why she was looking at Florida's weather.

"Cause I'm moving there," she said.

I pulled myself onto my elbows. "Wait. You're moving to Florida?"

At last Luce glanced in my direction. "Man, you're easy to mess with. Don't worry, nobody's leaving. I just wanted to wake your ass up. Now go get dressed, we're hitting the road in five minutes." She slid off the couch and trotted into the bathroom as if everything was perfectly fine.

Soon Luce and I were biking up to Broad Street. We got breakfast tacos from the little mom-and-pop truck that liked to hang out behind the self-serve car wash. We paid in quarters. The only cash we had was from the jar in the kitchen where we kept our laundry change. After eating, which helped a little, Luce said she wanted to hit up the one decent motel pool in Anklewood. I told her we should probably stop by the bank first, get new debit cards, take out some money. "Also we've been bounced out of that pool a million times. We'll never make it past the lobby."

"Wrong again," Luce said. "Turns out their new security guy went to school with Wilky. Got me and him in last month, no problem. Brought us a stack of towels, little cups of lemon water. We'll swing by for an hour or so and then head to our meeting." She looked at me. "It's warm enough you could even swim."

We biked over to the motel, the sun shining on our faces, the wind blowing our hair back. Luce had a point: if all the bad stuff makes you want to parachute right off the planet, the only thing left is to try and focus on the good. Soon it would be spring and after that, summer. Maybe by then things would have calmed down a little. We'd be back in our daily routine for starters, not to mention we'd have gotten our licenses restored and Luce's car in working condition. Once we were driving, we could apply for better jobs at better restaurants, which would help us earn some better dough. Take a class or two at Anklewood Tech, like we used to talk about way back in the beginning. Start playing a different kind of game.

But when we reached the motel front entrance, a woman we knew from the rooms told us Luce's security connection had been fired for stealing booze out of the mini-fridges. Carla worked in housekeeping, and though she always iced us out at meetings (Luce once called her the c-word when we first quit using), she must have forgotten she thought we were trash. We found her outside on her knees, scrubbing graffiti off the walkway with a little wire brush and a bottle of toilet cleaner. She'd gotten a lot of it already, but you could still see the faint outline of a dick, its dumb slit of an eye squinting up at us.

"Who's in charge around here," Luce said. "It's important."

"There something I could help you with?" Carla said.

Luce explained we were hoping to use the pool, try and

relax a little. "It's kind of a mental emergency, if you know what I'm saying."

"I thought you couldn't swim," said Carla.

Luce folded her arms over her chest. She was sensitive about that particular topic. "Where'd you hear that bullshit?"

"You shared about it, remember? The sheet of 10s, the water wings."

Luce gave her a grudging smile. "Right. I forgot I told that one."

"It's a classic. One of the best war stories ever." Carla squirted more toilet bowl cleaner onto the dick. "Listen, they been real strict here lately, but since it's you, I don't mind helping." Moments later she was opening the gate to the pool with a swipe card and waving us in. "Just be careful. We don't have a lifeguard on duty."

"Always," said Luce.

We strolled in giddy as schoolchildren. Kicked off our sandals, did a few stretches. Luce was going to dangle her feet in the shallow end, maybe work up to wading, and I was excited to practice my dives. Good thing I didn't take a running leap into the water. The pool was empty. Drained for the winter.

"Fucking cunt," Luce said.

If it had been just me, I would have slunk away in embarrassment, but one of the best things about Luce was she would never accept defeat, no matter how brutal. She dragged two deck chairs out of the nearby storage tent and set them up poolside like this was exactly what we wanted. No towels or anything close to lemon water, but at least the clerk had some decent music loaded onto his phone. For the next half hour we lay by that concrete abyss—Luce examining her waitress calluses, me messing around on Reddit—and listened to some of the doomiest doom metal you can possibly imagine. We're talking stuff like Pallbearer, Coffinworm, Witch Mountain. I'm not sure why no one came to shoo us away, but my guess is management decided a couple wrung-out-looking chicks sitting by an empty pool in winter was a pretty good joke.

We were between tracks on Electric Wizard's latest when Luce let out a sigh and rested a hand on her belly. "You know I like being clean and all, but the one bad thing is the weight gain makes me look preggo."

"Shut up," I said. "You're hot and you know it."

"You would say that. You and Wilky. Sometimes he'd talk to my pooch like it was hiding a baby. Played it lullabies on his guitar, told it stories. Dude loved kids more than anyone." She gave her belly a wistful pat. "We were even talking about trying for one, once we got to Florida."

"A kid." I hit pause on the music. "You and Wilky?"

"Well who else would I have a baby with?"

"I don't know," I said, flustered. "I never thought about it."

"Nobody ever thinks anymore. And now look at me. Fucking roofie-victim needle-using can't-even-swim junky-ass waitress. Closest I'll ever come to having a kid is this pooched-out belly." She picked up our remaining laundry money, gripping the sack of coins by its neck. "Guess I better go feed it. You want something? Vending machine's around the corner."

"Don't worry about the kid stuff," I said. "I'm serious."

She slid her feet into her sandals. "We could split one of those honey buns. Twizzlers if they have them."

"Get both," I said. "But just grab a couple bucks and leave the rest. For safekeeping."

She dug out a handful of quarters and dropped the bag onto my stomach. "Fine."

Once she was gone I restarted the music, lay back, and tried to picture Luce as a mother. I had to admit she'd be pretty amazing. She was smart, funny, and everyone loved her. Not to mention she had the kind of resourcefulness that could get you out of any situation, which was probably the number-one important quality for a parent. As long as Luce was around, you knew you'd be all right. Sure she had a couple of issues, but who didn't? She was working on them and getting better on a daily basis. Everyone slips sometimes. And okay, yes, the day before we'd probably set some new records in the slippage department, but already things were edging back to normal: Luce was on the hunt for sugar, the sun was shining safely out of reach above us, and even our doom metal soundtrack had veered from its typical growls and high-decibel rantings into some seriously blackened sludge—as if someone, somewhere, knew the exact medicine I needed. It wasn't long before I found myself growing drowsy.

A goblin scream, courtesy of Electric Wizard's lead vocalist, jerked me back from wherever I'd drifted. I looked around, blinking and groggy. Where was Luce? I couldn't have been out for more than a few minutes. If she was off eating all our Twizzlers, I was going to be pissed. I struggled to my feet and hurried around the corner thinking I'd catch her red-handed. No Luce anywhere. There wasn't even the vending machine she'd promised, just one of those industrial cigarette urns, its steel smoker pole watching me closely. Some days, the dicks won't let you alone. Annoyed, I tried to think what a resourceful person like Luce might do in this situation. Moments later I was sprinting across the lobby, past the elevators, and into the women's restroom. The only occupied stall had four legs in it.

"Get out here," I said. "Now."

Silence. The buzz of a zipper. The stall door whined open and a guy with a stringy half ponytail pushed past me and out into the lobby. Seconds later, Luce emerged. She went to the faucet, started rinsing her mouth out.

"I don't care what you did," I said. "Just hand it over."

She spit in the sink. "Hand what over?"

We watched each other in the mirror. With a wheezy insuck of breath, she reached into her shirt, pulled two bags out of her bra, and flung them in my direction. They bounced off me and landed next to the hand dryers.

"You're a cunt too," she said on her way out the door.

I scooped up the bags and hurried after her, but my body must have finally flushed out all the numbing poison seltzer because I hadn't gone more than a few steps when a hatchet-like pain drove itself into my kneecap. My leg collapsed and I tumbled face-first onto the lobby carpet. By the time I managed to pull myself up and limp outside, Luce was already flagging down a dirty white pickup. One of those coal-roller types with jacked-up tires. The truck stopped, she climbed in front, and though I called out for her to wait and that I was sorry, the truck went roaring down Broad Street and vanished into the distance, leaving me in a mushroom cloud of exhaust.

Biking back home with my knee was impossible. It was Carla, of all people, who agreed to help. Briskly she loaded me and Luce's bikes into the rear of her Honda. Drove me home, got me up the porch steps, eased me onto the sofa. Fixed me up with a baggie of ice and some ibuprofen before heading back to scrub more peen off the pavement. All afternoon I waited for Luce. I still had the clerk's phone, but with hers stolen, it wasn't like I could call or text her. She wouldn't have answered anyway.

It was dark out by the time I decided to make a quick post on Reddit. I only wanted some advice, maybe a little support in the process, but the responses that came in got me even more freaked out and angry. I hobbled into the kitchen and ate Luce's gummy vitamins by the handful. Chased them with another dose of ibuprofen, fought my way back into the main room, and got into it with a few more idiot Redditors until at last I gave up and turned on the TV. The only thing on was a bunch of game shows. The contestants looked queasy with panic, as if their big-money question had them thoroughly baffled, and the studio audiences kept yelling all the wrong answers—or was it all the wrong questions. I remember shouting, "Who is Pythagoras?" at the screen. It would have won me five thousand bucks if I'd been the one standing at the buzzer, enough to turn me and Luce's lives around and get us started in a different direction. But we were about a zillion miles away from that.

And even though my liver was soaked full of Advil, my knee wouldn't stop screaming. The area between my legs felt shameful and raw. At last I got out one of Luce's bags and tapped out a sloppy line of powder. It only took a couple sniffs before my mood lifted, but it still wasn't anywhere as good as IV.

Which is why I got into the second bag once the first one turned up empty. It's not like this particular Day 1 was working out the way I wanted. I'd start fresh the next morning. Soon a thick pudding-like warmth began oozing through my bloodstream and I gazed around the room with renewed pleasure. This was how life ought to be. One final sniff and my head got so heavy it toppled onto my shoulder. I tried to lift it but all the old opiate dreams were already loaded up and whirring. Super bright and saturated with pigment, sort of like those Technicolor movies Luce watched on weekends, except all the plotlines were completely mixed up.

I woke to find Wilky sitting in the BarcaLounger. He had on head-to-toe camouflage, like the day Luce and I first met him at the county fairgrounds, and a few lingering streaks of the Halloween makeup he'd worn the night he got busted. His acoustic guitar was lying across his lap. It was just an old roadhouse beater—I think he got it on Craigslist for a hundred bucks maybe—but the thing was pure beauty. Solid spruce top with a dark glossy finish, rosewood fingerboard, back and sides made out of wild cherry, and a neck crafted from silver leaf maple. It's amazing what you can build out of trees. Even someone like me, who had no musical skills whatsoever, could strum a chord and it would sound almost impressive. But Wilky, who had genuine talent, could pluck out the simplest of notes and have you all weepy before you knew what happened. If the stars had aligned for him a little bit differently, he might have had a whole other existence—one that took him far away from our unhappy mountain and all the bad luck that went along with it. Which is to say he might still be alive.

He began to play. Softly at first, then building to one of the rich, earthy tunes that always made me think of childhood summers. Red dirt, grass stains. The husky cries of cicadas calling out to each other. I listened so close I was hardly breathing. Like I was trying to decipher some secret message meant just for me. And though I could have listened to this part on repeat forever, somewhere along the way the music shifted, moving into something far more sad and spooky. Minor chords. Slowed-down tempo. The time signature went from a cheerful four-four to a drowsy three-quarter, like a drunken waltz or maybe even a heartbeat—if the particular heart in question was on its way out.

I wasn't alarmed by what was happening. Or okay, maybe I was a little, but it was more like I'd always known this other world was out there, tucked deep in the woods that had us all surrounded. On and on the music came out of Wilky's fingers and soon I got the uncanny sense that whatever existence he'd come from was the real one, while all the rest of us were blundering around this place like a bunch of dumb ghosts. When at last his song ended (not a cheesy fade but an actual ending), Wilky placed his guitar across his knees, his gaze tired but expectant. The time had come for me to hit the buzzer and answer his question. Only problem was I had no idea what he'd asked. It was then I noticed he had red mud all over his boots, as though he'd hiked a long way through the mountains to find me. Despite the warm fizz in my bloodstream this thought made me cry, and not a few childish sniffles either. "I'm sorry, I'm sorry," I heard myself saying.

"Me too," he said at last.

I didn't wake up again until the next morning. Alone in the house, still on the sofa, Luce's afghan tucked neatly around my shoulders. If this had been a scene from a movie, a muddy boot print would have remained by the BarcaLounger to make the audience think Wilky's visit had really happened. If you were to ask the Reddit crowd about the experience, no doubt they'd chalk the whole thing up to an overdose, saying I got lucky and woke up before my system shut down completely. I agree this explanation makes the most sense. And yet I swear on everything I believe and know to be true that Wilky really did come to see me. Not a chemical hallucination, not some dreamed-up version. He was there. For all I know he's still out in the woods, waiting, watching—along with all the others who are no longer with us. So I guess here's my big money question: How do we bring them back?

LUCE AND WILKY HAD BEEN DATING A LITTLE OVER a year and six months had passed since our Chicken Feathers encounter. Wilky was still at Fort Bragg but he'd gone back to using, which meant all three of us were in the game. We'd just hit the sweet spot too: perched at the top of the arc, between all the crap you go through as a rising amateur player and the inevitable plunge that follows once you hit pro levels. What I'm trying to say is, we were happy, happy! The evening in question was Halloween.

And that night we had plans to drop by a house party in Ribbins, where Luce had grown up and still maintained some connections. Dusk had just settled in when Luce and I decided to kick things off with the classic combo of Norcos and Somas. Responsible users, we did a cold-water extraction first. (Crush the tabs, chill the powder in water, strain out the APAP, drink down the goo.) The Somas we scored from a line cook at work who'd messed up his back unloading a Sysco delivery. The Norcos we bought from our elderly neighbor who'd fallen while trying to knock down a wasp nest, breaking her wrist and whatever they call that bone in your forearm. As soon as we caught a glimpse of that bright orange cast they gave her, Luce and I baked up some banana muffins and paid her a visit. Turned out her doctor had prescribed a month's worth of 10/325s. After Luce worked her sweet-talk magic, our girl agreed to keep a third for herself and sell us the rest. Her price wasn't as cheap as we wanted, but we managed to swing it thanks to our latest server hustle. If a customer ordered an iced tea or coffee and paid in cash, you just transferred those drinks to a table whose beverages you hadn't rung up yet, closed out the check, and kept the balance. It didn't come out to more than a few dollars a ticket, but on good days we were each walking with an extra forty, fifty bucks.

Anyway, we were in the bathroom doing our Halloween makeup when we heard Wilky's car turn into our driveway. Luce put her sponge down and checked the time on her phone. "Dude is always late. I told him eight thirty. It's ten after seven!"

"Um." I tilted my head. "I think that means he's early?"

"My point exactly. It's fucking weird." She went off to greet him, leaving me alone in our cruddy little bathroom surrounded by tubes of fake blood, scar wax, scab gel, and whatever else Luce had managed to cram in her pockets from the pop-up costume supply.

I took her spot in front of the mirror and rubbed primer onto my face in brisk circles. No doubt Wilky had failed to score anything from his regular Fayettenam clinics so he'd sped over to our place to see what we had going. Lately the Feds had been cracking down on all the strip-mall pain management rackets, lowering the supply and driving prices up even further. What was once our breezy little hobby had become a full-time enterprise. Still fun, but also stressful and demanding. Wilky. Why did he have to show up early? It meant less time for me and Luce.

He followed Luce back to the bathroom and stood in the doorway while we got ready. When I asked him how the pill mills were holding up, he claimed they were humming along like always. When I asked how he was feeling and if he needed anything extra, he said he was doing great. "Fact is, I haven't had anything since lunchtime."

"Wait, what?" Luce turned to him in confusion. "As in nothing?"

"You think you might get whiz-quizzed?" I said. As long as Wilky stuck to the meds his army docs prescribed and kept his numbers down, he could pop hot in all the random urine tests they gave him.

"It's not that." He glanced at Luce. "Just taking a little time-out is all."

Thinking back, that was the night Wilky started edging toward the exit. The three of us had been hitting it hard since the previous summer and though Luce and I were busy setting all kinds of personal records, you could tell Wilky's heart wasn't in it. Jumping back into the game, once you've been free of its clutches, is never as great as you think it will be. There would be a few more months before Wilky was ready to stop altogether, but soon he would be running regular practice drills for his second try at quitting. He was probably also testing Luce for her reaction. I can tell you from experience that there's plenty of shame when it comes to using—but there's also a decent amount when it comes to getting clean.

"Why tonight though?" Luce said, her voice turning pouty. "You're just going to get sick and we'll have to leave early."

"We'll stay as long as you want, I promise. I've got supplies in the car if things get uncomfortable." Wilky picked up a tube of fake blood and squinted at the ingredients. "Besides, you know how Ribbins parties are. Probably a good idea for one of us to be clearheaded in case something happens."

Luce whisked the tube out of his hand and put it on the back of the toilet where he couldn't reach it. "Things are most definitely happening," she said.

We finished getting into makeup. We were going as murdered death-metal rockers. It was all Luce's genius idea. The black lipstick and corpse-white foundation were pretty standard, but the ghoulish scars and wounds she painted onto our faces raised things to a whole new level. She'd watched YouTube demos all week, practicing on herself in the bathroom for hours, and by the time Friday rolled around she could give you razor slashes on your neck or an oozing bullet hole in your temple so real-looking it was like she'd gone and done the actual deed. That was one thing about Luce. You never knew what was coming. Even if you didn't like whatever surprise she flung in your direction, it was always invigorating. With Luce around, you couldn't help but feel alive.

Nogales, too, could fling a surprise when he wanted—but his rarely landed. Prime example: That night he showed up costumed in blue scrubs instead of the death-metal getup we'd all agreed on. This was back when the two of us were still seeing each other. I don't think anyone would have said we were a great match. Nogales didn't use, for starters, and while you could argue it made sense considering his place of employment, he also wouldn't drink except maybe a beer on special occasions. Most of the time he stuck to embarrassing things like unsweet tea, ginger ale, or god forbid, cranberry and soda. About the only vice he had was the random cigarette.

Partly this was because his mom, like mine, was a champion drinker. All his life she'd been in and out of twelve-step programs, bouncing from job to job, getting popped for shoplifting. Neither one of us had heard from our moms in over a year. In this way, me and Nogales made sense together. Sometimes we'd lie in bed, passing a smoke back and forth and comparing childhood stories, marveling at how lucky it was we'd found each other. Here's the thing. If you grew up with an afflicted parent and the accompanying chaos, being with an actual stable person can feel almost euphoric. You can't get enough of it. Other times though, it's like someone snuck in and switched your zesty prescription goodies for over-the-counter duds. I don't know. I guess the best way to describe Manny Nogales is he's the kind of person you figure you'll end up with eventually, but only after you've run through all the worst choices.

He knocked on the door at eight thirty, right as scheduled. Classic Nogales. Luce had finished our makeup a few minutes earlier and Wilky was taking a bunch of photos. I went to let him in.

"Whoa," Nogales said. "You look incredible."

I stared at him. "Scrubs. You're kidding."

"What's up, doc," said Wilky. He came over and gave Nogales a friendly clap on the shoulder. "The stethoscope really sells it."

"Blue's your color," Luce said. "Come get in a picture. Wilky's making an album."

"What about our plan?" I said. "Luce was going to do your makeup. That wig I borrowed for you?"

"I'm sorry." Nogales took off his surgical cap, embarrassed. "Watkins wants everyone on call. Thinks we might see some trouble. Figured I better wear something on the tame side in case I'm needed." He leaned over to kiss me, but I held my hand up to block him.

"You'll smear my zipper," I said.

Nogales and I rode to the party in his mom-style minivan, which he'd bought for cheap at one of those police auctions. Luce and Wilky went in the Subaru. Before we left, she and I swallowed down the last of our Soma/Norco cocktail, so even though I started out pretty mad at Nogales, it wasn't long before I was drifting way up above everything, all nice and floaty. Maybe this was what the afterlife was like. The idea made me laugh, considering my murder-victim costume, and I got my phone out.

"What's so funny?" said Nogales. "Who are you calling?"

"Hold on, I'm texting Luce." I told her my afterlife thought and added a bunch of skull and heart emojis, but she didn't answer. Probably she was drifting up above everything too.

Nogales looked relaxed as well, but for his own reasons. For once, he hadn't been stuck on traffic watch and instead he'd visited Anklewood Elementary and gone from classroom to classroom, passing out Halloween candy and giving scare-'em-straight lectures about drug use. "You should have seen them. Wide-open faces, asking all sorts of questions. And wow, so smart. Actually gave me hope for the future." He glanced over. "You ever think about having children?"

"Check please," I said, waving my hand at an imaginary waitress.

"Come on, it's just a question."

I pulled my hair off my neck. "You see the stab wounds Luce gave me? I'll be lucky to make it through tonight without croaking."

"Guess I was right to come as a doctor."

"You look more like a dentist," I said. "Got any nitrous?"

"Not tonight, but I did bring some candy. Trying to drum up business, you know. It's under your seat if you want to get started."

I reached down to find a giant bag of Sour Patch Kids— watermelon flavor. Sometimes even Nogales could play along.

Of course soon as you start thinking Manny Nogales is one of the few decent male humans out there is when things go swooshing right down the crapper. First he refused to go more than five miles past the speed limit, even though with his badge it wouldn't have mattered, and we lost sight of Luce and Wilky. Then he got all mad when his phone led us onto some twisty back road, like it was the satellites' fault they couldn't guide us through the remote wasteland of Ribbins. We drove around so many loops and switchbacks trying to find the right address I came this close to upchucking watermelon gummies all over his dash. By the time we reached the complex it was crammed full of cars and we had to park by the manager's office in a spot marked EMPLOYEES ONLY—ALL OTHERS TOWED 24/7. I told him we better not risk it and we should leave his car at the gas station up the road and walk back over. Nogales said we'd be fine since it was after hours.

"Guess we'll find out," I said.

We picked our way through a hopeless maze of apartments. The fog in Ribbins was that dense upslope variety you get in certain mountain passes, making it difficult to see anything until you got right on top of it. Even though we could hear bass thumping from several buildings over, it was impossible to tell where it was coming from.

"You sure you want to do this?" Nogales said. "Why don't we go back to my place. I'll make dinner, light a fire."

"You serious? Me and Luce worked doubles all week so we could get tonight off. We haven't been to a decent party in ages."

"Hey, it was just a suggestion."

"You don't want to be here, fine. I'll get a ride home from Wilky."

"Whoa now." Nogales shifted his six-pack of Canada Dry from one arm to the other. "You okay? Something going on I ought to know about?"

"Couldn't be better," I said, zipping up my coat.

But the truth was I had a bad feeling. Not just because Wilky was taking a pill break, though that was part of it. No, it was something else, something far bigger. I remember gazing up at the sky and thinking how it looked carved out and empty, and how that emptiness kept going on and on forever until it fizzled out into nothing. No matter how hard you tried, you'd never be able to see where it ended. Surely there was an end somewhere. After that, what?

At last we turned a random corner and found the party. Considering Luce's hype, it didn't look that great. Just a plain two-story building with a lone strand of orange lights over the main entrance. A few candle stumps flickering in windows. A pumpkin head on top of the community grill, grinning like a child. In the parking lot, someone had set up a portable fire-pit in one of the spaces reserved for disabled drivers. A crowd huddled around the flames, talking in low, confidential voices. No one I recognized.

Finally I spotted Wilky on the far edge of the group and soon after that Luce resolved into focus. She was chatting up this super-pale guy in a black TAMA tee, black jeans, and a cheesy black headband. He kept hitting his abs over and over with a pair of wooden drumsticks. You could tell by the tightness in Wilky's jaw that he wasn't impressed with Luce's new companion and when the guy tossed his sticks in the air and caught them again with a stagy flourish, I felt Nogales bristle beside me. He didn't like being around people on stims.

Luce saw us and waved us over. "My dudes! Guess who this is!"

Nogales and I made our way toward her. He ran his eyes over the drummer. "Anemic Don Henley? Depressed Phil Collins."

"Haha," Luce said. She nodded at the guy. "Go on, show them."

With a sly look, he put his sticks in his back pocket and lifted his T-shirt, revealing the name LARS ULRICH tattooed across his chest in the classic Metallica font you see on all their albums. The *L* and *H* stretched down into the yellow fur of his armpits. The ink must have been fresh because the edges looked pretty raw and swollen, maybe even a little infected.

"Is that commitment or what," Luce said.

For some time we stayed outside talking. Or actually Luce and Lars Ulrich drifted away and began a private conversation just out of earshot, their heads bent so close they were almost touching. Nogales and I chatted for an awkward minute or two until he couldn't take the drumming any longer and announced he was going inside to put his Canada Dry in the fridge. After that it was just me and Wilky, who kept rocking back and forth on his heels and staring into the fire. You could tell he regretted his decision not to use. I decided I'd wait, let him get a bit more agitated, and then give him a couple Norcos to smooth things over. No time for a CWE, but he could deal with a few stomach issues if he had to. Otherwise he and Luce might leave early and I didn't want that.

So when Wilky asked how work was going, I figured he was just making small talk before easing himself into the subject of my pillbox contents. I told him it was my dream job and I'd never been happier.

"Hey, good for you," he said. "Luce hates it there, but I guess that's no secret."

I looked at him. "I was kidding. I hate it as much as she does. More, maybe."

"Right." Wilky gave a funny little laugh. "Sorry, you're kind of hard to read sometimes."

I wasn't sure what he meant, but I didn't like it regardless. I stole another glance at Luce. Despite the bloody claw marks across her cheekbone and the gangrene that stretched from her forehead down into her collar, the glow from the fire lit her up with a rare beauty. Lars Ulrich must have seen it too, because he leaned over and whispered something into her hair. She turned toward him, smiling. As for Wilky, he kept talking and talking like he hadn't noticed anything at all.

"Yeah, I'll be glad when we can finally get her out of there," he was saying. "Next spring she's going to put in her notice."

I blinked up at him. "What notice."

He went on to confide that although they hadn't got the details worked out exactly, he and Luce had been talking about opening their own restaurant. "A little mom-and-pop café. The kind of place with paper on the tables and crayons for kids to color with. An outdoor patio where people can bring their dogs."

"She likes dogs," I said cautiously.

"Between us, I was thinking we'd call it Lucille's. What do you think?"

"Lucille's," I said, testing the name out. It sounded strange. She'd been Luce as long as I'd known her. "I mean sure, I guess. But what about the army? No way you can do that and also run a restaurant."

Wilky said he figured he'd taught enough people how to jump out of planes for one lifetime. In a few short months his commitment would be over and with an honorable discharge he'd qualify for a home loan through the VA with zero down. "Soon Luce and I can live pretty much anywhere we want.

We were thinking someplace warm, near the water. Florida maybe."

"Florida. Wow." I looked over at Luce in time to see Lars Ulrich withdraw a baggie of pills from his jeans pocket and press it into her fingers. With the grace of a seasoned cold-copper, she slid it into her coat. "Well, as long as you two are going to be there, I'm sure I'll get used to it. Any place has got to be better than here, right?" I had no doubt they'd hire me on at their restaurant—probably make me manager or something.

"Actually." Wilky hesitated. "Don't take this the wrong way, but we were thinking the two of us had better make a clean break from this scene. Start fresh. No temptations."

A tide of panic splashed through me, hot and frothy. "What do you mean, no temptations?"

"It's not that we don't want you around," he said quickly. "But it's probably not a good idea. Not if she's going to get clean. No offense, but you two aren't exactly healthy for each other. You want the best for her, right?"

I managed to nod yes, but it wasn't easy.

"Me too," he said.

Wilky went back to watching the fire, all relaxed and peaceful like he hadn't just exploded a bomb in my face without warning. My blood thundered all through me and my chest closed up so tight I had a hard time getting air. I groped around for the tin in my pocket, thinking I'd better go slow things down a little, and snuck a final glance at Luce. She must have felt me looking at her because she flashed a three-fingered *W* down by her side—our signal to meet in the bathroom—and then she swung around and headed into the party. Right away I got that beautiful calm that comes when you finally get well after a long sickness. Good old Luce. Meanwhile Wilky was so wrapped up in his dumb Lucille fantasy he didn't even notice his actual dream girl had gone trotting off without him. People like that you almost feel bad for. When I told him I was going to go find Nogales, he gave me a distracted nod and said he'd catch up with me later.

It wasn't until I got inside that I understood it wasn't just one apartment throwing the party—it was the whole lower level. At least a dozen units had their doors flung open with bodies spilling out into the hallway. I texted Luce asking which apartment she was in but she didn't answer. Twelve bathrooms and hundreds of people and nobody I knew, except Nogales of course. I ran into him in one of the many kitchens, leaning against the refrigerator and chatting up some woman decked out in a slutty-nurse costume that included a plunging neckline and white patent stilettos. She was examining Nogales's stethoscope with a look of wonder, as if he'd invented the stupid contraption himself. I went up behind him and jammed a finger gun in one of his kidneys.

"Whoa," he said, turning to face me. "There you are. I was looking all over."

"You see Luce anywhere? I can't find her."

He gave me that smug Nogales look, like he knew something I didn't. "Ah yes. Luce. Listen, I have an idea. Why don't you forget about her for half a second? Enjoy the party, meet some new people. This here is Natalia. She lives a couple buildings over."

"You can practically see my bedroom from the roof," Natalia said. "Did you know me and Manny both brought ginger ale to this thing? Isn't that funny?"

I turned back to Nogales. "If you see her, tell her to check her phone. I've been texting."

"Wait, hold up," he said. "Where you going?"

But I was already halfway out of the room, following a spiky-haired blond I thought was Luce, but who turned out to be a run-of-the-mill goblin happily grinding her teeth into chalk. When she caught me watching her, she let out a yelp of delight and came hurrying over, arms outstretched as if to hug me. MDMA-ers are so annoying. I had to move fast to get away.

For the next half hour I searched for Luce and her baggie. The party must have spread from the first floor to the second because soon there was a whole new set of apartments and bathrooms. Endless costumes, laughing faces, blurry washes of color. Music from Southern hip-hop to acid techno to, god help us, bro-country. The sickly-sweet odor of rose cologne in a bedroom turned into the funk of armpits in a crowded kitchen turned into a balloon of dank smoke by the fire escape. And yet I began to settle into the strangeness. Maybe it was the extra Soma I broke down and ate (you have to be careful combining muscle relaxers with Norcos), but soon I began to think of myself as traveling in a sleepy little boat on a river and around each bend there was something new to discover. In one apartment, a woman dressed as a fairy godmother was cutting a pan of brownies into squares and passing them out in orange paper napkins. Another unit had ballroom music on the turntable with a bunch of witches and wizards waltzing in sock feet on the hardwood, their shoes piled in an intimate jumble by the door. The next apartment was full of nothing but seniors arranged in a semicircle in the main room: shrunken white-haired folks in fleece bathrobes and slippers, watching a black-and-white movie on a giant flatscreen. No one was in costume, and I didn't see so much as a jack-o'-lantern or a string of paper bats taped over the doorway, but when I entered they all waved me in with the kind of excitement that suggested they'd been eagerly awaiting my arrival. A man in a wheelchair rolled himself toward me and held up a bowl full of individually wrapped packages of gummy worms and spiders. I took one of each for both me and Luce.

The upstairs corner unit had a litter of puppies shut up in the bathroom. I discovered this by accident, believing that the *Do Not Enter* note taped to the door meant this was where I'd finally find her, peeing out all the blue Gatorade she'd guzzled in place of supper. Instead, five tiny dogs were snoozing together on a plaid quilt laid out on the tile. I shut the door behind me with the gentlest click I could manage but they woke up anyway and came scrabbling over, yipping with excitement, their little legs all shaky and uncertain. My dopamine levels went flying skyward. No wonder Luce wanted a dog. I freshened their bowl from the sink tap, sat cross-legged on the floor, watched them lap up water. They had the pinkest little tongues I'd ever seen. I'm not sure how long I stayed with them, rubbing their ears and petting those soft round bellies, but at some point this Wednesday Addams–looking chick came in and tried to scoot me out, saying I wasn't supposed to be in there. "Can't you read?" she said, tossing an indignant black braid over her shoulder.

I pulled myself to my feet, apologizing and saying her pups were the cutest things ever, and that I'd just poked my head in for a quick second hoping to find my missing friend. "Her name's Luce. Makeup like mine, spiky blond hair, a funny tooth that sticks out a little?"

Wednesday gave me a puzzled look. "You hear that? Like someone screaming?" Without waiting for an answer, she pushed past me to the window and heaved it open. It was just the usual party chatter, the same chaos of music. Some people get so paranoid when they use.

"Well if you see her, tell her to check her phone," I said, backing out slowly. I was almost at the door when I had the idea. "You know, me and her were talking about getting a dog just this morning. We could take one of these puppies off your hands if you want."

Maybe if Luce and me got a dog together, she wouldn't be in such a hurry to run off to Florida.

"Sure, for three hundred bucks," Wednesday said, still looking out the window.

There went that idea. I'd worked doubles all week and I wasn't close to having that kind of money. A dollar a milligram adds up quick. "Any way you could go lower?"

Wednesday must have heard something in my voice because she turned and looked me over. "We could probably work out some kind of trade. You wouldn't have anything interesting, would you?"

I thought of Luce and her Lars Ulrich baggie. "Always. Let me find my friend and we'll get back with you." I had my hand on the doorknob when someone yanked it open.

"Kimmie!" a guy said to Wednesday. "Some girl fell out. You better get down here."

He was dressed as the Joker—purple suit, green wig—but despite the smile carved into his face he looked pretty panicked, as if this wasn't your basic nodding and someone had gotten herself in real trouble. An icy chill went straight through me.

Already I knew it was Luce.

By the time I got downstairs a crowd had gathered around her. She was lying in the dim little corridor that ran between the first-floor apartments. Her eyes were rolled way back in her head and her bandage dress was hiked up so far you could see her Hello Kitty undies. I pushed my way through, yanked her dress down, leaned over, and put my ear to her chest. She was breathing, but so shallow it barely counted.

"Call 911," I heard myself say.

After that, a woman holding a baby hollered for someone to go find some Narcan, but everyone just stared at her, mouths hanging open. A man dressed as the grim reaper asked if anyone knew CPR. Nogales would know what to do, or even Wilky, but they must have been off planning big moves to Florida and chatting up nurses. I glimpsed a dude at the far end of the hall, looking a little green around the edges. Lars Ulrich, I realized. He met my eyes and then he turned and slipped out the rear exit.

"I want whatever she ate," a man's voice said.

It wasn't until the whine of an approaching siren rose up in the distance that the crowd sprang into action. Quick as a flash everyone scattered into various apartments, locks clicking, bolts sliding.

The woman with the baby told me I'd better get a move on. "You don't want to be here when they show up. Good Samaritan laws don't work so great in Ribbins."

I told her I wasn't leaving no matter what happened. No way, forget it.

"Okay okay, stop crying," the woman said. "Then you better check if she's holding. Go on, hurry."

I went through Luce's coat pockets, hands shaking so bad I could hardly control them.

"And if the cops show, keep your mouth shut." The woman looked at her baby as if she was giving it advice. "You can't ever trust them, no matter what they say."

At last I found the baggie of pills tucked in the waistband of Luce's fishnets. When I held it up to show her, the woman backed away like I was going to fling fent all over her and her kid. "You crazy? Hide that shit in your underwear or something." She turned and hurried up the stairwell.

"Can you at least stay till EMS gets here?" I called after her.

Somewhere above me a door slammed, leaving me and Luce alone in that hall, life dribbling out of her body with no way for me to get it back inside or even slow down the process. I shook her so hard her head bobbled all over. "Come on, come on," I chanted.

No response.

And then Wilky was flying down the hall toward us. He

one-armed me away, tilted Luce's head back, pinched her nostrils, and gave her mouth-to-mouth the way he'd been trained in the army. Soon she was awake and gazing around in sleepy wonder.

"Where," she said.

"It was those pills that guy gave you," said Wilky. "I knew he was trouble."

"No pills," she said thickly.

"Luce," he said. "Hand them over. We're flushing the rest down the toilet."

"Don't have any." With effort, she pulled herself up to a sitting position. "Promise."

"It's true," I said, my mind scrabbling to come up with a believable answer. "We already tossed them. One look and we knew they were total fakes. This was just an asthma attack, plain and simple. Probably tons of mold in this building."

"Asthma," said Wilky. You could tell he didn't believe me, but at the same time he didn't want to call me out. "Where's Nogales? Did he see what happened?"

Before I could answer, two paramedics hurried through the front door. "Couldn't find the right building," said the first one. He leaned over and aimed a penlight into Luce's eyes. "Yep. You called it."

His partner set her kit on the floor with a hostile *thunk* and squatted next to Luce. "All right, what did you take? Be honest."

"Baby aspirin," Luce said, her voice groggy.

"Yeah?" The woman pulled some latex gloves out of her jacket and put them on with two harsh snaps. "Okay then,

I'm going to check your pockets. Any sharps I should be aware of?"

"Hold on," Wilky said. "You can't search her, not without her permission."

At last Nogales came charging through the rear exit. He must have sprinted from a few buildings over because he was having a hard time catching his breath. "Heard the sirens."

"Look who's here," I said. "We missed you."

He ignored me and bent over Luce. "You okay? What happened?"

"No searching," Luce said to the paramedics.

The woman sat back on her heels in annoyance. For someone as amped-up as she was, she looked pretty worn out. Her skin had the same gray waxy look that mine always got when Luce and I pulled an all-nighter and her right hand kept twitching. She tucked it behind her back and turned to her partner. "You want to tell her or should I?"

Her partner, an older dude with a Bicced scalp and JUST FOR TODAY inked on his forearm, explained there had been a rash of ODs that week due to a spike in bad presses. They needed to know what she'd eaten and what it looked like. "Don't worry, we're not required to report you. Good Samaritan laws and all that. We're trying to track this stuff so we can warn people. You don't want anyone else getting hurt, now do you?"

Nogales pulled his wallet out of his scrubs, showed his badge. "Anklewood PD. Here to help if you need it."

"Thanks," said Mr. Clean. "Hope we don't have to take you up on your offer."

"Fine," Luce said. "Feel me up if you're that desperate."

Thank god I'd gotten to the pills in time.

It was the woman who searched Luce's coat pockets, the lining, the zip-off collar. Ran her fingers along the seams of Luce's dress, made her remove her shoes, and still all she scored was a tube of Wet n Wild lipstick and a half-eaten pack of chocolate tarantulas. You'd think not finding any drugs would have satisfied the woman, cheered her up even, but it only seemed to annoy her further. Made you wonder what she did with all the pills she confiscated.

After that, Mr. Clean wanted to check Luce's vitals. I reminded Luce she didn't have to let EMS do anything, but once she found out their services were covered by her stepdad's insurance, she relented.

"I thought you and your family didn't speak to each other," said Nogales.

Wilky motioned me and Nogales back toward the stairwell so the paramedics couldn't hear. In a low voice he told us Luce and her mom still weren't talking, but her stepdad had recently come back into the picture. He was trying to convince her to go rehab. She'd get a full ride with his Blue Cross policy.

I looked at Luce and back at Wilky. Neither of them had ever mentioned rehab before. "She's not going, is she?"

"Won't even discuss it," Wilky said. "But after tonight? I'd say it's back on the table."

Nogales reached for my hand and held it gently. A comforting gesture, but it only made me feel trapped and anxious, and after a few seconds I pulled away.

The exam didn't take long. Luce's pulse was irregular and her breathing was sluggish—I think they said she was only hitting eleven or twelve breaths a minute. Whatever had put her down earlier wasn't done with her yet. Luce drew the line when they suggested taking her in for bloodwork, saying all she wanted was to go home, lie on the couch, and eat a big stack of toaster waffles.

"I hear you," said Mr. Clean. He pulled a silver thermos out of his kit and took a weary swallow. "Been a long night already."

The woman scooped up her kit and strode to the front door. "From the looks of things, it's only getting longer." She gave a final accusing glance in Luce's direction.

"Sorry to be such a letdown," Luce said. "I can hook you up with some blow if it'll help any. Addy, if you'd rather stick with something familiar."

The woman's face blotched into a telling shade of red.

We waited until we heard their van drive away and then Wilky announced he was going to get the Subaru and pull it up front so Luce didn't have to walk all the way to visitor parking.

"I think I'm ready to head out too," I said to Nogales. "I'll catch a ride home with them so you can hang with your nurse friend a while longer."

"It's not like that," he said, flushing. "I'll explain in the car."

Nogales went on to suggest we all finish the night together at me and Luce's. "Wind down a little, maybe watch a movie. I bet one of the Freddy or Jason ones is on. Luce, you like slasher stuff don't you?"

"More bodies the better." You could tell she was trying to act normal, but her voice sounded sludgy and she kept blinking in scary slow motion. From the concentrated look on her face, her breathing had switched from automatic to manual. I glanced at Nogales and Wilky but they didn't appear to notice anything unusual and instead they headed outside discussing Jamie Lee Curtis and her yogurt commercials as if there had never been any real danger at all.

Soon it was Luce and me again in the hallway. While she focused on getting enough oxygen into her system, I tried to figure out a way to bring up Florida. I couldn't imagine her leaving. The whole thing felt unreal. Maybe she was just letting Wilky believe what he wanted to keep him happy. I did the same thing with Nogales and even her on occasion. It's not a hustle if it's someone you love. I was debating whether to ask her straight up or go at it sideways when she looked at me and held her hand out.

"Take some if you want," she said, "but give me the rest."

I told her I had no idea what she was talking about.

"Dude. Don't fuck with me," she said.

If she hadn't been in energy-saver mode I'd never have been able to change her mind about getting her pills back, but as it was I convinced her without too much trouble that it was best if I held on to them a little while longer. "You know they always set up checkpoints on Halloween. Wilky gets stopped, it could turn into a whole situation."

"Right," she said. "This is about Wilky."

"Come on, don't be like that. Point is Nogales only has to flash his badge and we're back driving in no time."

She thought this over. "Makes sense I guess. Besides, if Wilky finds my stash he'll toss it. Sometimes he acts like such a normie. It's embarrassing."

"You're not really moving to Florida with him, are you?" I said.

At first she denied it. Said she hated hot weather and Disney was bullshit and of everywhere in the whole entire universe, Florida was the last place she'd ever want to live. "Can you see me in a beach house somewhere, wearing nothing but bikinis and stinking of coconuts?"

"Look me in the eye and tell me you're not moving," I said. Even though Luce had an incredible talent for pulling off hustles, she was one of the worst liars ever.

A long moment passed between us. At last she admitted that she and Wilky might have talked about relocating a couple of times. "But who knows what'll happen! You know how life is."

My heart was beating so fast I had to chew up another Norco right there in the hall.

Both of us probably wanted to get up and leave at that point, but seeing as we didn't have much of an option, we sat there waiting for Wilky and Nogales, trying to make small talk. Our GM at work and the giant packages of meat we'd seen him loading into his car after hours. The bodybuilder hostess and what you had to take to get that kind of definition—and how she might have some connections worth looking into. That went all right for a while, but when I asked if she'd thought about a timeline for moving, Luce announced she was sick of the entire subject. When I said all I wanted was for her to be happy, she told me to mind my own business for once in my life. By the time Wilky arrived, she'd already pulled herself up off the floor and was standing wobbly-legged by the mailboxes, giving me the silent treatment.

He held the door open. "You ready?"

She didn't answer, just went and kissed him on the mouth right in front of me, before heading out to the car.

Nogales didn't show up for another ten minutes, maybe longer. Turned out he'd gotten to his minivan only to find a tow-truck driver already doing the hookup. Had to do some serious talking to get her to unchain it and even then she made him give her fifty bucks cash and the rest of my watermelon gummies. I probably shouldn't have laughed when he told me, since it only cranked his anger up to eleven, but I couldn't help it. The extra Norco was kicking in hard. A few minutes later when we got turned around trying to find our way out of the complex, I had to angle my face to the window to keep from busting out in dopey giggles. Nogales glanced over. "I don't know what you think is so funny. They could at least put up some exit signage."

"Maybe you should give them a citation."

"Maybe I should," Nogales said.

Between that and getting lost yet again on the all the unmarked mountain roads, we were at least fifteen minutes behind Luce and Wilky. Ordinarily I would have decided this was a good excuse to pick a fight, but I was feeling pretty loose and I wanted to enjoy it. When he tried to explain about the slutty ginger-ale nurse and how it was nothing, I told him I didn't care and to please shut up already. Deep down I knew he wasn't cheating. Luce might have been a terrible liar, but Nogales was the only truly honest one of us all.

He put on some of his sappy shoegazer music, pausing the mix every so often to explain some lyrics or fill me in on a little band trivia. It was kind of nice hearing him droning on and on. Soothing even. By the time we reached the sign announcing the Anklewood exit, I decided maybe I wasn't in such a hurry to get home after all. I pointed out to Nogales it was early enough we could still make Bojangles' if he wanted, and he got so happy you'd have thought he was the one doing combos. He loved their all-day breakfast more than just about anything.

We were discussing if we wanted seasoned fries or Bo-Tato Rounds when we saw lights flashing up ahead in the distance. Some poor fool had gotten themselves pulled over.

I told Nogales they could handle a stupid DUI without him.

"My thoughts exactly," he said. "I vote we get both the fries and the Rounds, along with one of their jumbo family dinners. That way there'll be plenty to share with Luce and Wilky. She needs more than frozen waffles on her stomach."

He really was a good guy.

But as we got closer, something in Nogales's face shifted. He turned off the music. "Looks like we might need to pull over."

"Hope it's not another deer. That makes three since Monday."

"Hard to tell, but I think a car's upside down on the shoulder." He put on his blinkers, started braking. All at once the scene went from blurry to clear. I threw my door open while we were still moving.

"Whoa!" Nogales lunged for my elbow.

"Luce!" I said, jumping out.

WHAT HAPPENED WAS THIS: LUCE FELL OUT again on the way home, slumping forward in her seat belt. When Wilky tried to pull over he was in such a panic he almost slammed into a station wagon full of trick-or-treaters and though he was able to swerve away at the last moment, he ended up skidding off into a ditch and flipping the Outback. It being Halloween the roads were thick with cops. Two highway patrol cars came roaring onto the scene and soon a whole new set of paramedics joined them. At least the adrenaline jolt of the accident woke Luce up enough so she didn't need to get Narcanned. Even better, both she and Wilky came out of the wreckage with nothing worse than matching seat belt–shaped bruises that didn't emerge until the next morning.

By the time I sprinted over, Wilky was standing with two state troopers, blowing a cool zero on his BAC field test. Luce was sitting on the rear bumper of the EMS van, insisting the whole thing was nothing and that she'd had messed-up lungs since she was a little kid. You could tell the paramedics didn't believe her, but if she refused treatment they didn't have much say in the matter. After recommending she see a doctor for a physical, they excused themselves for a quick vape. Even from where I was standing, you could smell the young chunky chick's Froot-Loops-and-milk e-juice, while the old skinny one with three silver rings in her eyebrow had what I swear was watermelon-gummy-bear flavor, which told me all I needed to know about her.

Nogales went right to the senior trooper, a petite dark-haired woman with a sly-looking expression. He showed his badge and volunteered his assistance, saying he happened to know the involved parties. After a doubtful glance at his scrubs, she steered him off to the side where they could talk in private, saying maybe he could clear a couple things up for her. Clearing things up for people was one of Nogales's most cherished pastimes and though his back was to me, I could tell by the look on the trooper's face that he was doing a pretty good job. When she turned away to speak into her radio, I sidled up beside him and said we probably ought to get going.

Nogales rested a hand on my shoulder. "We're about done, don't worry."

I went and sat on the van's bumper next to Luce.

Soon a flatbed truck had arrived and two bearded guys in reflective yellow vests tried to get the Subaru flipped back over. It took a while for them to wrangle it and there was one tricky moment when they almost sent the whole thing careening down the side of the mountain. At last they got the wheels on the ground. The senior trooper put her arm in the air. "Don't load her up yet, boys. We got K-9 coming."

Luce and I exchanged uneasy glances.

"You good?" I said.

Within seconds she was making a clumsy beeline for the Subaru. She was almost there when the junior trooper, a guy who looked to be about the same age as Nogales, stepped between her and the car. "Can't let you do that."

"Sir, I just want to get my chapstick. It's so dry out, my lips are about to start bleeding."

He told her to go stand by his squad car and zip it.

"But officer—"

"You hear me?" Junior took a menacing step forward. "One more word and I'm shutting you in the back." He had a blond buzz cut and the puffed-out physique of someone who spent all his free time pumping weights alone in his basement.

Luce, who knew that type a lot better than I did, gave him a look of pity. "Whatever, guy," she said, backing away.

Still, you could tell by the way Luce kept watching Wilky that she was worried. When the sniffer hound showed up a few minutes later, she tried to get in the Subaru one more time, claiming she'd left her inhaler in the center console. Again she was warned to stay back or else. Soon the dog was alerting and the K-9 handler was holding up an envelope of pills in triumph. They handcuffed Wilky and folded him into the senior trooper's car, while Luce shouted that the pills were hers and she was the one who should be arrested.

"You'd be willing to swear they're yours?" said Junior.

I hurried over to Luce and told her to keep quiet. The sniffer dog turned to look at me, his head cocked in suspicion. He must have gotten a whiff of the presses I'd stuffed in my pants. "I mean it. They'll twist whatever you say against you."

Luce just put her wrists behind her back and demanded they cuff her. "Do it, motherfuckers. I'm serious."

They were all too happy to oblige.

After they recited Luce's rights to her, the senior trooper went on to say that even if the pills were hers, them being in Wilky's car still counted for possession. "Class 1 felony," Junior said. He took Luce by the arm and steered her into the back of his cruiser.

I tried to signal to Luce that I'd meet her at County, but either she couldn't see me from inside the car or else she ignored me. I went up to Nogales and pleaded with him to stop what was happening, but he held his hands up and said there was nothing he could do. Soon both Wilky and Luce were taken away. I watched until their taillights vanished.

Nogales drove me home in silence.

It wasn't until we were turning into the driveway that he finally glanced over. He said Natalia was from his meeting.

"What meeting."

He pulled in behind Luce's Impala, put his car in park. "I told you before, on the way to the party. I knew you weren't listening."

"You spent the whole time blabbing about music!"

"I also said I've been going to Al-Anon. That's where I met Natalia. You know, the nurse? We'd never spoken until I saw her drinking ginger ale in the kitchen, but it turns out we have a lot in common. Her mom's just as much of a mess as ours are."

He kept talking but my head was roaring so loud I couldn't understand what he was saying. When he tried to take my hand, I pulled it away and tucked it under my leg. I didn't even try to hide how disgusted I was with him.

"Irene," he said. "I didn't have a choice back there. You know that."

"Why the shit are you going to Al-Anon," I said.

It took some time for him to explain, but I guess what it came down to is Nogales wanted me to quit using. Said it hadn't been so bad at first, but lately it had been making him pretty unhappy. He'd been going to meetings to try and figure things out. When the state trooper asked him about the car accident and if there was a chance drugs were involved, Nogales insisted the word *yes* fell right out of his mouth before he could stop it.

"Or maybe not," he said. "Maybe part of me thought if the cops scared you and Luce bad enough, things would change. Let's be real, you're never going to get clean as long as she's using."

"Yeah? Guess what." I pulled out my pillbox and chewed up a Soma right in front of him. "You and your know-it-all bullshit only make me want to use even more."

Nogales gave me a stricken look, like I'd stuck a knife into his chest and carved out something important. He lowered his eyes and gazed into his lap. It took a solid half minute or longer before he recovered enough to speak and even then his voice had a drained sort of quality. "All I want is for us to have a normal relationship."

I gave him the sweetest, most tender smile I could summon. "Problem is, we don't have any kind of relationship at all."

I got out of his car, went inside, and listened at the door until I heard the crunch of tires pulling out of the driveway. I got the spare key for Luce's Impala from the junk drawer in the kitchen. My body felt like a giant sandbag I was being forced to lug behind me, but I needed to go spring her and Wilky. I knew from the whole Mom-getting-arrested experience that bail bondspeople took Visa. If Wilky didn't have enough savings, maybe he had room on one of his credit cards. I would have made it there too if the extra Soma I'd eaten during my fight with Nogales hadn't decided to get all cozy with the extra Norco I'd chewed up at the party. Muscle relaxers and hydrocodone are amazing together right up until they turn into a complete horror show. I woke up in the hospital with a broken collarbone and my own possession charge after nodding off and steering the Impala headfirst into a drainage ditch a few blocks from the sheriff's.

It took a few months for our court dates to arrive, thanks to a public defender shortage, but in the end Luce and I both got suspended licenses, thousand-dollar fines, and two hundred hours each of picking up trash on the highway. Even that last part wasn't so bad, since she was right there beside me with her state-issued grabber, bagging up used condoms, used pads, used diapers, and other assorted grossness. If we hadn't been a couple of white chicks, no doubt our punishment would have been way worse. I've heard it said the system is fucked, but the way I see it, it's working the exact terrible way they planned all along.

Only Wilky took any real hit. Though he passed his BAC field test like a champ, the arrest was reported to the bigwigs at Bragg, triggering an investigation. Along with the sixty percs the army medical center signed off on every month, a little digging revealed that Wilky had gotten scripts from at least seven different pill-millers in the Fayetteville area at one time or another. Things escalated fast. He did all he could to fight it—self-reported to the army's substance abuse program, hired a fancy lawyer to represent him at the hearing—but it didn't matter. Wilky found himself chaptered out with a Big Chicken Dinner, a.k.a. Bad Conduct Discharge. The post-separation benefits he'd been counting on went up in smoke.

While this ended the whole Florida scheme, at least for the moment, it didn't break him and Luce up the way it did me and Nogales. If anything, it brought them closer, and in more ways than one. Before long Wilky was moving to Anklewood and getting a job not far from where we waited tables. And though it took a few more months for them to make the commitment, at their next Valentine's Day dinner they agreed it was time to get clean. Started going to meetings, working the steps, doing service. It wasn't easy, but it wasn't nearly as hard as the other—at least most days. As for me, I was right there beside them, racking up time and sharing stories and being the best little recoverer you could possibly imagine. I had to if I ever wanted to see Luce.

A ND THEN JUST LIKE THAT IT'S THE FOLLOWING year, as if time has looped around and tied itself off all nice and efficient. Wilky is gone forever and Luce has run off in a filthy white coal-roller with a *University of Margaritaville* sticker on the rear panel. According to the clerk's phone it's already midmorning. Maybe Teena is awake.

Half an hour later she was driving me to the bank in her smoked-out Mercury Cougar so I could get a new debit card and some cash from my car fund. Once that was finished, I bought some supplies. It wasn't like I was sick or even close to withdrawals, and thanks to my little two-bagger the night before, my knee felt almost normal. I just wanted to turn my brain down a couple of notches. After that, I'd go find Luce. Maybe some time apart had made her realize how lucky she was to have me.

So after I copped a bun from Teena and she fixed me up, we drove out to Wilky's old bar at the far end of Broad Street. I felt almost cheerful on the way over, but once we pulled into the parking lot the day took on a deflated quality I hadn't expected. Even the air felt all sucked out and empty, like there wasn't any air there. I guess I had it in my head we'd find Luce waiting for us on that saggy green sofa, like in the old days. No such luck. My chest got so tight it was painful and even after I undid my seat belt I had a hard time breathing. I looked over to find Teena watching me closely.

"You better not start punching my car again," she said.

We went and sat on the couch and this time she fixed herself up. I paid attention to how she did it. "Number one thing to remember," said Teena, laying her works on the cushion between us, "is take care of your needles. I'm not saying you can't reuse them, but keep them clean as possible. Bottled water when you can, fresh cottons. And if it hurts going in, pull that puppy out. Means you hit a nerve or a muscle and not only will it waste your shot, it can mess you up something awful."

She passed me her cooker—a bent spoon with a bunch of flowery swirls on the handle. "Hold this. My ex once got an abscess on her thigh the size of a Granny Smith apple. Thing stunk so bad I thought they were going to have to chop her leg off. Okay, steady now." She tapped in powder, a dribble of water. "And no sharing your spike or you're asking for trouble. That's how my ex got hep C. Watch your fingers." She held a lighter under the spoon. "I like 31 shorts with a 1cc syringe, but I'll use one of those 23 harpoons if I have to." When the stuff bubbled, she unwrapped a tampon, pinched off some cotton, added it to the mixture. "For filtering."

After tying herself off with her phone charger, she got out her needle and held it up to the light to show me. "Easiest way to get your spikes is online, long as you don't mind the government or whoever having your info. You want to buy them in person, avoid the mom-and-pop pharms cause they'll give you a harder time than places like Walmart who could care less if you live or die. Or adopt yourself a diabetic cat so you can get a needle prescription. Maybe one of these days we'll get an exchange around here but I doubt it. Now remember, eye down when you draw it up, eye up when it goes in. Like so. Oh and don't forget to untie yourself first to help with the bruising."

She pulled back on the plunger a little and red swirled in the barrel. "You don't see any blood, it means you missed your shot and you need to redo it. Spurting blood means you hit an artery and you better stop fast or else. You with me?" She glanced over to make sure I was still watching and when I nodded yes, she pushed the plunger down. A moment passed and she withdrew the needle nice and steady. Held a finger to the crook of her arm. A few more seconds and she closed her eyes and leaned her head back. "There."

And afterward, she wasn't so chatty. We did talk a little, though. Music. Our favorite drug movies, crime dramas. She told me some stuff about prison, which would have been pretty depressing if I hadn't been loaded. All the violence. The inside prices. Making rigs out of ballpoint pens, paper clips, those little eye-drop bottles. Being on lockdown for weeks on end. What it was like having a control freak for a parole officer back when she was still on paper. "Bitch had me doing UAs on the weekly."

"You mean you had to stay clean after they let you out?"

Teena gave me a disappointed look. "You don't know shit about shit, do you?"

That was when I learned about buying fake piss in head shops, buying clean piss from your friends' kids, detoxifiers, dilution methods, and other urine-based hustles. When she brought up the Female Whizzinator, I laughed so hard I almost wet my pants. Turns out it's this contraption that lets you hide synthetic pee in your undies and release it into the cup as needed. Even includes heating pads to make the temperature more authentic.

"Wow," I said. "That's one scam I bet even Luce hasn't heard of."

"Luce Luce Luce," Teena said. "You sure you don't got a thing for that girl? You only talk about her every other second."

I informed Teena that Luce was my best friend and I'd do anything for her, but it must have come out a little hotter than I wanted.

"Chill, guy," Teena said. "No need to get all up in anyone's face."

We didn't say much after that, just enjoyed the warm cuddle of afghan brown flowing all through us. It lasted longer than I thought it would. The sun was practically resting on the ground when I asked Teena if she'd rig up another shot for me.

"You paid for it," she said. "But try fixing yourself this time. Anything happens, I'll be right beside you."

The only thing she had to show me was how to tie a slip-knot one-handed. Otherwise, I did it all on my own.

•

The smell of vinegar. The prick of the needle. I swear, you can feel the warmth travel from your arm on up to your chest. And then when it gets there, my god.

"Well?" said Teena.

"It's beautiful," I heard myself say.

By the time we were ready for round three, it was full-on dark out. The bar had opened and a few customers had come out for a smoke break, so Teena suggested we relocate, find a more private place to duck into. Out on Broad Street, folks were already nodding in doorways and on the sidewalk, though I knew from walking home after dinner shifts that it wouldn't hit peak junky for a few more hours. Every once in a while you'd glimpse the flare of a lighter, the bright orange of a syringe cap. Up above, the sky was this deep velvet blue with just a few pricks in the fabric where the stars had once been.

Despite what our fellow users were up to, getting well out in the open isn't the smartest move ever. After failing to get into the bathrooms at Burger Hut, Sub World, even Quik Chek (the idiot managers all refused to give us the key for some reason), I suggested we go hang at my house where we wouldn't be messed with. Privately I was hoping Luce would be there, though I wasn't about to admit that to Teena.

"I'm down," she said. Her gaze shifted to the Quik Chek ATM in the corner. "You good for another dip?"

Unfortunately I could only get two hundred more dollars, but Teena assured me the daily limit would reset at midnight. My new balance wasn't too cute. At least my knee hadn't hurt all day, which meant I could probably get through a dinner shift with maybe a tiny bump or two for assistance. I made a mental note to call the restaurant first thing in the morning and ask Marshall if he could please forget the whole suspension business. Once I was back on the schedule, I'd be able to replace the money without too much trouble. Maybe Luce would be ready to go back to work too.

We got in Teena's car, started driving. The idea of being home again, sitting with Luce on the couch, watching one of our shows and eating ice cream sundaes together made me feel better than anything I could have loaded into a needle. I lay back in my seat and turned my face to the window. Over and over trees rushed by. Even at night you could identify them by their silhouettes—and this too felt incredibly soothing. Oak, hickory, loblolly pine.

So when Teena zipped by the road that led to our place, I was so relaxed it took me a few seconds to understand what had happened. I struggled to sit up. "Wait, I think you passed it."

"Yeah, I got to meet someone." She kept her eyes on the road and her voice was hard and toneless.

How did I not see that coming. I sank back into my seat and tried to hide my disappointment. "Sounds great."

We kept driving. Down the mountain and up over the next one. We swooped onto a ridge that looked almost pleasant—twinkling lights on porches, blooming camellias— but swooped right back out again. It wasn't until it hit me that Teena was meeting her connect for more powder that I felt somewhat encouraged. I sat up again and tried to pay attention. If Luce and I could cut Teena out of the middle, we'd be able to get our dope for even cheaper. Then I felt the heat of Teena's gaze on my cheek. I glanced over.

"Don't even think about it," she said.

We ended up in a sad dump of a town. No working streetlamps anywhere, no neon signs or lit-up billboards, just a TV flickering in a window every so often. A flapping power line, countless potholes. The rotten-egg stink of a leaky septic tank. Teena rounded a corner and up ahead stood a woman clutching a trash bag to her chest as if it contained all her worldly possessions. As we got closer, she shifted the bag to one arm and stuck her thumb out, smiling broadly despite the painful-looking cuts on her cheek and forehead. When we sped by without stopping, she picked up a rock and hurled it at us. It hit the bumper with an angry thud.

At last we reached a small split-level cottage. The bars on the windows weren't too comforting and neither was the handwritten *Beware of Dog* sign propped against the rain barrel. The kid's tricycle parked by the front steps made me feel a little bit better, even though I knew dboys with families were often way worse than the single dudes. Teena knocked on the door and we waited. One of those baby monitor getups was mounted above our heads. It wasn't long before a sullen-looking teenager, sixteen maybe, opened the door and stared out at us.

"Hey Brandon, how you doing?" said Teena. Suddenly she was nothing but a warm liquidy syrup.

Brandon clearly had experience with the Teenas of this world. Without bothering to acknowledge her or her question, he swung around and headed back inside, up the stairs, and soon we heard the classic start-up sound of a Sony PlayStation.

"Fucking brat," Teena said.

We let ourselves into what turned out to be a cozy wood-paneled room with a nice blue couch and a matching armchair. Framed photos on the mantel. The distinct smell of stewed chicken hung all around us and before long a man in an apron that read *Hot Stuff Coming Through* walked out of the kitchen gripping a wooden spoon. After a quick glance at me, he turned to Teena. "You get my texts?"

"I told you," she said. "It's not happening."

"Left you a couple voice mails too. There was some good stuff in there. Real good."

"Yeah, my phone died," Teena said. "Look, me and my friend here are short on time, so can we do this?"

Hot Stuff didn't answer, just kept watching Teena. At last he slid a phone out of his apron pocket and punched a few buttons. Somewhere in the house a different phone started ringing. One of those electronic melodies that are always going off in old men's pants. When it finally stopped, Hot Stuff spoke into the receiver. "Got you a couple custos. Okay. Yeah, sorry. I know. I know. I already said I wouldn't, I promise." He hung up and stared at the screen for several long seconds.

"Everything cool?" said Teena.

Hot Stuff looked up at her, his face vibrating with anger. "You're good to go. But next time I reach out, you better answer." He swung around and went back into the kitchen.

Teena and I exchanged glances. Dudes everywhere were always the same.

She led me to a door by the staircase and opened it, revealing a basement. All at once the whole doctor nightmare began flashbulbing before me in a series of hot stabby explosions. A sweat broke out all over my body and soon I got so lightheaded I had to rest my hand on the wall for balance.

But either Teena didn't notice or else she chose to ignore it. She leaned in close, her breath warm and damp in my ear. "Only rule is you can't say anything, no matter what. Don't worry, this stuff is worth it." She headed downstairs, expecting me to follow.

And I did.

ON THE MORNING LUCE CAME HOME THE SKY WAS this gorgeous Dreamsicle color, pale orange with a few milky ribbons. Already I knew something good was going to happen. Sure enough it wasn't long before she was walking up our gravel drive, head bent, black hoodie slung over her shoulder. I lowered the pack of frozen peas from my nose and cranked the BarcaLounger up to a sitting position. She eased open the door. She had a puffy eye and a greening bruise on her cheekbone, but from the face she made when she saw me, I must have looked worse than she did.

"We leave now, we can make the 8," she said. "If you're interested."

I nodded. "Let me just change my shirt."

Almost three days had passed since Luce and I had seen each other. I'd been with Teena for most of that time and by the end all I had left was a pocketful of ATM receipts and a busted nose. The basement hadn't even been the bad part. Once we got down the stairs all we found was a private shooting gallery with a dozen or so women collapsed in a circle of beanbag pillows, enjoying their ecp in blissful silence. No, the bad part came a couple nights later after I nodded out on Teena's toilet and tumbled face-first onto the edge of her bathtub, my pants twisted up around my ankles. Blood everywhere. When Teena heard the crash she came running in panic, but once she saw I hadn't ODd, she got so enraged at the mess she grabbed my feet and dragged me outside and left me to spend the night on her porch with nothing but an old dog blanket I found scrunched up in the corner. Which of course made me think of the dog leash.

In a groggy haze I pounded on Teena's door with as much force as I could summon and when she didn't answer I went staggering around to each of her windows, smacking the glass over and over, pleading for one last hit to get me through till morning. At last she came outside, eyes sparking with fury. Shot me up with what felt like nothing but baking soda, loaded me into her car, drove me back to me and Luce's, and left me at the end of the driveway next to the mailbox. From a certain distance it's almost funny, but at the time I was scoring a perfect ten on the pain scale. Good thing my bank account was on *E* and I couldn't get any more powder, otherwise I would have needled myself into oblivion and then some.

Luce and I went to the meeting. Although I was no longer hopeful about any sort of recovery, it meant we would spend an hour together. You take what you can get. We were both still a bit faded—not so much that anyone would notice, but enough so the sharp edges felt sanded down to a manageable level—and while we didn't say very much on our walk down the mountain, I distinctly recall slipping my arm in hers as we trudged up the church driveway. She flinched a little, but at least she didn't pull away completely.

And oh, that 8 a.m. meeting. These days I take a deep pleasure in the cool dim of sunrise, but back then I made a habit of sleeping late as possible. Even though Wilky had gone to the early Eye-Opener group pretty often, the 1:30 was the only time slot Luce and I had ever attended. When the two of us walked into the church basement that morning, we found ourselves staring down a whole new crowd. People with tucked-in shirts, ironed dress pants, polished heels and loafers. The room smelled like spice deodorant and lemon shampoo. There was still a crushing line for the coffee, but once everyone got their fix they didn't clump up by the table and instead they went and sat in the circle, chatting politely.

"These here are the pros," Luce said.

I suggested we take the chairs nearest the door in case we wanted to make a quick exit. A few people gave us the whole newcomer once-over, but they were pretty discreet and it wasn't too terrible. Even so my stomach felt queasy. Ever since Wilky, things had been getting worse and worse no matter what we did or how hard we tried to stop it and it occurred to me that maybe the wise thing was for Luce and me to make a run for it while we were still able. Then she leaned over to fix a sock that had gotten bunched up around her ankle and I got a whiff of the sweaty tang she always took on after working a double in summer. It calmed me somehow.

The woman who ran the 8 a.m. was nothing like Greenie. Tall and slim, with short brown curls and little stud earrings. I'd seen her around Anklewood on a few occasions and I was pretty sure she worked in admin at the hospital. Billing, maybe. Beside her sat a woman who turned out to be the guest speaker. Some rock n roll chick I'd never seen before. Dyed black hair with a few electric-blue highlights. Aviator glasses that managed to look more cool than stupid. Black sweater dress, ankle booties, and black tights that had these weird cartoon clocks all over. On anyone else the tights would have looked even dumber than the glasses, but this chick, who-ever she was, pulled it off. I was trying to see what time it was on the clocks when I felt Luce's elbow. "Dude, check out her necklace."

She had on a gold pendant shaped like Florida. My stom-ach rolled over.

"Maybe it's a sign from Wilky," Luce said.

The meeting started. Despite this being the profes-sional version, it turned out to be a lot like the 1:30. Same announcements, same readings from the Big Book. If any-thing, the war stories here were more hard-core. Stuff like ripping shots in the hospital bathroom while a parent lay dy-ing. Sucking d for sub wrappers. The guest speaker, Ms. Flor-ida, shared about scraping bags at her kitchen table while her baby looked on from her high chair. Although her story was one of the worst I'd heard in ages, when she got to the recovery part it turned out to be pretty inspiring. Obviously her bottom had been way lower than me and Luce's, and now look at her.

We took our Day 1s and that wasn't so terrible either, not really. We introduced ourselves, got our key tags, everyone applauded. The 8 a.m. leader gave us a Whitestrips smile of approval and so did Ms. Florida. Even Luce turned to me with a hopeful expression. It struck me that the two of us might actually get through this—and out of nowhere I started laughing. Not a big laugh, more like one of those secret ones where you keep your face as still as possible so no one can see it. Although she'd gone back to watching Ms. Florida, I felt certain that Luce was secretly laughing too. We were both in on the same inside joke together. We always would be, no matter what happened. Only problem was the joke hardly ever seemed funny anymore.

It wasn't until the very end that things veered off in a new direction. We'd finished up the formal part of the meeting, done the whole group-hug thing and said our goodbyes, when Ms. Florida approached us by the percolator. Luce was refilling her cup for the walk home. "Hey you two. Congrats on Day 1. How you feeling?"

"You know. Hoping it sticks," I said. "Thanks for the share by the way, it was helpful."

"Why does this place always run out of sugar?" Luce said. I turned in time to see her fling the empty Domino box back onto the table. Clearly her dopamine levels were starting to plummet. "Like how hard can it be to keep this shit in stock? It's not fucking powder."

"You need some sweetener?" said Ms. Florida. She reached in her purse—a sleek leather bag that would have cost me and Luce a month of weekends—and pulled out a ziplock crammed full of sugar packets. Not the cheap white kind either, but the fancy brown. "Learned years ago to bring my own supply whenever I travel. Stuff's a real hot commodity in the rooms. Take as much as you want, I got plenty more in my suitcase."

"Wow, thanks, man," Luce said, helping herself to a handful. She snuck another look at Ms. Florida's necklace. "I'm guessing you're from the Sunshine State?"

"You know it. Born and raised in Tallanasty, went to school in O-town, now coming to you live from Delray Beach. I'm here for work but I'll be heading home this weekend."

"Right on." Luce took her time stirring her coffee. "Actually I had plans to move to Florida last month. Course it all went sideways at the last minute."

"Oh yeah?" Ms. Florida said.

After that, things moved pretty quickly. Luce confided that her boyfriend had ODd out of nowhere and now the two of us were hoping to get back on the clean-time train after slipping. Turned out Ms. Florida worked for a treatment center that had exactly two empty beds. "Most likely they'll be spoken for in a few hours, but it's a pretty sweet setup if you can nab it. Inpatient, women only. Less than a mile from the beach. They even waive any out-of-pocket fees, long as you have insurance. You have insurance?"

Luce said she was still on her stepdad's policy. "The dumbass."

"I got one of those myself," Ms. Florida said. "But seriously, why not take advantage? They got this place tricked out. Daily massages, guided meditation, a freaking world-class chef. And of course you'd be detoxing with professional supervision."

"Sounds good," said Luce. "But I'm more of a Gatorade and Imodium girl, if you know what I'm saying."

"How much is it if you don't have insurance?" I said. "Any scholarships available?"

Luce turned to me. "No way. You'd do it?"

I told her if I could afford it, I'd think it over. After everything that had happened, I'd take whatever would help us get clean. "But only if you're going."

"Huh," said Luce. For the first time, she appeared to consider the possibility. She looked at Ms. Florida. "This isn't one of those six-month deals is it? We got jobs to think about."

"Most people graduate in twenty-eight days unless they backslide. And after that there's a sober-living option." Ms. Florida pushed her aviator glasses higher on her nose. "We don't have any scholarships, though. Insurance only."

It hadn't been something I'd wanted or even known about five minutes earlier and yet the old familiar lump of disappointment formed in my stomach. Money, money, money, money.

"I get it," I said.

I turned to Luce, thinking we'd say goodbye to Ms. Florida and head out already. Our run hadn't been very long, so we probably wouldn't have the worst withdrawals ever, but it would still be a good idea to swing by the store, get some food in the house, restock our children's chewables. And then I saw Luce's hand. It kept opening and closing, like some kind of sick mixed-up flower. I filled my lungs with air, let it out slowly.

I told Luce she should still go.

She looked at me funny, like maybe she didn't hear me.

"I mean it," I said, louder this time. "You go get better there, I'll get better here, and we'll meet up again when it's all over."

"You're okay with me going to Florida," she said. "Without you."

I said if it helped her get healthy again, then yes. "Anything you need. I'm here for you always."

For the first time in a long while, Luce looked at me the way she did back in the beginning. So warm and tender it was like god herself had shot me up with the pure stuff.

"You're a good friend," she said.

We got a ride home from Ms. Florida. Luce handed over her insurance info. Ms. Florida took a photo of the card with her fancy iPhone and forwarded it to her boss. Said as long as they didn't hit any snags, approval shouldn't take more than twenty-four hours. "They'll send a plane ticket and we'll get started."

"A plane ticket," I said. "They fly people down there?"

"What kind of snags we talking," said Luce.

"You know." Ms. Florida zipped up her coat, draped her purse over her shoulder. "The usual corporate hassle. Have to make sure your coverage lines up. And then once you're checked into our center, we'll need a dirty urine test so we can prove you need treatment."

"Shouldn't be a problem," Luce said, following her to the door. "Though I do have a pretty good metabolism. Stuff rips through my system. You think I'll still pop hot by the time I get there?"

Ms. Florida turned back to face her, cool as ever. "Testing clean is an easy fix. We got a guy. Don't worry."

Two days later, Luce was on a plane for the first time in her life, heading south to Delray.

My favorite memories of Luce:

Driving across the mountain in her grandma's Impala, taking the hairpins as fast as possible, listening to her CD mixes and singing our heads off

Gulping Monster Energy drinks every afternoon while we changed into our work uniforms, trying to amp ourselves up for another night of serving

Stringing a week's worth of the empty cans onto a clothes-line and shooting them up with her BB gun

The way she'd steal all the best tables from all the worst servers

The way she'd help out if she saw you were slammed, refill-ing iced teas and coffees and taking dessert orders

How if a customer gave you a hard time, she'd walk over and pretend she was the shift supervisor and tell them if they said one more wrong word, they'd be 86ed

I made endless lists like this when she first went to Florida. What else was I supposed to do? Stare down all the giant Luce-size holes in the air around me? Ugly, gaping things.

It wasn't like the two of us could talk to each other. Before she left, we destroyed the clerk's shitty burner with her BB rifle and bought the cheapest of cheap Tracfones, but aside from the texts we exchanged when she switched planes in Atlanta, I didn't hear from her no matter how many messages I left or how often I tried calling. *The person you are trying to reach is not available.* How many times I've heard that in my life. When I called the treatment center to talk to her, the man who answered said unfortunately this was impossible, that phone usage was forbidden in the early weeks of recovery. When I tried to argue, saying I just wanted to make sure she was doing okay, he assured me Luce was great and I shouldn't worry.

"A star patient," he said.

Even this scrap of news kept me happy. Sober. Strangely, I didn't think all that much about using once I got past the first week or so, though I did think about Luce more than was probably healthy. It was like the song of her had become stuck on a loop in my head. It got so I was always imagining what she was doing at any given moment. Lying in bed, gazing at the pink lollipop sun outside her window. Knuckling sleep out of her eyes in the bathroom mirror. Sitting in the dining hall and forking one of their fancy omelets into her mouth.

From what I knew of rehab, I figured she'd have group right after breakfast and as I sat circled up in the church basement from 8 to 9 every morning, I took comfort in the idea of Luce sitting in her own meeting, sharing her stories. The doctor in charge, who I imagined as a sensible-looking woman with a notebook full of tiny immaculate writing, would know exactly what to say and when to say it. Chores would come next and lunch would follow. Maybe one-on-one therapy after that. Later she'd get a bit of afternoon free time, which is when

Luce and all the other residents would ride bikes along a sandy little path down to the ocean. Seashell collecting, volleyball, Frisbee. Maybe someone would even teach her how to swim. All this and more played out in my mind like a movie with the best soundtrack ever: Luce getting better, little by little. By god I was going to get better too.

I still wasn't ready to face Greenie, so I put my 1:30 home group on hold and added the 7 p.m. meeting to my daily schedule. Stay busy they kept saying and it's true this helped stop my mind from roaming to dangerous places. It also gave me the chance to hear a bunch more stories from a whole new set of people. I shared a few stories too. When the night crowd heard about me blowing up my savings during my final run with Teena, a couple of them came up after and offered me part-time gigs as a dog-walker. "To help keep the wolf away from the door." Another one loaned me a high-end neoprene knee brace with fancy hinges and cutouts, and soon I was going on afternoon hikes all over our mountain with a little collie mix named Bella and a huskie/mastiff combo named BooBoo. I couldn't wait to introduce them to Luce. The smell of loblolly pines, gauzy light, a pair of dogs trotting beside you. Walking through the woods, I've come to discover, can help remind you what's important.

> Luce's pink toothbrush in the cup in the bathroom
> Her eyeshadow palette with the secret compartment
> Her black hoodie slung over the back of the sofa
> Her glorious dogtooth

•

Meetings twice a day might sound like a lot of commitment, but it's not so hard when you don't have a job to deal with. It's nobody's fault except mine. When my suspension ended it took me a few days to return Marshall's messages and with both me and Luce out of the picture he had no choice but to hire replacements. He did promise to work me back into the schedule after I put six months' clean time together. I think he would have too.

Before Luce left, I'd never been the type to share much at meetings, but once she was no longer sitting beside me, for some reason I started talking more than usual. Probably because I was trying to make sense of all that had happened. Also, I was lonely, lonely. Except for the occasional grocery store clerk or a random neighbor encounter, meetings were the only time I talked to anyone. I shared about how Luce and I met, our job at the pool hall, getting revenge on Ronnie Ankle, working that Buck-a-Dog booth. Copping pandas from Chicken Feathers and his blocked-up mother. Being screwed over by Gayle Crystal. A little bit about getting roofied, though it would take a few more years before I was ready to dig into all that. None of it was easy, but once it was over I was almost always glad I'd spoken up.

It wasn't until I told the story about Luce flying off to rehab in Florida that a girl approached me after the meeting and asked if we could talk for a second. This was at the 7 p.m. New in the rooms, she couldn't have been much older than sixteen, seventeen tops, with a fierce junkyard-dog way about her that let you know she'd gone through something pretty horrific. She kept shifting her weight from one leg to the other like she was nervous—and right away I knew she was going to ask me to be her sponsor. I admit I was flattered. I'd never been asked that before.

"First things first," I said. "You should know I don't have much clean time."

Something in the girl's face jumped around a little. "Yeah, same."

She had on a backward Korn hat with a few dark pieces sticking out from under. Brown eyes. Bunched-up shoulders. The flush of pimples on her cheeks combined with her bitten-down fingernails made her look even younger than I'd first thought. A child, when you got down to it.

She motioned me over to the percolator. While she took her time refilling a giant red thermos, I launched into all the newcomer advice I could think of. Stuff like ninety meetings in ninety days, letting go, keeping busy, taking things one day at time or even minute by minute. How willingness, honesty, and open-mindedness were the keys to recovery. And sure, it was nothing more than a bunch of twelve-step stuff all strung together, but it felt good to say it. Greenie always insisted that being of service was a huge part of staying sober. What if this was my Higher Power telling me it was time to level up in the program?

"Look," I said as the girl stirred in powdered creamer. "If you want me to be your sponsor, I'd be honored."

She glanced up from her coffee. Once again her face got twitchy. "Yeah, that's not why I wanted to talk to you."

I felt myself redden. "Okay. What then."

"You ever hear of the Florida Shuffle?" she said.

The way Luce would pick all the marshmallows out of our Count Chocula and then complain we got cheated by the cereal fat cats

The elaborate ice cream sundaes she made for us every night once we quit using

Her strawberry-kiwi shampoo and how it made my nose tingle

The sound of her lungs pumping air in and out

The girl said she didn't want to scare me, but she figured I should probably know what was happening down in Palm Beach County. "There's some real fucked-up shit going on where your friend's at."

As politely as I could, I explained that she was either confused or mistaken. Luce was in one of the best rehabs in the country. She was coming home in nine days, clean and sober and better than ever. She was learning how to swim! Still the girl kept on talking. You could tell she was pretty worked up about whatever she was trying to tell me, but the truth was she wasn't making any sense.

Not wanting to hurt her feelings, I tried to listen, but soon I couldn't take it a second longer. I excused myself and went upstairs to the church restroom. Peed, washed my hands, splashed water on my face. As a last-minute thought, just to confirm how depressingly mixed-up that poor Korn kid was, I did a search on my phone for this Florida Shuffle business.

Next thing I knew I was dry-heaving into the sink.

Laughing at r/opioids sub threads together over breakfast

Upvoting all the best war stories, downvoting trolls and idiots

Congratulating the people celebrating their cake day

Posting a . for a moment of silence whenever an OD was announced

The hustle works like this: In exchange for a hefty payout, a body broker like Ms. Florida finds someone struggling with addiction who has health-care coverage, usually under their parents' policy. She offers them a free bed in a treatment center and promises all sorts of perks and amenities. Who wouldn't want to get clean in a fancy setup next to the beach? But the place turns out to be little more than a flophouse. No perks, not even treatment, just wake up and piss in a cup every morning. Instead of a chef, you get candy bars and frozen burritos. Maybe a group session once a day if you're lucky. Many of your fellow patients will still be using. Your bedroom is locked from the outside every night. Meanwhile the flophouse owner charges your insurance these epic amounts for your so-called treatment—we're talking tens of thousands of dollars—and when your claim runs out they stick you in a cheap motel for a couple weeks, give you free dope every day so you stay there, and then file a new claim with your insurer saying you relapsed. The moment it's approved, the cycle starts all over. The only way out for most patients is a fatal overdose—and once your tolerance is back down to amateur levels, that part's a cinch to pull off.

My head pounding with blood, I sat on the floor of the bathroom trying to buy a plane ticket to Palm Beach International, but the last-minute prices might as well have been a million dollars. I wasn't eligible to get my driver's license back for another week and a half, so I couldn't rent a car. I thought about asking Greenie for help, but I'd been dodging her so long I felt too ashamed to call her and instead I phoned my mom and left a long message saying I was in trouble and I needed her advice and could she please please call me as soon as possible? I never heard back.

Which is why I finally texted Nogales. He didn't respond right away and that wasn't like him. I texted him a second time. I'm at the church, I said. It's important! Can you meet me? It took a few minutes, but at last he got back to me with a stupid thumbs-up emoji.

It's urgent, I wrote back. Hurry.

All that got was a like.

I was waiting on the steps out front when his cruiser rolled into the parking lot, all nice and casual like he was hitting a drive-thru. I hurried down to meet him. "What took so long?"

"I was grabbing a slice with a friend," he said, climbing out of the car. "You okay? What happened?"

As fast as I could, I told him everything I knew about the whole rehab-shuffle situation. Pulled up some articles on my phone. "She's fine, right? All this is nothing but clickbait."

He didn't say anything, just scrolled through, reading in silence. At last he lifted his head. His face was the same greenish color as when he told me and Luce about Wilky. "I don't guess you feel like taking a drive, do you?"

Soon the two of us were speeding to Florida.

Nogales used his sirens the whole way.

86thepervontable3

.

THERE'S SO MUCH MORE I COULD TELL YOU. YOU never heard the full story about Luce breaking her elbow that one winter and how impossible it was to get anyone to prescribe her the pain meds she needed. Or about me trading our TV for a half dozen blues during a moment of desperation, and then pretending we'd been burglarized when Luce came home and saw it was missing. One of the many times I lied to her, I'm ashamed to say. Us stealing another TV to replace it is a whole other story—nursing home, craft hour, rear exit—and so is us making amends to the facility and its residents once we got clean and started working the steps. You also never got to hear Luce's favorite story. Or maybe *favorite* isn't the right word exactly, but it's the one I heard her tell more than any other and I'd bet any amount of money it's the one she'd share if she were sitting here with us.

I wish she were sitting here with us.

Anyway. I can't tell her story for her. I wouldn't want to. Once upon a time there was magic, there was music, and then: nothing. Even now, years later, there are days when the world is little more than an empty scraped-out bag. And the with-drawals, let me tell you, are a real motherfucker.

•

Facts then? Okay, something easy.

College. Not right away, but after another year or so of serving I decided I should probably look into another option. Something that required a little less brainpower. A few more months passed until one night, after getting written up for being rude to a grabby regular (hi Ed, remember me?), I was so angry I went online, filled out the FAFSA, and got student loan approval. Turned out I also qualified for a Pell Grant and the following month I sent off two applications. Got flat rejected by one school and wait-listed by the other, which eventually turned into an acceptance. I enrolled.

Not that this made things easier. Even with the loans I still had to wait tables while taking full-time hours. A small mental health incident occurred during my second semester (February is always a hard month to get through) and I transferred to a different school the following year. Dropped out of the second school not long after and did another lengthy stretch of food service until at last I eased myself back into the system with what they call distance learning, a.k.a. online education. The first class went better than expected. I signed up for another. And another. Eventually my transcript wasn't quite so embarrassing and I managed to squeak into a big state university in Florida. Well, you probably don't have to have a degree in psychology to understand why I applied there.

I take classes like everyone, I get grades, I have professors who respond to my emails. Unless something unexpected happens I'll get my degree next May. Oh and here's something funny: instead of math, I'm studying English. Partly because after all these years in the rooms I've come to love stories. Partly because nothing adds up anymore.

Something else funny. With maybe one exception, everyone here at school thinks I'm a normie. Of the many skills I learned from the old hustle, the ability to figure out what someone wants has been the most valuable. Once you understand that, it's not so hard to let them have it. To them I'm just some harmless older woman trying to get herself a little education. I think a few of them feel sorry for me. Hey, if it makes them happy, I don't mind, not really. For the most part I'm glad no one here knows about my former life and all that happened—though it does make me feel even more alone.

Which is a big reason why I still go to meetings. Online ones, mostly. If you're interested, there's a good site called In The Rooms. But full disclosure: Although I haven't used pills or h for eight years and counting, I'm not completely sober. It probably doesn't qualify as official medication-assisted treatment, but having a beer or two every night helps keep me steady. At least it has so far. I admit I did steal a half sheet of Oxy 5s from my mom after her car accident two summers ago (DUI, broken ribs, broken pelvis), but they're still under my bathroom sink, next to the toilet bowl cleaner. Haven't even broken the foil. I can't say why for sure, but maybe the idea of getting into it without Luce here to join me is too depressing.

Luce.

•

I'll come out and say it.

She died in that Delray rehab the morning before Nogales and I got there. Did a shot packed with fent while sitting on the edge of the bathtub. Just like that, her lungs clicked off and she stopped breathing. Instant release. I'm told a fellow resident found her collapsed on the tile after breakfast. You'd think a treatment center would be the last place where people could get loaded. Not in Florida. Or California, as it turns out. Arizona, Texas, and others.

She was twenty-two years old.

Since I wasn't on any of Luce's paperwork—she'd listed her stepdad as her emergency contact—no one called me. If Nogales hadn't driven me down there, who knows when I would have found out what happened. Months later, when I was reading everything I could about the whole rehab hustle, I came across several interviews with parents who said they were never notified that their child had died.

A lot of what followed is blurry, and most of what I recall is little more than ghostly flashes: The odor of pizza drifting in from the back room at the funeral parlor, the shock of the open casket, the old-lady dress Luce's mom and stepdad decided to bury her in. The online obituary that called her Lucille. The fill-in-the blanks eulogy from a minister whose phone kept buzzing in his pants all through the service. "She's in a better place now," I remember him saying. "God needed another angel." It was like he copied his speech off wikiHow. One of my biggest regrets in this life is I didn't stand up when he asked if anyone wanted to add something further. Not even one small story about what an amazing human she was and how much she meant to me, and how life will never, ever, be the same without her. Luce, I'm sorry.

The night before the funeral, I called my mom to tell her what happened. It had been almost three years since we'd spoken, so it wasn't like I thought she'd answer. But sometimes even leaving a message helps a little. I've left countless messages over the years. So you can imagine my surprise when she not only picked up, she sounded happy I'd phoned her.

"Irene, that you? I've been calling and calling but you never answer."

"Mom! Oh my god."

I knew she hadn't tried to call me, but I was so glad to hear her voice I didn't care if she was lying. I told her as much about Luce as I could handle.

"Oh my goodness, baby," she said. "That's heartbreaking. I wish I was there with you."

"Me too."

A long pause followed. A TV was playing in the background. Applause, cheering. A game show most likely. Seconds later, the TV clicked off.

"Now listen," she said, coughing a little. "I need to ask you something important."

When I'd told my mom about Luce's drug use, I was hoping she wouldn't want to know if I'd gotten mixed up in all that business. She had a lot of shame about her own drinking and if she found out I'd inherited the same problems with addiction, it would hurt her. This much I knew. Then again maybe it was time for both of us to face the hard questions.

"Okay," I said. "What is it?"

"There any way you could loan me a hundred bucks?"

But if there's someone good in this world, it's Nogales. Not only did he drive me to Florida and back again the next day when I was too wrecked to do anything but weep into the passenger-side door, in the eternal Day 3 that followed he made sure I was putting food and water in my body on a regular basis. Kept me from sleeping for eighteen-hour stretches. Gave me a ride to the 8 a.m. every morning to make sure I stayed with the program, and at my request, he held on to my phone for the first couple of weeks to make sure I didn't text anyone I shouldn't. Which of course made me think of Luce.

When I got my thirty-day key tag it was Nogales who sat beside me in the circle, clapping the loudest. It was Nogales who took me out for Bojangles' when I hit the sixty-day mark. At ninety he brought over a chocolate Bundt cake from the Food Lion bakery. We ate it with our fingers as we drove to the meeting. On our way back, I invited him over for a home-cooked dinner that Saturday. To thank him, I said. He turned me down at first, saying he didn't need any thanking, but at last I got him to agree to come over the following Monday.

"Won't be as good as an eight-piece box," I said, "but I promise you won't leave hungry."

He said he was looking forward to it.

I was too. I'd gotten my driver's license back by that point, which allowed me to get a new job waiting tables at this horrible little "American" place that had opened up on the edge of town, not far from the highway. Baby-back ribs, chicken tenders, fried-shrimp platters. Having no seniority meant being scheduled a double on Sundays, but I spent all of Monday tidying up Luce's and my place, grocery shopping, prepping. The eggplant parmesan I made turned out pretty great. The secret is dipping your salted eggplant slices in egg batter and fresh bread crumbs and then frying them like cutlets until they turn brown and crispy. One thing about getting clean is you have a lot more time for your other interests. I never cooked for Nogales back when we were together, and after he finished, he patted his belly and smiled at me from across the table.

"Wow," he said. "Where'd that come from?"

I told him there was a lot about me he didn't know.

When he asked if seconds were a possibility, I said he could have as much he wanted. As I watched him dig in, the question came out before I'd really thought it over.

No. That's not true.

I'd been considering it for several weeks, months even.

"What do you think about us trying again?" I said.

Nogales didn't answer right away, just kept chewing, eyes lowered. At last he swallowed. Wiped his mouth with his napkin. Folded the cloth into a tidy square. By the time he looked up I already knew what was coming.

"Thing is, I'm seeing someone," he said.

He went on to explain that he hadn't meant to hide it. He'd

just never found a good time to bring it up. When I asked if I knew her, he said he didn't think so. They met at his Al-Anon meeting. She lived out in Ribbins. "Oh wait, you did meet her once. Natalia. You know, the nurse from that Halloween party."

Why did I ever think Nogales would want to be in a relationship with a stupid barely sober ex-junky waitress?

"Right," I said. "I remember."

We didn't see each other again.

Not so long ago, I did an online search for *Manny Nogales*. I found two profiles with the same name on Facebook, but they were both older guys living out in California. It wasn't until I typed his name into Google Images that his face appeared in my phone. His wife, as I soon found out, posts a lot on social media. A rundown of her various accounts tells me he's married with a little girl and a second baby coming. The wife isn't Natalia, but another woman. Round face, good haircut, pretty. Belongs to a bike club and a group called Mountain Hikers. The outdoorsy type. I also learned that Nogales quit the sheriff's department a while back and enrolled at UNC Charlotte. Got his associate's in nursing and then his RN license, capped off with a certificate in substance abuse counseling. These days he works at an in-patient behavioral health center in Western North Carolina. I bet he's great at it too.

Out of everything that went down, the biggest unanswered questions have to do with Wilky. Why did he use again.

Where did he get the pills they found in his jacket. Was it the first time he'd slipped or had there been others? How much of it was my fault? From everything I've heard in the rooms and read online, there are people all over this unhappy country asking themselves these same impossible questions. None of it makes any sense. Where do people go when they die? And why do they have to leave us in the first place?

I'm sorry, Luce. This last part, I'm screwing up completely.

All I know is, if anyone ever tries to tell you they have the answer, put your hand on your wallet. You're about to get hustled. Sure, the sky might look pill blue from a distance, but once you're actually up there in it, strapped into your parachute and jumping out into nothing, it becomes a whole new thing altogether. Years later, I'm still trying to figure out what exactly it is. As they say in the rooms, there are some things you never recover from, no matter what happens—and even now there are times when I can hear Luce cranking the volume on one of her mix CDs, blasting music from her bedroom, and singing her lungs out the way she used to.

"Ireeeeene!" she calls out between tracks. "Where are you?"

I'm right here, I say.

Acknowledgments

I waited tables in eleven different restaurants for over twenty years. Though the server nightmares endure, so does the love and admiration I have for the many brilliant, talented co-workers I met in those houses. This novel wouldn't exist without them.

It also wouldn't exist without the incredible Amelia Atlas and Leigh Newman, for whom I am infinitely, weepily, giddily grateful. Megan Fishmann, you are a freaking dream. Thanks to all of the amazing individuals at Catapult Books for taking on this project. Fellow readers, please support independent publishers. They're saving us.

Mark Winegardner, a one-of-a-kind triple-threat writer/professor/mentor at Florida State, helped me from the first clumsy page to the end and beyond. Other FSU dynamos include Dr. Maxine Montgomery, Elizabeth Stuckey-French, Skip Horack, Janet Atwater, Dr. Trinyan Mariano, Dr. Alejandra Gutierrez, and Dr. Jeanette Taylor.

David Haynes, my extraordinary thesis adviser at Warren Wilson College, taught me mountains about literary craft, while modeling leadership, generosity, and activism. Support Kimbilio! Thanks too, to the ever-brilliant Maud Casey, Christopher Castellani, and Megan Staffel.

The best writing group on the planet consists of SJ Sindu, Laurel Lathrop, Colleen Mayo, and Amy Denham, and I'm damn lucky to know these gifted people. Dear readers, please read their work. And then there's Nathan Ballingrud, my fellow Western North Carolina fiction writer/server/friend. Read him too, people!

I went back to school pretty late in the game, with no undergraduate degree and little confidence. Many creative writers helped me in workshop and out. Thanks to Misha Rai, Sakinah Hofler, Clancy McGilligan, Marianne Chan, Alex Jaros, Sean Towey, Obi Calvin Umeozor, Tiffany Isaacs, Whitney Gilchrist, Rita Mookerjee, Shaw Patton, Laura Roque, Zack Gerberick, Casey Whitworth, Brandi Bradley, Jennifer Adams, Gary Sheppard, Mikayla Ávila Vilá, Daniel LoPilato, Latifa Ayad, Munib Khan, Damian Caudill, Maddie Kahl, Jess Cohen, Feroz Rather, Dyan Neary, Zach Linge, Jayme Ringleb, Aram Mrjoian, Iheoma Nwachukwu, Rebecca Orchard, Geoff Bouvier, Dorothy Chan, Alex Quinlan, Matthew Zanoni Müller, Denise Delgado, Matt Roesch, Matt Bondurant, Seth Brady Tucker, and Luke Hankins. Special thanks to Kevin Weisman for the earliest encouragement. Toodles for Chris.

I'm grateful to Sue Mancuso, Dr. Leigh Edwards, and P.E.O. International for their support of this project back when I was still drafting. Thanks too, to *The Missouri Review*, *The Yale Review*, and *Boulevard* for publishing early excerpts of this work.

Deepest thanks to Daniel Wallace, Bland Simpson, and Marianne Gingher for giving me a job during a global health crisis and for welcoming me into the UNC community.

Final acknowledgments go to family: All the love to Lynn Tucker.

All the love to my mom. Dad, I miss you and love you.

All the love to Melanie Lipof and Merle Weber. Joel, I miss you and love you.

All the love to Jared Lipof, always.

© Jared Lipof

KAREN TUCKER was born and raised in North Carolina. Her fiction has appeared in *The Missouri Review*, *The Yale Review Online*, *Tin House Online*, *Boulevard*, *Epoch*, and elsewhere. She lives in the Blue Ridge Mountains with her partner and multiple cats.